The American Painter Emma Dial

A NOVEL

The American Painter

Emma Dial

 SAMANTHA PEALE

W. W. NORTON & COMPANY

New York • London

"Walk the Line," words and music by John R. Cash, copyright © 1956 (renewed 1984) by House of Cash, Inc. (BMI), administered by Bug Music. All rights reserved. Used by permission. "The Lambeth Walk," music by Noel Gay, words by Arthur Rose and Douglas Furber, copyright © 1937 by Richard Armitage Limited and Cinephonic Music Company Limited for the United Kingdom, Ireland, Australia, Canada, South Africa, and all so-called reversionary rights territories. Copyright © 1937 by Richard Armitage Limited for the USA. Copyright © 1937 by Cinephonic Music Company Limited for the world (Ex United Kingdom, Ireland, Australia, Canada, South Africa, and all so-called reversionary rights territories and the USA). All rights reserved. International copyright secured. Rights by permission.

This is a work of fiction. Characters, businesses, institutions, and organizations in this novel are either the product of the author's imagination or, if real, are used fictitiously without any intent to describe their actual conduct.

For information about permission to reproduce selections from this book, write to Permissions, W. W. Norton & Company, Inc., 500 Fifth Avenue, New York, NY 10110

For information about special discounts for bulk purchases, please contact W. W. Norton Special Sales at specialsales@wwnorton.com or 800-233-4830

Manufacturing by Courier Westford
Book design by Charlotte Staub
Production manager: Julia Druskin

Library of Congress Cataloging-in-Publication Data

Peale, Samantha.
The American painter Emma Dial : a novel / Samantha Peale. — 1st ed.
p. cm.
ISBN 978-0-393-06820-7 (hardcover)
1. Women painters—Fiction. 2. Painters—Fiction.
3. Triangles (Interpersonal relations)—Fiction.
4. New York (N.Y.)—Fiction. 5. Psychological fiction.
I. Title.
PS3616.E235A8 2009
813'.6—dc22

2009004322

ISBN 978-0-393-30455-8 pbk.

W. W. Norton & Company, Inc.
500 Fifth Avenue, New York, N.Y. 10110
www.wwnorton.com

W. W. Norton & Company Ltd.
Castle House, 75/76 Wells Street, London W1T 3QT

1 2 3 4 5 6 7 8 9 0

For John
and for Tina

ONE

1

WHEN I TURNED AWAY from the painting on the wall,
Michael stood right behind me, hands on his hips, at the
base of the wooden scaffold, watching me add a coat of
glossy blue to a corner of the sea. Perched four feet in the air,
a row of warm incandescent lights over my head and the
remains of a cheese sandwich at my knees, I felt like a pet
bird. A red-footed falcon or a hooded crow. Or a gull. An
unlikely pet. I made the painting from a collage of photographs Michael took on a trip to France. Leaden darkness
blankets the horizon and there is no land in sight.

A pair of Los Angeles collectors had been watching us for
half an hour, leaning against the radiator in their fur-
trimmed down parkas. They were in New York to celebrate

Christmas and ring in 2006. The Breslauers owned five
Michael Freiburg paintings, three that I made, one painted
by a previous assistant, and an early one, from 1978, that
Michael did himself.

Unobserved, my postprandial painting could get downright languid, so the Breslauers' presence kept me alert,

hustling along, swigging coffee and dangling a cigarette
between my lips like an old master.

Michael was in the midst of a cunning performance. He
had cleaned himself up: an expensive cut to tidy his gray
hair and loose black clothes I had not seen him wear before.
He looked sleek and handsome chain-smoking my cigarettes and giving me a piece of direction each time I loaded
the brush with paint. I obeyed beautifully, reverently, at
moments overzealously brandishing the brush as if a giant
feather quivered at its end: my own performance. Michael
oozed appreciation.

"Think of gliding below the surface of the water, like a
fish. Emma, apply the paint as though you were a fish."

"A barracuda."

"Emma, a piranha. Loads of piranha in Corsica."

I thought the piranha was a South American fish but did
not want to correct him, or even hazard a contradictory
guess, in front of the Breslauers, who were charmed by
everything he said and did, though they were uncertain how
to react, if at all.

"How about a cormorant? Or a goat." My job was to keep
the talk jocular, fleshly, skidding between oblique associations.

Catherine Breslauer looked ready to jump in but remained quiet. She and Lewis behaved so carefully with Michael, which was too bad because I had seen them be quite funny on their own.

"No goats." Michael frowned. "No."

We both felt the picture was special, the spooky 96-by-111-inch seascape had consumed us for nearly three months, though for entirely different reasons. The picture held me personally, it contained sensations of my own physical and mental effort; Michael knew it was a hit. I often imagined gently tipping into the vast two-dimensional Mediterranean water, swimming lazily, turning my body over and over, neither coming nor going. Last week Michael thought the sea was finished but then decided to exert some last-minute control in front of the Breslauers. They would probably buy it, or another painting from this new series.

Michael's wife Gerda kept calling the studio and his cell as she approached the building in a cab but neither of us picked up the phone.

"Emma, just a little tiny, tiny bit heavier. Right?"

"Okay."

I continued with the same brushstrokes, moving my hand more deliberately. The Breslauers salivated over Sea-shadow, its austere colors and monumentality, the lack of human presence.

"Emma, we brought you a little holiday cheer," said Catherine. She placed a gold box on the glass-topped table beside the colors I had mixed for Sea-shadow. They gave me vintage Krug each year, which I saved in a cabinet above my fridge.

Lewis Breslauer moved the gift to the ratty yellow recliner where Michael often sat and oversaw my work.

"Why don't we wait for you in the office?" he said.

The Breslauers had seen enough to feel proprietary about the picture, which was the purpose of allowing them to spend the afternoon in the studio.

I paused so the door opening and closing did not jog my hand. No mistakes. Not even tiny ones. Michael took the gold present from his chair.

"Stop, thief. That's mine."

"It's in the way, Emma. I'll bring it up front for you. While I'm on vacation the lawyer is going to deliver some papers. You have to sign for me."

"As me or you?"

I did a perfect forgery of his signature, incorporating the inconsistencies of his letters, the way he gripped a pen with his fist. I could copy any mark made by a human hand, though I never let on how proud I was of it.

"As me. It's my will, Emma. Don't forget."

Gerda had threatened to hide his passport until Michael updated his will.

"I'll try to remember: I'm you."

"It needs to get notarized too. Send it all back by messenger. Also, don't let anyone from the gallery in while I'm away. Don't climb off that scaffold unless it's someone hugely important."

If Michael could have his way, I would spend all my con-

scious hours up high, painting something enormous on his
behalf. Six and a half years ago he hired me straight off the
scaffold of a commercial studio in Chelsea where I worked
for a few years after art school, painting displays in department stores and trompe l'oeils in townhouse foyers, and a
ceiling mural of an African sky in the American Museum of
Natural History. I loved that one still. Michael's previous
assistant had walked out after a fight that came to blows
over stolen materials. I was on the top rung, painting a hundred yards of Greek key pattern on sheets of plywood for a
construction barricade on Forty-second and Fifth. Michael
shook one of the legs to call me down. He said he had seen
the museum sky, another mural in Bloomingdale's of Mont-
parnasse in 1965, and watched me whip a brush across the
plywood for a few minutes while he negotiated the fee he
would pay my employer if he took me on. I met him at his
studio the following morning and showed him slides of my
own work—views of my grandmother's house on Cape
Cod, the hummingbird feeders filled with dyed red sugar
water, my mother's old bedroom that was turned into a TV
room where I had spent millions of hours playing video
games—as well as art school reproductions and studies. He
stood with his feet planted shoulder-width apart, bending
over the light box to look through a loupe. My mother, a
professor of art history specializing in nineteenth-century
painting and sculpture, railed against Michael Freiburg. She
pronounced his work soulless and market-driven and it
maddened her that so many of her students at the Maryland
Institute were smitten with him and his celebrity. That her

daughter would paint for the man was more proof that my impulses to work were wrongheaded, because I had to be activated by someone else, to use her parlance. At that time, I refused to see her point on the topic of me not being self-motivated. I would improve the work, I had thought, no matter what it was. And how could the company of Michael's genius not do me some personal good? He gave me a test: to copy one of his pencil drawings, a decently rendered portrait of the painter Therese Oller, his first wife, and then a detail of Velázquez's portrait of Philip IV. He sat at his desk reading travel magazines and talking on the phone while I worked for seven hours. Right away we were not in any hurry to get away from each other.

The telephone rang but neither of us reacted. My brush barely touched the canvas.

"You heard me, right? Don't let those people in here."

"I know."

"Don't read the will to see if you are getting anything because I'll fire you and then sue."

"Just be generous."

Michael's concentration on *Sea-shadow* began to loosen. He dialed Gerda's number, shifting his weight from one leg to the other, his new sneakers shuffling on the gritty floor. Dinner with the Breslauers would be served at the artist Philip Cleary's studio and I wanted badly to be included. The Breslauers should know me better, I decided. I needed to think of my own career, which should benefit from my connection to Michael. Plus Philip Cleary was a painting hero of mine, and despite his long friendship with Michael, we had never met.

"Emma, get down. That looks good for now." He pointed to the six square inches I had been working on since the Breslauers showed up two days ago, and then waved his arm grandly at the entire picture. "That should last forever."

"Eternal."

"Right, that's the word."

Before leaving for dinner Michael intended to sign the last painting I had finished, a field of lupines and absinthe being searched by sixty-seven uniformed police, executed in the signature style I developed for him: painstaking layers of glazes, a gauzy view of both color and form; the movement and possibility that exist outdoors revealed. It had been drying in the front of the studio for almost a month.

"Come on, Emma, I have to hurry up. Catherine and Lewis are waiting for me."

"I am you, remember?"

He laughed and patted my rump when I jumped off the scaffold.

"I'm famished . . ." An indirect approach worked well with Michael. Sometimes.

"Me too. Phil puts together a fantastic spread."

"Like what?"

No answer. My time was running out.

Spring Field with Police rested on felt-covered blocks in the front office, the image facing the wall. Michael liked a ceremony to be made of the signing and the Breslauers waited patiently, ready to revel in every detail.

"I'm going to placate Gerda. Go and keep our guests company, will you?"

"I'd be delighted."

"Enough with the sarcasm for today. It's annoying. Fucking goats."

"Take a joke."

Now I had to switch gears to scratch the Breslauers behind their ears until they purred. Maybe no dinner for me. During my tenure as Michael's studio assistant, I had learned to give and receive lavish, sometimes embarrassingly intimate attention on Michael's behalf. It required exceptional dexterity to quickly and gracefully step aside the instant he was available to fawn or be fawned over without leaving a wake or feeling jilted, to smooth the abrupt transitions.

The Breslauers heads jerked up at the sound of the door opening.

"Michael had to meet Gerda upstairs. He won't be more than a few minutes."

"Of course," said Catherine.

Catherine had pulled up her hood, framing her face with chocolate-colored fur. She leafed through an auction catalogue she had selected from Michael's shelves. Lewis looked over his wife's shoulder at the contemporary art that was auctioned in New York last spring and where, I recalled reading in the newspaper, they had sold a few pieces from their collection and added another Philip Cleary painting to their stockpile.

"Tell me, will you spend the holidays in the city?" Catherine returned the book to the shelf.

"I never go anywhere."

She laughed easily. I liked Catherine; I wished there were a way to be myself with her.

"I hope that's not true. Both of our daughters live in Manhattan so it's a special time for us. Get a dose of the real cold and see our five grandchildren."

"Soak up the city," added Lewis.

"Frederich set up some studio visits for us, which is so nice. He basically acts as our private advisor." Frederich Hecht Gallery represented Therese Oller and Michael. He showed Philip Cleary until the mid-eighties, when Susanna Mackie lured him to her then modest gallery. "One of the great pleasures of collecting is having that close bond with the artists," said Catherine.

"It's an important relationship."

I thought of all the champagne the Breslauers were depositing at studios throughout the five boroughs. They probably had a private advisor at Sherry-Lehmann too. Michael had taken my gold box upstairs, so I would swipe one of the two that had been arranged around a potted poinsettia on his desk.

"Very rare, very unique," said Lewis.

"We're going out to Williamsburg, Brooklyn, tomorrow. Which is always such fun."

"That's where my studio is." This made a very nice impression on the Breslauers, who both rushed to me halfway across the room, inadvertently wedging me into a corner between *Spring Field with Police* and a row of filing cabinets.

"Is that a fact?" said Lewis.

"We had no idea," said Catherine, gripping my left bicep. "You never said a word. You're a devil, not to have invited us."

"We've known you forever," said Lewis.

"We're a family. You must have us over immediately. Right, Lew? I'm sure the pictures are outstanding."

"You've been holding out on us, kiddo." Lewis gave my shoulders a gentle squeeze.

"I have so little time to work there. It's an endless battle."

Before I could kick myself for admitting to the Breslauers that painting was not an utter cinch for me 24/7, Michael threw the door open and bounded in, smelling of scotch and nicotine.

"You should definitely come see the work. Anytime." But it was too late, I no longer had their attention.

"Let's get the show on the road!" He strode up to *Spring Field with Police,* pulled it back from the wall, and began to very deliberately examine a nail in the crossbar of the stretcher.

Catherine found a spot sitting on the edge of my desk, then realized it did not afford a good enough view and moved to Michael's side. Lewis paced in the center of the room. Outside, a man and a woman argued in front of the building over who took whom for granted. Their voices grew more rapid until after a pause I heard the woman coolly announce, "You've lost your credibility now." He yelled still: that he did nothing but support her, that he had not told her a single lie; that she never thought of him, only of herself. Then it died down. Inside, we all pretended nothing had happened.

I took out this sketchbook intending to record the incident but instead I wrote: *Credibility: approaching seven-year anniversary with Michael. I'm nearly thirty-two.*

Michael pushed up the sleeves of his new sweater and took the king-size permanent marker I extended to him. I kept my desk drawer filled with ten-packs of black markers; each pen would only be used to sign a single painting. I laughed at him, at the way he made the completion of each picture significant by ceasing all other activities, at his gestures of making history. I enjoyed the ceremony too. It did not take place without me. He stooped at the lower right-hand corner and signed the back of the canvas: *Michael Freiburg, 2005.*

The Breslauers made some light applause, gathered up their shopping bags, and flung their scarves over their shoulders. Michael glowed. He gave me a wink.

"Okay, you three. Gerda awaits." He tossed the marker toward the garbage can beside his desk.

Three meant me. At last!

Lewis stood in the hallway holding the door open when my friend Irene, flushed with alcohol, suddenly appeared at the center of our little group, dressed in jeans and a sweater that accentuated her figure. She gathered her black hair away from her face and held it up, away from her neck, for a moment before letting it fall.

"I ran all the way. You have to come with me." She waved a red cigarette lighter and, implausibly, a mimeographed tract written in a bold, foreign-looking font, which she hid behind her back when she noticed me trying to read it. "Don't look."

Then she spun around on one foot.

"Irene Duffy, how do you do?" She shook hands with both Breslauers. When she turned to me again Michael and the Breslauers seized the opportunity to check out the back of her.

"Won't both you ladies join us for dinner?" said Lewis Breslauer.

If Irene joined the party my thunder could be stolen by a simple twirl of black hair around her index finger.

She grabbed my hand. "Now."

Delight emanated from Irene; there was no way to slow her down. Even the Breslauers looked ready to follow her.

"We have to go. People are waiting." She pulled harder on my arm.

My invitation, wasted.

"Catch up with us later." Michael made way for us to pass.

"Give my regrets to Philip Cleary."

We were downstairs in an instant and racing to a tapas bar on First Avenue, Irene's new favorite haunt. Despite below-freezing weather, she wore no coat.

"You just ruined my big chance with those collectors. I wanted them to do a studio visit."

"So call them up tomorrow. But don't be so pokey. They might not stay put."

"Who? Who's waiting for us?"

"I met these guys. From Spain. Two from Madrid and their friend from Chiapas."

Chiapas held massive allure for Irene since she and her boyfriend Idris, an earnest, hardworking sculptor and magnetic provocateur, spent half of their first year together there. They had lived in a sand-floor *cabaña* at the edge of the jungle, making friends, making art, rolling joints on the cover of a *London Calling* LP they picked up from a pair of Global Exchange's witnesses for peace at the end of their stint eyeing the Mexican military. In the intervening four years, Europe, Africa, and Asia had received Irene and her cameras. She had been prolific, in her own scattered, undisciplined way. Irene's Chiapas plot entailed being awarded grant money and returning with Idris to make a film. Undercutting our friendship was my top secret desire for Irene to stay put, stop racing off. I could become privately unhinged listening to her plan to leave me behind.

Of course they were still there—three angular brunettes with big noses, bony ankles, and a sheaf of Zapatista tracts—eager to take Irene anywhere she wanted to go, even a meeting with Subcommander Marcos. We ate white asparagus and calamari. Soon Idris arrived from his studio, amped up from an afternoon of cutting big timbers.

"I started building a catapult today." He described how he would assemble it and all the heavy things that could be hurled, including his electrical tools. "It's going to be about the size of a golf cart."

Our new friends were all poets who worked as laborers and like Idris they wanted to throw the tools of their day jobs away.

I took off my shoes, tried not to think of Philip Cleary and the Breslauers with regret, and drank two giant glasses of Rioja.

2

I TOOK THE L TRAIN out to Brooklyn. It had been raining on and off; during a lull the slick streets filled with people walking toward the Bedford Avenue stop to go into Manhattan. Bundled up in my usual woolen uniform, a soft navy turtleneck and men's trousers beneath a narrow black overcoat, I walked in the opposite direction, navigating the islands of sooty ice that lay along the curbs, looking for someone I knew. The door to the Metropolitan Avenue Pool swung open and shut, busier than when I used to do laps there; often I had had the place to myself. I bought cigarettes and chocolate cookies in a bodega on Grand Street and continued south. Rain began to fall again.

I had lost the early part of the day to my computer, where

I perused the Web chasing my twin obsessions: wildlife photography and the Föhn site, a small clothing company in St.
Moritz that posted strange and enigmatic images from the
farthest reaches of the earth. For the holidays Föhn had
posted an eerie alpine castle nestled in snowy woods with
dark attic windows and puffing chimneys. The inky sky
showed no moon or stars. Despite how I had come to jus-
tify the habit as an exploration of possible painting ideas, it
had an anesthetizing effect.

Hideki waited for me in the doorway of the old factory
building on Berry and South Third where he rented a 400-
square-foot corner of a floor divided into painting and
sculpture studios. He had moved to New York from Kyoto
to go to art school and started managing Therese Oller's
painting studio about the same time I hooked up with
Michael. The professional rivalry between Michael and
Therese made my friendship with Hideki feel inevitable and
illicit, and because we both had our own aspirations as
painters, competitive.

We rode the freight elevator up to the fifth floor.

"You haven't been here in a while." Hideki stifled a smile
and I pretended not to notice. He had new work to show
off.

"I'm not in the neighborhood much."

"You're working hard?" he said.

"Kind of. Michael's show goes up in November. Ten new
paintings."

"Good stuff?"

"Big. You should come by and see. He'll be away all of January."

Usually I did not have friends visit the studio, but Hideki respected the work and he never let on to Therese that he saw what Michael was doing. Indiscretion would cost my job.

"I'm sure they're beautiful, you just won't say so. How many have you done so far?"

"Six down, four to go."

"That's not so bad; one every two and a half months."

"How's Therese?"

"Same deal: big paintings, autumn show. September."

"Therese, then Agnes Martin, and Michael in the bronze position." I had not thought of this before. There was no way Michael would stand for his show following Therese's and risk being compared to her. "Is this a new development?"

"They've pushed back the date twice already, she can't meet a deadline to save her life. Smart of Frederich to have them flank someone awesome and dead."

"Hell of a lineup. Groundbreaking stuff?"

"Therese is in the blue-chip phase of her career," Hideki said in his best American accent. "It doesn't matter what she makes now, it all gets snapped up. You know."

I had always liked Therese's paintings more than Hideki, who found them too fussy. Her last show included pictures of lightfall in mountainous landscapes that contained stunning, magical shadows.

"Can I see?"

"Definitely. Come when Therese is around. She loves the potential for Michael drama."

"Don't we all?"

I followed Hideki down the low-ceilinged Sheetrock corridor until we reached the final door. He had a row of clip lights hung from the ceiling, a combination of fluorescents and expensive full-spectrum bulbs. A twelve-foot workbench with shelves of supplies below and cans of brushes on top, a vinyl couch, a bookcase, and a wooden chair with a hot plate where the coffeepot boiled all lined the exterior wall. Cracks in the small panes of the old awning windows had been taped up. Few things in the studio did not have paint drips on them, even the sheet of newsprint pinned to the wall where he wrote possible titles for paintings had smudges and streaks of yellow. A 3-by-4-foot canvas leaned against the north wall, before the row of lights, and two other similar-size paintings, in earlier stages, hung opposite. He had been painting bright landscapes, inspired by trips to the house he and his boyfriend Shiro owned on the North Fork. These pictures were more stripped down than his previous work; they used very few colors applied in fat, brushy lines. The position of blue relative to green gave the colors natural forms, trees, sky, water.

"Fantastic." I sounded like Michael, though Hideki did not notice.

I filled the two mugs with burnt coffee, opened the cookies and left them on the couch. We both grabbed two

at a time from the plastic tray. In the southeast corner, a
careful arrangement of nine colored glass bottles stood in
a diamond pattern around a gold plastic owl with a candle stuck in the top of its head. This was new. I found the
way Hideki stored and displayed all the crap in his studio
much more interesting than the paintings he actually
made there.

"You know, they are turning the lower floors into condos?" said Hideki.

"I noticed the new windows when I walked over."

"They are trying to throw us out of here so they can make
condos on this floor too. Our lawyer said if we win, and
there is a chance we could win, then we'd have rent stabiliza-
tion."

"Does that ever work out?"

"Not for anyone I know," said Hideki. "It's just another
test."

"What are you doing for New Year's?"

"I might run the midnight five-kilometer race in Central
Park and then go to a couple of parties in Brooklyn. What
are you doing?"

"Dinner at Remiz. Irene and Idris are coming." Remiz
was a little bistro on First Street, down the block from
Irene's apartment, that became our local when we were
roommates.

We tore through the bag of cookies.

"How's Irene holding up at her nine-to-five?"

Hired by Magnum as a black-and-white printer, Irene

had begun her day at eleven. Even though she worked until seven, she had been fired after a week. A short week.

"She's not."

"She should stick with something for a change and stop fucking up her career."

"Irene doesn't want a career. You know she steers clear of anything with a usual progression." I was protective of her. Irene could not sustain interest in the work she did for money. Only creating pictures consumed her; she approached filmmaking and photography as though she had nothing to lose, which I envied and believed to be elemental to making art. Hideki was a businessman first, constantly doing math in his head. I flopped on the couch, stretched my legs in front of me, yawned, and changed the subject. "When's your next show?"

"I don't know. The gallery hasn't seen these yet. I'd like to get them out of here soon."

My eyes flashed along the canvases, registering the colors, measuring the pigments and mediums in my mind. My coffee tasted like mud.

When about an hour had passed Hideki stood beside his chair.

"Okay, time for me to get back to work."

We polished off the last two chocolate cookies and Hideki walked me down the cement stairwell to the street.

"The elevator is always busy now. People are moving in." He looked west, toward Manhattan. "It's clearing up. Are you going to walk over the bridge?"

The sky was the same smooth gray as when it rained.

"I wasn't planning on it." I used to walk over the bridge to my studio all the time, but not anymore. "It looks like it's going to pour."

Packs of dogs used to roam the streets by my studio. I remembered watching their silhouettes trot through the dark and the rain, stopping to smell garbage cans and bird carcasses and then pissing on them.

3

Teenage boys set off fireworks on the handball courts across First Street. The bursts of light could not be seen from Remiz's small dining room but the whistles of cardboard rockets taking flight made festive end-of-the-year music. After igniting a brick of firecrackers and some Roman candles the boys began to scatter. They were neighborhood boys I knew by sight from when I lived on the block. I waved from the door and called into the street, "Have a drink before the cops show up!"

Four flutes of champagne waited for them at the bar when they ran in, each wearing a stuffed backpack. None of them was older than eighteen. A police car rolled along First Street and the entire restaurant applauded.

"Come in for a warm-up later, guys," said Stuart the owner.

The boys downed their drinks and ran back to the park and the whooshes began again.

"We used to buy stink bombs and cherry bombs to light off my grandmother's dock."

"Who did?" said Idris.

"My dad and me."

The nights at my grandmother's house were completely dark. I lay on the crooked dock watching light leave the sky and listening to fish jump and crickets and whatever creatures crawled through the bushes until I was too scared to move. I hatched a lot of plans on that dock; it was where I decided to move to New York, an idea my grandmother planted. "That's the city for an artist," she told me when I was twelve. She introduced me to painting, Baudelaire, and keeping secrets.

Irene, Idris, and I tossed around mean jokes about our laziness and procrastination and the bad art we sometimes made. What was continually in the air between the three of us, our strongest bond, was how we would do our work. I called Idris a quintessential Midwesterner because he worked so diligently, without neurosis or irony. Also he would not pay more than twenty dollars for anything and used hilarious phrases like "We sure don't," a favorite he referred to as "the positive negative." Idris had two older brothers and he knew how to take a joke. We teased Irene less because she bruised easily.

They quizzed me on state capitals, lines of dialogue from

Network, my grandmother's house in Wellfleet, old telephone numbers, allergies, broken bones. What did I know about the world and myself that had nothing to do with Michael Freiburg? I played along.

"I fractured my left ankle climbing in Chamonix." I hung my head. "No, that's Michael too. I've never been to Chamonix."

I answered their questions in a fine imitation of Michael's wily growl, leaning way back in my chair, scratching my chin and stomach, rambling about recent interviews, trips abroad, upcoming shows, making quotation marks in the air with my fingers.

"Who influenced you?" Irene extended her fist like a microphone and held it beneath my chin.

"Me? Me? I remember Bill de Kooning taking my arm as we walked through his studio on Long Island." I craned my head in mock distraction, boldly looking over a passing woman.

"Aha!" Irene snapped the imaginary microphone back to her own mouth, "The working-class immigrant. Artistic success after much suffering in the mother country."

"Crap," said Idris. "Romantic middle-class crap."

A server appeared. "Do you want bottled water for the table?"

"We sure don't," said Idris. "Tap water's fine."

"There it is: the positive negative. That could be the name of our political party," said Irene.

"My brother was killed in an ambush in Vietnam." I kept Michael's voice and posture.

"Quit your bitching," said Irene.

"And shut up because here they come," said Idris.

"They?"

Michael said he might stop in for a drink but I was surprised to see both of them, especially for dinner, since they were leaving the next day for Sils-Maria. Gerda wore one of her impeccable black couture ensembles and Michael was also very dressy, which made me wonder where they had been earlier. It was after ten, so maybe the theater. They slid onto the banquette beside Irene and Gerda commenced ignoring me. She immersed herself in the menu. "Here's something new," she said in a ravished voice. When Stuart came by she ordered food for the entire table, never having uttered a word to anyone. Gerda tolerated me because I predated her and she probably felt she had no choice. Michael and I broke off into a separate conversation about *Seashadow*.

"I'm worried about the water. I don't think it's sexy enough," he said. "Maybe we need more highlights."

"The colors are perfect."

"Do you think the colors pop, Emma? I don't know if they pop enough."

"Don't get cartoony. Please."

"You're right." He looked into my eyes. "Have you ever noticed that Therese communicates with me through her painting titles?"

"No. I haven't noticed that."

When he took a Therese tangent in front of Gerda it made me squirm.

"She's always told me important things with her titles. *Yesterday's Volcano.* That's for me."

I had expected him to complain that his show was scheduled to follow Therese's, to confide in me that he minded exhibiting after her.

"I know my paintings reach her on a subconscious level. How could they not?"

Idris told a story about working in a frame shop as a teenager where he met a photographer who was phobic about small white buttons. He only wore crewneck and V-neck shirts in dark colors. If he absolutely had to wear a shirt that buttoned down, his wife tied his tie for him and helped him into a jacket to hide all the small buttons.

"All small buttons or just small white ones?"

"All smalls, with small white ones being the worst." Idris glanced around. "Why am I the only black man in this restaurant?"

"The chef is black."

"What's his name?" Idris challenged me.

"Claude. He's from Paris. Or outside Paris."

"We've met him before." Irene had been sizing up everyone in the room while she ate her food and picked at Idris's plate and then mine. She leaned lazily against the banquet.

"Don't get snoozy on me, baby," said Idris.

"When I was growing up my mother always fell asleep at the dinner table," said Irene. "She still does. She works nonstop all day: five daughters, now eight grandkids, cooking, cleaning, sewing—sewing I don't know what—more cooking. She's very proud."

Irene was proud of her, too.

"Mine was disappointed." I considered my own mother, her eyelids cranking down after a few barbs about my so-called lack of enterprise. "She's still disappointed."

"You ended up with her white hair," said Idris. "That's what you get for hating her."

"I don't hate her. I feel sorry for her. Her hair's not white." My grandmother had a glamorous head of thick silver hair, which I suddenly assumed at the age of twenty, upon her death. Irene had photographed me each morning to record the transformation. Within a month my brown hair disappeared and I assumed a dramatic appearance, ghost-like, young and old at the same time. It took some getting used to but I courted the resemblance to my grandmother and never dyed it brown. My mother, her daughter, a dedicated brunette, was a romantic who held dear the idea of the persevering artist being responsible for making every fucking brushstroke, a subject I had debated with her enough for one lifetime.

At midnight a man at the next table made a toast to his girlfriend, the other diners, and the city. He spoke with an Italian accent and looked familiar but I could not place him. Maybe an ex of Irene's, though she did not let on.

"Raise your glasses to 2006," he said, and everyone in the restaurant did.

Michael kissed Gerda, Irene, and then me, clutching a hank of my hair. He began to loudly describe his latest Internet acquisitions—some original David Bowie LPs and a deco chess set he declared "would be great for kids," as if

he would ever part with an object he had purchased. Now
he wanted to buy two Balthus drawings "on a whim."

"His drawings are better than his paintings."

"His paintings are excellent," said Michael.

"People love the sensational ones of naked girls. The rest
of them are pretty unspectacular. Ugly, even."

"Come on, Emma. You've seen *The Mountain*."

The Mountain, part of the Metropolitan Museum's permanent collection, was seven figures on an alpine walk, one
of the two women in the foreground raised her arms over
her head in a sensuous stretch, the other sprawled bare-
legged, clutching a walking stick, her eyes closed. In school
I had been taught to see Courbet's influence and we read
that some of the figures were based on Swiss women Balthus
knew. I considered Balthus overrated and it irked me that
Michael thought otherwise. I was being reductive, but I
wanted to get a rise out of him. Gerda's presence subdued
him, which I minded.

"I can't tell if you mean it, if you really like him." I was
emphatic despite a clear lack of interest in Balthus from the
rest of the table.

But Michael had turned to ask the server about the
roasted marrow bones with parsley. We tended to agree on
what paintings were good and who was worth watching; he
even permitted me to instruct him now and then as long as
he did not have to admit it. He had not even described the
Balthus drawings, which proved my point. Balthus made
them and so they were desirable.

I drowned my meal in wine and had smoked an entire

pack of cigarettes between sundown and twelve-thirty. Gerda excused herself and inched across the cramped room to the bathroom downstairs. Irene and Idris had a party to go to on Clinton Street. I followed them to the door.

"We're going to drive out to Chicago next weekend. Come with us," said Irene.

"I'll pass, I think. I have to work."

Irene nudged Idris; she had predicted my answer in an earlier conversation with him.

"When was the last time you got out of town?" she said.

Idris could not care less; he looked ready for more action.

"Time to move, babe." He pushed the glass door open an inch and the cold air filled the tiny vestibule.

"We're going dancing. It's not New Year's without dancing. You should come too, said Irene."

"Can't."

"Nice night," said Idris. He gave me a friendly shove.

The door closed between us and I watched them step out of view. Then I took Irene's old seat on the banquette beside Michael. He looked far away and I wondered what he was thinking about. His eyes flitted from table to table where handsome young people in beautiful dark clothes clinked glasses and laughed. The two men next to us resolved to give up alcohol for the entire month of January. "After this holiday season I'm pickled," one of them said.

"I just ordered another bottle. You'll join me, won't you, Emma?" said Michael.

"Count on me."

This was the kind of New Year's Irene and Idris eschewed

as too staid, but I felt completely at ease, sated and buzzed, sitting with Michael in the pretty bistro where we were regulars. We had spent many hours together at Remiz talking about painting. Alone with him I was capable and important, attributes so at odds with the role I played in my family as a dreamy person who lacked direction and tended to be short on facts. I kept thinking sadly about my parents, whom I missed but who were by and large too displeased with me to visit during the holidays.

"Do you make resolutions?" said Michael.

"I smoke so I'm off the hook for giving up other bad habits."

"Some years I try to begin something new. There are always things I should do more of."

"Me too." He had forgotten about Balthus.

"Therese and I spent a New Year's Eve in Los Angeles. Nineteen eighty-one, I think. She gave up cigarettes that night. Enormous willpower." He drank water thirstily. "I would like to do the best paintings of my life beginning this year. I want to bump it up a few notches, kick into high gear. I feel as if I am getting close to really having it." He drank again and put the glass down hard, sending a knife to the floor. "What do you think?"

"Easy. It will happen if you want it." I got a surge of energy when he planned demanding work, accompanied by a flash of fear that our symbiotic relationship would one day collapse.

Gerda sat across from Michael. She was pale and rumpled. She may have been sick in the bathroom.

"What's happening now?" she said.

"We're waiting for a special bottle to be delivered," said Michael.

He seemed happy. He took Gerda's hand and kissed her palm. The three of us were quiet.

"It's great they're letting us smoke in here tonight," said Michael.

"I think they enjoy breaking the law."

"Who doesn't?" Gerda giggled.

I noticed the music for the first time that night. It was Brahms, a favorite of Michael's. Despite hearing this symphony many times at work, I had never gained any appreciation or feeling for it. This was Michael's music. Neither he nor Gerda showed any recognition of the piece, which made me feel slightly hostile. Surely they had listened to recordings of this symphony hundreds of times. I could not think of a word to say to either of them, about Brahms or anything else, which would not betray my displeasure in our threesome and some unearned self-pity. An hour into the New Year and it was time for me to go home.

There was a traffic jam by the door followed by a gust of shocking cold air. Grumbling halted nearby conversations. A man entered alone and came to a full stop. He was physically magnificent, powerful and bearlike, his hands plunged deep in his trouser pockets. Everyone's complaints about the cold ended. His eyes passed over the candlelit room. Though not as tall as I would have guessed, this middle-aged, barrel-chested man was unmistakably Philip Cleary. He stepped in further. He had a head of luscious black curls and wore a heavy charcoal suit and a black Föhn sweater with an almost imperceptible line of green—the catalogue called it yucca—at the throat. My skin was suddenly ablaze with interest.

"Hey, Phil!" Michael called out. He had been waiting for Philip Cleary the whole time.

"There you are." Philip Cleary pronounced "you" like "ya" in a sonorous bass. He kissed Gerda on the side of her head. He shook Michael's hand and Michael beamed.

No woman, collector, gallerist, museum director, or magazine editor could please and impress Michael as Philip Cleary could. He was from Odessa, Texas, the son of an oil entrepreneur, and he had a way of leaning back on his hips and surveying a scene as though he controlled everything his eye settled on. He had often been photographed in this becoming pose and I could understand why he cultivated it. These days Philip Cleary painted voluptuous portraits in a classic seventeenth-century court style. Anytime his name was mentioned Michael said, "I love Phil. Did you know he's had a show at the Met?"

"I'm glad you invited me. I've been meaning to come here for a while." Philip Cleary sat down across from me and raised his chin playfully. "Emma Dial, at last we meet."

He knew my name. The lore about Philip Cleary, Therese Oller, and Michael coming to New York in the early 1970s to make painting relevant again had inspired me and scores of other teenage painters to move to the city. It was impossible to behave normally around him. He made me nervous. I had the bizarre urge to shake water out of my ears because

I was afraid I could not hear him well enough. I was attracted to him and did not want to miss a word.

Stuart appeared with two dusty green bottles and opened one. Michael took a noisy sniff and swallow. He reached for my hand but then withdrew.

"You have to try it," he said to Philip Cleary. "This wine has a lot of percussion. Fantastic!"

When I was an art student, I tacked postcards of Philip Cleary's paintings to my dorm room wall, *A Woman and a Blackbird* and *Golden Birds*. We had almost met many times over the years but instead there had been a tortuous series of near misses. I stared at him openly, memorizing his face and voice and body so that when I got home I could make a record of him in this sketchbook I have been filling.

Gerda barraged him with proprietary questions; she knew about his life. "How is Isabelle?" she began.

"I'm worried about the moron my daughter is out with tonight. Akkk!" He stuck his tongue out, as though he tasted something foul. "He's horrible, but what can I say? I'm her dad." He laughed. "I just came from a party she and her friends put together in a gallery space they opened off Canal. Everyone is real nice, says hello, how are ya. Isabelle introduced me to the meathead; he's too cool to shake hands with the old man. I can only hope he won't last longer than any of the other ones." He laughed again. "My little girl."

"How's she liking Columbia?" said Gerda.

"She likes it. She's painting all the time and she's good. Could be really good, I think, if she stays with it."

In Philip Cleary's *Wardour Street,* which hung in Michael

and Gerda's living room, a dark-haired, dark-eyed woman sits alone on a bench outdoors in a green and secluded spot; she wears blue and has a self-satisfied expression. I assumed the woman was Isabelle's mother, from whom Philip Cleary was divorced, though I had never asked. Michael also had a drawing of the two men together, when they were young artists at the beginning of their careers, and the pencil lines held the excitement and confidence of that time, or so I felt whenever I saw it. Many years ago my painting teacher Meredith Davies said, "There is nothing sexier than a well-drawn line." Philip Cleary's lines possessed all the sensuality and power that a mark could possibly contain. My mind slipped sleepily between these two images and returned to a photograph I had seen of Pinto Canyon Road in the Föhn catalogue. The caption read: *Thirty miles of dirt switchbacks with expanses of ranchland and mountain vistas.* That was close to Philip Cleary's original landscape, within a few hundred miles. I glanced quickly at the yucca green encircling his throat and he caught me.

"I saw what you've been doing," he said. "Impressive work."

I enjoyed his compliment, though it galled me to be flattered by someone famous.

"When were you at the studio?"

"Yesterday evening. You were walking down Christie when I pulled up." Philip leaned over the table and lowered his voice. "You and Michael make me think of a sex scene in a film. Are they really doing it? There is an enormous crew on set but it's an overdetermined situation. The audience can still get into it and be moved by the actors. Is it real? Is pleasure experienced or is a script being followed, a task accomplished?"

In his pause I heard our breathing change. I did not know what we were really talking about but I was annoyed with myself for having to meet Philip Cleary as an assistant, which suddenly felt lowly.

Gerda goaded Michael to remember where he had put his passport. He insisted she had kept it for safekeeping.

"It's no sex scene. It's a day job." My repartee may have been wanting but I managed to remain unruffled. "I get to paint all day. I mind that you are making me slightly defensive."

"I don't mean to." He was apologetic, I think. "So it's not making art?"

This should not have been the first thing we ever talked about. Assistants were standard practice; even he hired people sporadically for simple or menial aspects of his work.

"I accept Michael's way of working—it's very different from mine," he said. "I'm curious about it. What is really happening? I wonder about you and what it's like to be making this great work."

His hair fell over his forehead after he raked his hand through. I wrote "magnificent" but perhaps I mean "resplendent." I could not help myself.

"Not the same as doing my own work, but there are definitely times when I get caught up, in the beauty of it, or the challenge."

Michael and Gerda quietly argued and the coast was clear for me to change the subject if I could pull it off.

"But you get to avoid the crises," said Philip.

"Well, I am in a position to cause a crisis or to be blamed for one."

"When did you start?"

I prepared to launch into my vetted spiel about what Michael made without exactly speaking on his behalf or explaining the work in an obtuse way.

"Six years ago." I rounded it down by half a year; he probably thought I would be Michael's assistant forever. I wondered if he knew how competitively Michael felt toward him. Even I had considered Philip Cleary while I worked, what he would think when he saw a finished picture of Michael's in a show. Now I wished he were meeting me in a different context, where he could see me independently of another artist.

"I meant when did you start painting? How did you come to it?"

I was accustomed to everyone wanting to talk about Michael, but Philip already knew about Michael.

"When I was a kid. Before I can remember. I started painting watercolors with my grandmother."

"Were you always good at it?"

"I think so. I remember it made me feel competent. I painted to get that feeling."

"Me too," said Philip. "It's harder to achieve the older I get."

I agreed even though I felt the opposite, though in front of my own canvas it might be a different story. I could have talked about my grandmother all night. But it would be severely out of place for me to tell Philip Cleary about the flowered cups she served tea in, the bay stretched out below us, a few motorboats fishing on the glinting blue. I had a plastic box with four Woolworth's brushes. She and I each made one picture before anyone else in the house stirred. I zeroed in on a detail that might amuse her, a piece of paper she had crumbled and pushed an arm's length away, the blackened remains left in the fire pit, the same osprey she had painted. Then I took my first swim of the day, running off the end of the dock and plunging in. By the time I rounded the hulking gray rock I nicknamed "the hippo" and returned to the house, everyone was awake and breakfast and newspapers covered the table. No one saved all those pictures we made. When my mother examined some paintings I made as a teenager she accused me of being a show-off.

"None of this means anything, Emma, if you simply loll around all day and then dash off a few eagles when your grandmother sits you down."

"I didn't dash."

"You've only been out of bed for an hour."

"I had the eagles in my head long before I got up."

She could not seem to appreciate the way I did things. She struggled as an academic and believed in seeing the sweaty effort from hard work. But I never believed that about painting.

Michael kicked the leg of my chair.

"You don't mind if I smoke your cigarettes, do you, Emma?" He never asked first.

Anyone else might have tried to hold Philip Cleary's attention. But I was a painting assistant in the company of her boss and his wife and I refused to make a fool of myself and jeopardize my position attempting to bewitch someone who had not come to meet me. I did my best to meet Philip Cleary's eyes. He rubbed his hands together and held them up to his face and blew into them. He looked at me closely, as if I could not see him, or I was not really present, or not even alive. He may have considered me as he would a painting he worked on, or he simply took note of me, the way one might take note of a *Starry Night* poster in a dentist's office. I could not tell which. He looked over his shoulder at the table of four people speaking Italian. Both women turned to him with delight. He half raised an index finger in Michael's direction.

"Hey, how long are you going to be in Sils?" he said.

"Just two weeks." Michael was different with Philip Cleary, quieter, more serious, I think because Philip Cleary was serious. Michael stopped making quotation marks with his fingers.

"Then we're going to visit my sister and her husband in Amsterdam," said Gerda. "Then I would like to go to Provence, since we'll be in the general vicinity."

"We've also got to go to the Adirondacks next month," said Michael.

"And snorkeling in March," said Gerda. They went to the Caribbean every year.

"Sounds like you'll miss my opening. That's a shame," said Philip Cleary.

"No, no, I won't miss it." Michael lit a cigarette. "Dammit, Gerda, I can't go traipsing all over Europe, I have to work. Plus I have that AIDS benefit I'm chairing."

"Can't I do a drawing for that?"

"Visiting my family is not traipsing."

"Only if you cut two eyeholes in it. It has to be a mask."

"Ridiculous," said Philip.

They agreed that masks were ridiculous, though Gerda differed and said that people liked masks because they served a purpose. I considered chiming in as a great appreciator of purposelessness but I did not want to seem like an ass-kisser or draw attention to the fact that Michael's participation in charity events meant he cajoled or bullied me into making something for him to contribute.

"I may have Emma bug you about it," said Michael.

"Please do." Philip Cleary looked at me again.

Once I saw Philip Cleary with Isabelle waiting for the uptown 6 at Union Square and I heard him proclaim his love for Velázquez. She laughed and said, "You're not alone, Dad." Dismissing his passion as common. It had made me smile to hear his daughter speak to him as though he were an ordinary man.

I studied him speculatively. I smoked, filled my glass, and guzzled it down and filled it again. All my appetites welled up. I wanted to hear him speak, to know how he looked at things. I wanted to eat another meal and then race around the city, up and down streets I had never seen before, followed by an endless night's sleep. I began to fidget and to try to hide my fidgeting.

"It's going to be a really nice event, Phil. You should try and make it, we'll have a good time."

"I'll be in Miami all next month. When my show opens I'll come back for a few days."

Now that we had met, the idea of Philip Cleary migrating gave me a jolt. The winter would be long without a chance of seeing him.

Michael said good night to some people who had stopped at the table. It was time to go before I felt bad about being by myself. I pushed my glass toward the center of the table, gathered my cigarettes and matches, readied myself to say goodbye.

"Definitely come and see the new paintings, Emma Dial," said Philip. "I think you'll be interested." He stood to shake my hand.

I waited, excited and confused, for more information. We had not talked about me seeing paintings in his studio. Would I actually get to see him work? Speak to me, just me, Philip.

"You don't have to do that, Phil. Just have Emma pick up the mask from your assistant," said Michael.

Philip Cleary did not say another word.

"I insist, Phil. Don't let Emma disturb you."

Michael's slight mortified me since I had basically been yearning to meet Philip Cleary for most of my adult life and had not bargained on the anguish that being Michael's assistant would cause me when I did. Being shit on publicly should not have been part of the equation. I would call public humiliation, my own and others', a bête noire, and I con-

fess here that I hung my head slightly as Michael helped me
into my coat and we walked outside.

"It's going to be a good year for us, Emma."

The wind howled down First Street. At the corner of First
Avenue Michael found a taxi for me and opened the door.
He ran his fingers through my hair and made a sweet hum-
ming sound, proof that he was oblivious to my feelings. I
tried even harder not to be angry with him. If Michael had
not joined us I might be dancing on Clinton Street right
now and years could pass before I met Philip Cleary, if ever.
Remorse had to be out of the question.

"Mind your head," he said.

The car stunk of exhaust fumes. I closed my eyes, thrilled
to be alone and able to think about Philip Cleary without
maintaining any composure. It was uncomfortable to
breathe. The taxi window reflected a calm, sleepy-faced
young woman. But absurdly, my heart was racing.

Something wet sloshed around in the footwell that I
could not bring myself to investigate; what a mistake not to
walk home. We had circled the block and now sat in traffic
on Second Avenue. Philip lived on the West Side, overlooking the Hudson. I bet he would walk tonight, never mind
the cold.

"This corner is good. I'll get out here."

The amount of traffic made no sense, there had to have
been an accident somewhere nearby. It was after two in the
morning and all the bicycles and cars headed home toward
the bridges and the Holland Tunnel. Plenty of other people
walked alone.

I went over my conversation with Philip but I could not locate a lapse or misunderstanding. How would I see him again? He had gained an idea of me since he visited the studio, I was certain of that, and his attentions confirmed my thinking that Michael's paintings were the best anyone was doing. He knew my name. He would remember me.

People bolted across the street at any break in the cars, though it looked too close each time. The traffic lights stayed green in all directions with no police in sight to direct the traffic. A few years ago a neighbor was hit by a car at that intersection, crossing from the northeast to the northwest corner, which was what I wanted to do. I kept tracing my memories of Philip Cleary and waiting for the traffic to slow down. Like Michael, his perfectionism was legendary. There was a story about him painting late into the night at a *Kunsthalle* and the pictures still being wet at the opening. There were the typical debauched episodes when he was new to the city in the 1970s, also like Michael. In an interview he had described a road trip he had made to Central America and the gallons of lead housepaint in supersaturated colors he drove back to the States. On top of being a superb draftsman, Philip Cleary was a supreme colorist. I should get to be alone with him because I too am a supreme colorist. Birds of a feather.

Along with a few others I ran across Bowery. Houston was easier at Elizabeth, where there was a median. Broken champagne flutes littered the sidewalk across Elizabeth Street from my apartment, and a few friends out on the second-floor fire escape passed a bottle around. I hurried in the door before the revelers spotted me. I wanted to be alone.

Each aspect of Philip Cleary that I recalled—the way he sat hunched over the table, the thickness of his hands, the bravura and languor of his paintings—was vivid and captivating. Michael could not keep me away from him. Philip Cleary knew how good I was. I wanted him to feel me breathing down his neck.

4

MICHAEL SHOWED UP at my apartment before noon, as I
knew he would.

"You look peaked."

"You look like crap too, Emma. Come and take a shower
with me. It'll make us feel better."

The hour I had been awake had been aimless; I realized I
had been waiting for him. Michael turned up without pre-
arrangement. How many times he had pressed the buzzer
when I was out would always remain unknown.

"Last night ended strangely." Which was already not what
I meant. "I've said that to you in the past."

"We drank too much," he said. "I drank way too much."

We fucked under the hot water. I bent at the waist and

Michael held my hips but we kept slipping and I hit my forehead against the tiles. Physical gaffes were easy between us, thankfully. Our first sexual foray took place at the studio, leaning against the wall between canvases, and was harshly overlit. Beds and showers entered the equation later and, though not without their charms, heralded conventionality. Routines developed.

We soaped each other up and he said he was sorry if he had been a jerk at Remiz and I told him it was fine, because I was unprepared for this line of conversation, naked with lavender-scented bubbles close to my eyes.

"I'm kind of 'possessive,' I guess." He made quotation marks around "possessive" with his fingers.

"Possessive?" This was unprecedented from him.

"Of Phil." He stepped out of the shower. "You shouldn't nag him. He doesn't like people in his studio."

I backed under the spray so that I could not hear his voice. He had treated me dismissively, in front of Philip Cleary. That was bad enough. Worse, after a night's sleep he still could not admit that Philip Cleary might have been coming on to me instead of the other way around. He stood before the mirror checking out his widow's peak, which was dramatic, hardly receding, and a major attraction for me. I shut the water off.

"Don't worry. I could never steal Philip Cleary from you." What was it about me that could not let it go, even in the interest of a smooth send-off?

"I know." He squeezed my hips.

I needed to be done with this topic, lest it turned into an

actual argument over my worth. The waters between us were now officially troubled.

We dressed and went to the living room and Michael poured two glasses of wine from a bottle he had brought with him.

"Cheers." He knocked his back.

I drank mine back, too. This was me trying to be easygoing. Red wine made me feel horrible, I always slept badly when I drank it, even a single glass.

"Did I give you my passport for safekeeping?"

"It's in my desk."

"Why didn't you say so last night? Didn't you hear us arguing?"

"I don't want to keep your passport safe."

"Well, you have, in your own peculiar way. Walk me down, will you?"

Historically, our postcoital separations elicited genuine longing in me, but this time I was ready to fly solo. Gerda, who as far as I knew overlooked her husband's relationship with me, would be at home packing their bags. She took good care of him. Her existence precluded serious involvement and any wearying conversations about serious involvement between Michael and me. If Michael had ever made monogamous overtures in my direction I would understand that he did not think much of me as a painter, or maybe that was just the story I told myself when I walked home from work alone. Gerda knew she had hitched her wagon to a powerful man with a fearsome ego; I tried not to let her bother me. I had ambitious plans to spend the day puttering around my apartment, facing the music in my neglected kitchen and perhaps organizing a few of the monstrous piles of crap.

It was not snowing when we hailed him a cab on Bowery. Michael was in good spirits and gave me two long kisses, really good ones, before he got in the car.

5

MICHAEL FREIBURG'S PAINTING STUDIO was on Christie
between Delancey and Rivington Streets in a flatiron building he had owned for twenty-five years. The storefront was
leased to a pair of cabinetmakers from Vermont, Michael's
studio was on the second floor, he and Gerda, his second
wife, lived on the third floor with their Great Dane, Mar-
lene, and the top floor was storage space and a darkroom
that was only seldom used, and then covertly, by Irene.

Someone had tagged the front door with green spray
paint. The bulb on the landing had blown. Inside the studio, I punched the code into the alarm beside the door. I
kicked off my boots and padded across the cold sheets of
gray-painted plywood Michael had laid to make the floor

level, to my desk in the front corner. I kept a pair of running shoes in a filing cabinet drawer.

Each floor was 6,000 square feet, with fourteen-foot ceilings and walls of ten-foot windows overlooking Christie to the east and Bowery to the west, in other words, a palace. Half of the studio was an office where Michael sat at an L-shaped desk, custom-made from white Formica in the eighties by the bearded Vermonters. My desk was a smaller L, about a quarter of the size of Michael's, built to fit his assistant at the time, a guy from Minneapolis who left to teach painting to undergraduates in Chicago.

It was 8 a.m. I entered the date in the diary I kept—January 2—a history of the progress I made on the paintings. Each record began on the day I signed Michael's agreement for a new piece, followed by a description of his maquette and how the work would be executed. I made notes on the type of canvas, stretcher, gesso, and sandpaper I used. I kept recipes for colors. I listed the hours I worked, the date I finished, the date the conservator came to varnish the painting and the name of his assistant, the date Michael signed the back of the canvas with one of the new black markers; the date the painting was photographed.

Michael might flip through the notebook pages after a piece sold or was included in a special exhibition, reminiscing about its origins. Occasionally someone from the gallery called to double-check a detail. Had Michael dated *The Fifties* 2005 or 2006? What were the metric conversions for a particular work? I kept his handwritten list for the current series in a plastic sleeve, tucked into the center of the diary:

Emma, here is the painting list for my November 2006 show:

1. *Spring Field with Police,* 108 × 102"
2. *Phu Quoc,* 108 × 84"
3. *Stand of Evergreens,* 114 × 113"
4. *Persuasion and Coercion,* 91 × 77 3/4"
5. *Arriving in Munich,* 56 × 61"
6. *Elemental Earthy,* 108 × 102"
7. *Substitution,* 88 × 87"
8. *Sea-shadow,* 96 × 111"
9. *Interstices (Rusted),* 108 × 108"
10. *The Fifties,* 61 × 67"

Pantone color #'s (from the book of uncoated tints) are attached. Emma, please remeasure dims.

I rarely consulted these books myself but I tried to be exhaustive and perfect about the records, for posterity's sake.

I drank my coffee at Michael's desk, surveying the new piles and torn pages he had arranged along the L. I read him like a newspaper, starting in the upper right-hand corner. He was shopping for a new computer and scanner; he was planning a diving trip; he collected a few telephone numbers at holiday parties, Karen, Hannah, Audrey. His penchant for clipping magazine pictures of teenagers in bikinis had flared up. I had learned to ignore the habit, it was bland and commonplace and it did nothing for our relationship for me to be serious about it. He and Gerda would buy a new car; she wanted a Mercedes and he wanted something titanic. Two neatly clipped images of the same black coupe lay half buried beneath ads and brochures for supercabs with full truck beds. On a sheet of white paper half obscured by the phone he had written my home number and the date May 8 over and over, in two columns that filled the page. This could only mean one thing: more work for me.

I UNLOCKED THE DOOR separating the office from the painting studio in the back, turned on lights and the radio. *Sea-shadow* was drying. I pushed the wooden scaffold across the room to begin work on *Stand of Evergreens*. Michael had left me some Post-it notes: *Emma, please don't leave cigarettes burning on the color table. Emma, please call the gallery so they know when you are here in case Frederich wants to bring people over. Emma, call me so we can talk about the next painting.*

When we met Michael had just begun a new series of pictures, and as he discovered what I was capable of he painted less and less. Instead he concentrated on the visual descriptions I worked from, which he deliberated on for months. He made drawings and collages. He photographed still lifes. He chose colors from the Pantone catalogue and I mixed paint to match them. From his library he found images to show me exactly the style he wanted me to paint in. He tore pictures from magazines, flagged pages in art monographs. At lunch he sent me to see exhibitions he liked, usually the work of friends or the younger artists he said he influenced.

"You think everyone is influenced by you."

He laughed.

"They are."

Michael arranged the lighting and decided where the canvases were hung while I worked on them. He dragged the yellow recliner across the floor, positioning himself to get a good look at the work, directly behind my scaffold or twenty feet away or beside me to watch the paint applied in raking light. Once, while keeping me company, Irene had burned a hole in the arm when she fell asleep with a cigarette.

At the beginning, he yelled at me about colors, accused me of working from batches of paint he had not approved. I told him he was color-blind. I painted my name into the first two pieces I made for him—in the cold surface of a lake and in the lean trunk of a spruce—a reminder that it was my hand that made them. Only Irene knew.

Within the first six months I worked for him, we were having sex in the evenings. He said it would connect us and I would be able to paint more the way he wanted me to. He said I was a treasure he stole from someone who could not recognize I was a virtuoso. He said I had hips like a matador. I was twenty-five and wanted to fuck someone who was written about in art history books, who had met presidents, who had known Warhol.

He was right, too. It took no time for us to find a sexual rhythm, with room for other relationships and, in Michael's case, marriage. These days I made five, sometimes six paintings a year and earned about twenty thousand dollars per painting, depending on the size and amount of detail. I did not participate in the conception of the work at all. Michael's method of working suited his subjects—the distance between human beings and the environment, the natural and the man-made. The only thing that surprised me about his system was that he did not spend any time painting. Any time at all. He told me he did not miss it either. I had always loved holding a brush and the moment before I touched a canvas or paper for the first time with a color I had specially devised. I could not locate where the excitement was for Michael, why it was paintings. And not something else. This bothered me for a long time until I decided it did not matter. It was a job.

AT THE COLOR TABLE I prepared paint for *Stand of Evergreens* to match the Pantone chips Michael had selected. Tony the superintendent brought Frederich Hecht in at eleven, about the time I began to entertain the idea of a nap.

"Hello, my dear." Frederich was breathless from the stairs. "Don't stop what you're doing." He waved his hands before his face to clear my cigarette smoke away. "It's downright foggy in here."

Frederich Hecht, Michael's New York gallerist, was a seventy-year-old shark from Frankfurt who opened his Greene Street gallery in 1975 and swiftly forged modest yet international careers for Therese Oller and Michael. I had been listening to Michael grouse about Frederich and Therese for years, it was a central part of our relationship and his personal lore. Frederich and Therese used to speak German in front of Michael and he was always quick to feel excluded. At the time of Michael and Therese's divorce in 1982, articles about "the current scene" mentioned "a fierce shouting match at the El Quixote bar that turned ugly" after she exhibited a canvas titled *Limits of Reality,* which "Freiburg alleged" borrowed imagery from photographs he

had taken on their honeymoon in Greece. The police had
been called, the episode ended in a "teary breakdown," and
Michael was banned from the bar. Since then Michael suspected that anyone associated with Frederich Hecht Gallery,
including art school interns who catalogued slides and
painted walls a few hours a week for a single semester, was a
spy for Therese, whom, he contended, served up damning
stories about him for prominent art writers and regularly
stole his ideas for her paintings. How she did this, and why
Frederich would partake, I did not know or inquire.
Michael's lawyer had drawn up confidentiality agreements
that forbade Frederich (who signed an addendum on behalf
of his staff), me, the half dozen painting assistants who pre-
ceded me, and Gerda from discussing the production of his
work in any of the ways which, according to the four-page
document, could be construed as public, forever.

Frederich worked nonstop. I used to find him interesting,
his dandy clothes and industrial-strength German accent,
his superhuman tolerance for champagne and marijuana.
But more than once I had been the butt of his machinations
by repeating something Michael had said about the progress
of a painting or a personal relationship and then it had come
out that I was blabbing. Silence, or near silence, was the
only way.

Frederich sought to impart or, more likely, uncover a particular tidbit and I had to be still, even though it was excruciating to be alone with him when he was mining for
information, and let him do whatever he came to do.

He cleared his throat and snorted phlegm in his nose.

Give into it, I thought.

"Where's our boy?"

He was insulted not to find Michael waiting and I did not intend to apologize on his behalf.

"Switzerland."

I stopped working and glowered at Frederich to keep him from looking appraisingly at me. He had a horrible wet-eyed stare.

"I met the fellow who walks the dog. He spotted me before I could press the buzzer." He coughed.

"You know Tony. He takes care of the entire building. He's called a superintendent."

Frederich pretended not to know people's names or to forget them. It was his obnoxious way of assigning importance. He used to do it to me but we had known each other too long for him to be able to keep up the charade.

"Michael didn't mention he was leaving." Frederich coughed again. "He asked me to come by to talk about moving the show up to May."

He had decided his new show date while he cut out pictures of pickup trucks; that was why he had not complained about Therese on New Year's Eve.

"May 8, right?"

"Yes," said Frederich. "Every artist I have ever worked with wants more time. More time and more money. Michael wants less time."

"And he's not even here."

"Precisely! He stands me up. The bastard." Frederich sat in Michael's dirty armchair, tired, coughing. "He's our bastard."

I adjusted my position at the color table so that he could not see what was on the palette. The first time I met Frederich, he told me to call him when I had some of my own work to show and he would come to my studio and take a look. He probably thought I would not be with Michael for long, since none of the assistants before me lasted more than two years before they left to do their own work. At this point, I presumed he considered me a talented loser.

"How's everything going?" said Frederich.

"Fine. Fine." I kept looking at him so that he would hurry up and leave. He seemed small in Michael's chair, yet he made me feel like an ant. I wanted to be cruel to him. "You sound phlegmy. You look weak."

"Never better, thanks." He flashed his shiny old teeth. "Now, which one is this?"

"Stand of Evergreens."

"On schedule?"

"Always." Not that I would ever tell him otherwise. Michael once said that among the reasons Philip Cleary switched galleries was he could not bear the way Frederich dropped in unannounced and insinuated that there was something wrong with not spending every moment bustling productively.

"For the first week of May?"

"No sweat." A lie.

"You're a good little worker." Frederich stood abruptly

and shook out his frail-looking legs so his trouser hems fell just so over his shoes. "Tell Michael I was here and now he has to come to me."

"I'll let you out."

"No. I don't want to interrupt you any longer."

"I'm going to smoke a cigarette, Frederich."

"If you insist."

"Then I'm going to take a nap."

"Ha! You wouldn't dare. Too much to be done." He snorted again.

Asshole.

He strode ahead of me through the studio, past *Sea-shadow*.

"Fantastic. Spectacular." Snort.

It was really a sinister, murderous picture, and like all Michael's work, it was about domination, not natural beauty, but people loved landscapes, despite themselves.

AFTER LUNCH I FINISHED drawing out the bushy ever-greens in the foreground and began the underpainting, building up nearly transparent layers of blue-gray. The telephone rang twenty times throughout the day: the gallery wanted to bring someone by later in the week. Michael's sister Susan in Minnesota. His drunken roommate from forty years ago wanted to borrow money. Patrice Awofeso, the art handler, ready to move *Spring Field with Police* over to Frederich's. Three separate invitations for drinks and dinner from a Milanese clothing designer, Michael's attorney, and Philip Cleary, who had the Breslauers in tow. The constant

stream of magazine assistants and graduate students request-
ing permission to reproduce images of paintings and foreign
curators wanting to borrow pieces for their exhibitions.
Everyone wished him the best for the holidays. I worked
until seven, when my eyes felt dry and tired.

6

WITHOUT MICHAEL watching over me I slacked off and returned to my old digs on First and First. Idris worked around the clock in preparation for a solo exhibition in Chicago in February, so no one minded me showing up with an overnight bag.

Irene hunched over an array of manila folders, brown envelopes, magazine clippings, and snapshots laid out on the long table. Another pile of books and more paper covered her lap. Behind her the upper panes of the kitchen window were cracked and had been patched over for the winters with various widths of masking and duct tape. The ends of her hair were still wet from the shower and her toenails were freshly painted a red-orange color. Irene wrote by hand in a spiral notebook. Her gold rings knocked together as her hand moved across the page. I poured coffee from the pot and waited for the heater to stop blowing.

First and First was a terrific hovel, a long uninsulated attic with a skylight over the bathtub that was covered with birdshit. The kitchen and living room were one open space and the bathroom and two bedrooms were partitioned off with heavy velvet theater curtains stolen from NYU where Idris taught a course, "Painting and Sculpture in New York: A Field Study." First and First was as drafty and dusty as ever, cluttered with unmatched furniture, stacked with old newspapers and secondhand books from the Strand that reflected the range of our passions and curiosities over the years, beginning when Irene and I were eighteen years old, fast friends since our first day at the School of Visual Arts. Goya, Josef Koudelka, nineteenth-century Russian novels, the French New Wave, Eva Hesse, poker and whist, frog calls, Peter Doig's StudioFilmClub, animals of the Kalahari, Brazilian rainforest, porpoises, all of it strewn with sweaters and T-shirts and jackets. A Vija Celmins catalogue that I reclaimed. Dirty dishes filled the sink. The living room ceiling leaked in three places where it met the exterior wall and small chunks of plaster rained down on us on blustery days.

When the Modine went off we could hear each other and the traffic on First Avenue.

"How's it going?"

Irene dropped the books from her lap to the blue carpet and folded her legs beneath her.

"Too soon to tell. Are you hungry?"

"Yes, but I don't feel like eating yet."

I put on a pair of dirty socks and my peacock blue Föhn turtleneck. The damp wool smell conjured images of me going out and doing something productive or physically heroic, summiting a peak in a different hemisphere.

I sat at the opposite end of the table, Irene's bright roses between us. From my bag I unpacked two art magazines, a clip to pull my hair back, and this sketchbook. Once I drew habitually in a book, whenever I rode the subway or sat alone for more than a few minutes I made a drawing. After college I became self-conscious about drawing in public because people (men) often tried to talk to me about what I was doing, what a picture "meant" or "represented," a way of thinking about pictures that never held interest for me. I never quite got back to working easily in a book and the pictures no longer unfolded for me as though I were decoding a special language. But for a long time I had been buying and carrying sketchbooks around, just in case, though they remained mostly empty except for a place to write a note or telephone number. Now I write things down.

The photographs Irene had taken out were of Hideki and his ex-boyfriend Yuji, from years ago, when Hideki first got his studio. He proudly posed beside the sheets of plywood and Sheetrock he bought to build out the place.

In college Irene and I made up an interview game, we took turns being the subject or holding the imaginary microphone and speaking in a loud continental accent, the voice of *Artforum* or BBC Radio. Irene would say, "We are here today with the American painter Emma Dial, whose work is currently on view at the Tate Gallery." I flipped brilliantly back and forth between English, German, and Japanese, my paintings were in the best museums and private collections and Irene quoted critics about my formal and stylistic achievements. It was all accolades from Irene and witticisms from me until she hit me with a question no one would ever ask: "Why are you seeking your mean mother's approval?" or "What if you fail, if the institutional art world doesn't notice a girl painter from Baltimore who makes brushy pictures of her friends?" I told her: "I'm not going to fail." Watching Irene work, I was uncomfortable remembering those old questions. They were torture then, but fun, bearable torture because we had every confidence that we would make great art and a completely manageable and rewarding public life would ensue.

"Let's make a dinner for your birthday."

"Can we do it here?" said Irene.

"What do you want to eat?"

"Pork chops. I haven't had a decent pork chop since I was in Chicago last summer. Lots of garlic. However you and Hideki did them before, the big, thick chops and the chocolate cake. Or ribs and the cake."

"Who do you want to invite?"

"Us, Hideki and Shiro, Jennifer and whoever she's going out with now."

"The Bosnian guy?"

Jennifer, our friend from school whom we never saw, was the art critic for *TimeOut* and she was always busy.

"I think so." Irene poked at a pink petal with her pen. "Let's have it on the weekend so everyone can come."

The heater went on again. No more talking.

Irene worked, filling line after line with her fat capitals, paragraphs and outlines and lists, dialogue. I smoked cigarettes and scratched at the dry skin on my forearms and read articles about two of Michael's friends and a review of work by an ex-boyfriend who had moved to Los Angeles soon after our breakup and now had tenure at UCLA. He made enormous diorama-like installations, with painting and wooden and wax figures, all relating to his childhood in rural New Jersey: the Pine Barrens, the shore, summer concerts at the Meadowlands, an alcoholic father, a long-suffering mother, etc. During a fight over money—he was a charismatic sponge—he said I was pathetic when it came to relating to men and that I did not live in reality, proof of which was my refusal to pay his rent two months in a row and my paintings, which he called "old-fashioned aspirations to purity and genius." At the time I confided in Irene that he might be right.

Irene ordered pad see ewe with beef and spicy mint chicken to be delivered. She shuffled her pages while we ate in silence. At dark she moved to her desk to type at the computer and I walked up to St. Mark's Books and bought a massive book of Philip Cleary's paintings, *Intransitive/Unlimited: 1979–2001*, and blank CDs to burn music from a guy in an open stall on the corner of Bowery and Third Avenue.

When I returned Irene was writing by hand again. I called Hideki and Shiro and Jennifer to invite them to dinner. Hideki agreed to cook if I paid for everything. Jennifer was going to be in Miami. At midnight Irene's sister Ethna called from Chicago.

"I can't believe we're thirty-two this year," said Irene.

Ethna knew whom "we" meant. She told Irene a story about the restaurant she managed on the Gold Coast that Irene relayed to me while they were still on the line: when a valet got into an accident pulling an illegal U-turn in a customer's car, the police discovered he had a suspended license. Restaurant stories bored me but I liked Ethna. I did not have the guts to tell Irene how constantly I thought of Philip Cleary, studying his art like an undergraduate, searching for some link between us. Irene would track my progress with Philip Cleary if I told her what I was thinking. I wanted to be able to forget about him if I could not get any closer.

We sat at the table until three in the morning smoking Irene's cigarettes and drinking bottles of beer, *Intransitive/ Unlimited: 1979–2001* concealed in the bag at my feet.

7

THE WOMAN BEHIND the counter at Fortunato Brothers bakery took an order over the phone, what to write on a birthday cake. *Buon Compleanno Luigi!* Marble café tables were arranged against the windowed wall; two old men speaking Italian sat with empty espresso cups and pastry plates in front of them. I paid for the black forest cake with thick shavings of chocolate layered on the top, no writing. Irene's favorite.

I walked along Metropolitan Avenue holding the cake box carefully to my chest. A car service was letting someone out at the subway entrance. I peered in and the driver raised his eyebrows to convey that he would give me a ride after he made change. The passenger was a woman I had seen

around the city since the opening of the first paintings I
made for Michael. She walked with a wooden stick, a shillelagh, Irene had called it when we once spotted her together.
We recognized each other but neither of us said a word, just
a long expressionless look. I slid into the backseat and rested
the cake on my lap. What had been happening in her life
since that show?

The car made a U-turn and headed for the bridge; my
studio was exactly sixteen blocks away. The buzzer was still
labeled *Meredith Davies*, though the white had faded off the
raised letters of the name. It was Meredith's studio before
she gave me the lease in the spring of 1997. The floor-
through apartment had five rooms, including the kitchen
and bath, in a row house on South Eighth Street. Three rear
windows facing the Williamsburg Bridge and the constant
hum of traffic and trains were my favorite features. Across
the street Gabila's Knish Factory took up half the block. A
few early mornings a week they unloaded a semi of potatoes
into wooden crates on metal casters, making a disturbing
sound, thousands of potatoes falling out of the truck, which
unfailingly evoked images of being buried alive.

The brick façade was painted light pink. The stoop, fire
escape, cast-iron gate, and banister were a faded emerald
green. No one took care of the building. All the paint
peeled; the wooden sashes rattled in their frames; none of
the buzzers worked anymore.

Joyce Barnes, a legal secretary, lived in the garden apartment. A trust-fund poet from the Upper West Side lived on

the parlor floor with his two cats. The second floor belonged to me. A couple of Pratt adjuncts rented the top.

In the springtime the narrow yard was overgrown with heirloom roses. The parlor floor was six feet longer than the second and third floors, creating a short porch outside my rear windows. Meredith's hibachi, two plastic lawn chairs, and a dog bowl still sat out there. She used to climb down the metal ladder to cut roses from the yard. Her pruners had long since melted into the roofing tar.

Meredith Davies was an artist. She lasted twenty-three years in New York. She was also my teacher at the School of Visual Arts for three semesters, my mentor for three years. Not a friend. Meredith had three solo shows before she got tired and fed up, fell in love, married a carpenter, and moved to the West Coast. She left two wooden easels large enough to hold an 84-inch canvas and floor-to-ceiling birch plywood bookcases, stained orange and red. In the afternoon light the living room was on fire. She also left a map of Madrid on the bathroom wall, the cards for a group show she was in at International with Monument and a solo show at Brand Name Damages, a postcard she bought at the Prado of Goya's *Colossus* taped to the fridge, empty Café Bustelo cans for storing brushes and sponges and rags under the kitchen sink. The floors in every room were covered with Meredith's paint. Drops, specks, smears, spills, color tests, footprints—woman and dog. All violent and melancholy shades of vermilion, plum, white, every blue I could think of. I had swept the floor, cleaned the bathroom, and

moved my stuff in. The shelves overflowed with old art
magazines and yellowing newspapers, T-shirts to tear into
rags, tubes and jars of paint and pigment, linseed oil, Damar
varnish, gallon tins of turpentine, dozens of brushes, a mor-
tar and pestle, boxes of unsharpened pencils, rolls of canvas,
wood for stretchers, shards of beveled glass for palettes,
squares of Masonite, textbooks and handbooks from college, catalogues for art supply stores, old Manhattan and
Brooklyn telephone books. Things I would never use.

I used to imagine living on South Eighth Street. Meredith had kept a futon laid across two wooden palettes in the
windowless middle room and in the daytime she followed
the light. The floors were grooved from the easel legs being
dragged back and forth. She had kept her painting rack and
flat files in the tiny room over the staircase. Meredith
worked constantly from the time she moved to New York to
go to the Cooper Union until the time she left when she was
forty-one. She painted people, mostly women, in couples
and trios, on smallish, LP-sized canvases. For a while I
copied her a lot.

When she moved from Church Street to South Eighth in
1981, Meredith was the only woman in the neighborhood
on her own. The men, prematurely graying and balding and
softening painters and sculptors from nearly every conti-
nent, rode their bicycles or drove rusty pickups from their
studios to Williamsburg Paints, the Polish diner near the
subway, the bar down the block from the laundromat, the
drug dealers on Havemeyer Street. "Some wonderful men,"
she said with a sly look. But most of those artists were gone

within the next decade. The whole point, Meredith had emphasized, was to spend as much time in the studio as possible, not to make a career outside of being an artist. Even before she left town the neighborhood had become absurdly popular and expensive, and now it's a place where restaurants with enormous plate-glass windows and serious wine lists thrived.

I used to walk over the Williamsburg Bridge or take the bus to the studio. In the summer I rode a bicycle. I was trying to build my world around being a painter. I worked tirelessly, fantasizing about the picture I was making, all the pictures to come, and what it would be like when they took on another life out in the world, apart from me. I never doubted that painting was my future. I was so proud of my studio, of what I made there, and of my solitude, which felt essential, too. I painted every night until I was racked out. Or I was with Irene. I was not a person who spent thirty dollars on a cab ride to pick up a twenty-five-dollar cake.

CIGARETTE SMOKE SWIRLED in the hallway and the radio still played NPR loudly. Irene and Idris slumped into the couch, the case of wine I had fetched from Remiz at their feet. Hideki knelt on the floor in front of them, picking olives and almonds from a ceramic dish. Except for the light from First Avenue and a few candles, the room was dark.

"I had to open some. I was getting older every minute." Irene poured generously from a second bottle. She looked radiant in the same jeans and sweater she had been wearing for a week.

I shoved the cake in the fridge.

"I got the money to make the documentary in Chiapas," said Irene.

"We have a glass for you here," said Idris.

That meant they would be away for months. I kissed Irene's cheek and congratulated them both. Idris poured me a brimming glass of Syrah.

"Where's Shiro?" I sat beside Hideki on the floor.

"Working."

"After this doc, I want to make a fiction film about a cinematographer whose canyon house in Los Angeles burns down during the Santa Anas," said Irene. "Actually, I want to make a film about a girl who gets driven out of her family's home in Mexico City. For having sex. She crosses the border and heads up the coast, surviving one misadventure after another—a tempest, a shipwreck, an earthquake—with her former tutor, maybe her ESL instructor, as she makes her way to Chicago, the home of her childhood sweetheart. I think he works on a huge building site, plastering walls in ugly granite-countered condos. He's had his share of trouble too. Gangs, prison, being an illegal. But the three of them will live happily ever after, growing corn in the front yard of their shitty frame house in Pilsen."

"Your *Candide*." A new idea for a film brewed in Irene's head every hour.

"Yes. Can the earthquake be in San Francisco instead of Lisbon?"

"I think it has to."

What would I do without Irene for months?

"How far are we from eating?"

"What do you care? You don't even like food," said Idris.

"I like it when I don't make it."

Irene and Idris sounded as though they were about a bottle ahead of Hideki, a cautious drinker. Hideki gave advice on how to begin a project that could be completed.

"It can't all be spontaneous and fun." He pointed his finger at them.

Irene hid behind her drink, laughing, and Idris shook his head, his hand on his stomach, as though what he heard made him sick.

"I'll check on the meat," he said.

Hideki pressed Irene to relay the Chiapas plot. He kept asking her, "Then what's going to happen?" Determined to hear a logical plan.

"Hideki made this drawing for my birthday," said Irene.

She passed me a cardboard portfolio, handmade from the backs of two drawing pads and tied with a gray silk ribbon. On a square piece of heavy cotton paper he had drawn patterns of eyes and mouths, flowers and leaves, windows. I studied the drawing with feigned interest; it was pretty clumsy. Corny, really.

"Hideki has been extolling the virtues of slowness. How I need do some careful planning to build my career," said Irene.

"A business plan for your artwork."

"You want to skip to the end. The result. The success," said Hideki.

"We're going to make a film. Why are you taking it personally?" said Irene.

Idris banged a wooden spoon against the edge of a steel pan.

"Because I worry about you," said Hideki. "Why do you want to ruin things for yourself?"

"Idris and I need to pack our bags and get on an airplane. We're a team. We don't need to use someone else's method."

She was triumphant; she could make fifty thousand dollars go far in Chiapas.

Idris banged the pan again, this time it got Irene's attention and she scowled at him.

"Let's sit down. I'll help serve." How to derail Hideki and find out what was wrong with Idris?

"No. Me," said Hideki.

Irene lit tapers. I refilled the glasses and took a seat beside her. She had set a beautiful table using her beloved antique plates, chipped ivory china with gold-painted vines. Amid the candles and place settings were six arrangements of white roses in peanut butter jars. She took a stem from one bunch and laid it beside her knife.

"I don't believe someone gave you money without seeing a real budget. Idris, did you prepare a real budget?" said Hideki.

"No." Idris sat opposite Irene.

"To prepare for the future you have to do budgets. I still do budgets for Therese."

"The future. All you care about is the future." Irene narrowed her eyes at him.

"I don't want you and Idris to blow it," he said.

"Lighten up. It's her birthday."

"You protect her so she doesn't have to face any consequences," said Hideki.

I pointed the CD remote at Hideki to lower the volume on his criticism.

"This is so tasty." Irene swayed her shoulders. "Have you ever been to Mexico?"

"Once. For Therese. At this point you can't be abandoning projects halfway along, or more than halfway along." Hideki would not relent. "If you would make plans you wouldn't run into so much trouble."

Irene, impervious to being forced onto a hot seat, never solicited art advice. I think she always knew her energy for making things came back around. She thought of a million ideas for projects and nosed around each one until something stuck.

"You have so little to show for yourself," said Hideki.

"I met Philip Cleary on New Year's Eve." It felt like a good time to shoot my mouth off.

Hideki looked up from his food, he had served us all mountainous portions.

"He came into Remiz after midnight."

"What was he doing?" Hideki devoured celebrity gossip; no crumb was too small.

"Talking about his new paintings." I paused for reactions;

all three of them stopped eating. "You reminded me, your advice that Irene do further preparation."

"Any preparation," he said. "What about his new paintings?"

"He invited me to see them in his studio." An image of my own quiet studio began to form and then quickly dissolved again.

"Alone?" Irene asked, reading my mind and savoring the opportunity to encourage me, make me talk, maybe say too much. Balancing on a tightrope together was an old game for us. "When will you go?"

"What was he doing at Remiz?" said Hideki.

"He was pacing like a lion, waiting to be fed."

"A hungry lion." Irene wrestled the cork from a new bottle. "Is he patient or will he pounce?"

"Philip Cleary is more horse than lion," said Idris. He was laughing, which was a relief. "You're right." This could be a truce.

"He is a horse looking for a rider." Irene refilled all the glasses. "Giddyup, friends!" She finished her drink in two gulps and refilled it again. "Hideki, this is super good." She ate roasted cauliflower garnished with currants and pine nuts with her fingers.

"I'm a recipe follower. Just like Emma," said Hideki.

"Whatever the fuck that means."

"Didn't you used to do studies for paintings?" said Hideki.

"Yes. Beautiful ones. Remember?" said Irene. She gave me a tender look that I found mortifying.

"I drew because I was taught to and I always liked drawing, having a book to work in. You don't. It's nothing to do with recipes. Where would I get recipes?"

Hideki could not render anything for shit. Without a camera and overhead projector he would be a goner.

"No I don't. Therese does endless studies."

"Michael likes intimate drawings, in his own way."

"I think Irene should try a different approach."

"Irene's not a painter. You can't compare. I'm not involved in the preparation of images for Michael at all. My work is purely technical. It's easy to face someone else's blank canvas when you have a complete map to work from."

"What about Philip Cleary?" said Hideki.

"I think he draws." But I did not know. I wanted him to draw, to be free of electricity and lenses, to be able to do it all alone. Echoes of my mother, I knew.

"Philip Cleary and Therese and Michael. Do you know what you sound like? What about what you think? What do you do?" Idris pushed his plate away. No truce.

"I have been making Michael's work for a long time—it's a major experience for me."

"But why are you still there?"

"She gets paid a ton," said Irene.

"I paint or draw, for Michael, nearly every day. It's like drinking coffee. I want it that way—daily."

This was overly simple for Idris's tastes. I meant it was my addiction—painting all the time was what I did—but Idris rolled his eyes, ready to run me down. There was no point

in going into detail for him after such an untheoretical first
principle.

"In order to be good at our jobs we have to subvert our
ambitions," said Hideki.

"That sounds hellish," said Idris. "Like a little death,
Monday through Friday."

"It's impossible not to assert yourself now and then. You
can't be in service every moment."

Hideki shrugged. Maybe he could be.

"Be realistic. At work you have to maintain the distinc-
tion between being a painter and being an artist," said Idris.

Doing my job well was important to me, yet as the years
passed, the chance had grown slimmer that at the end of the
day I would trudge out to Brooklyn and do something for
myself.

"I only think of what I want to do, what interests me. I
think I am a better still photographer than filmmaker but
we want to make films now. It's more fun for us." Irene
swiped at her plate with the white flower. I think she
expected Idris to agree with her or chime in but he was
quiet. She swatted his wrist a few times with the rose and
petals began to drop off between their plates.

"Fun for a while," Hideki slurred.

"This is all very romantic now," said Idris. "You are determined by your famous bosses and their famous friends. I
don't know how you can go there day after day and call
yourselves artists. What about making art? What about
being able to stand alone?"

"Now who's the romantic?" But he had stung me.

Many months had passed, I was afraid it could be a year, since I had worked in my own studio, and before then, not so much. Not for several years. There was no painting under way there. I had vivid memories of other artists discussing how long one could go without lifting a brush, developing an idea, before the need and the desire slipped away, before one simply became deluded, a quitter and a fake.

Irene and I used to drink in a bar on Kent Avenue where everyone who painted or sculpted hung out. People a few years ahead of us had figured out a way to live in New York and have the time and space to make art, which fascinated me. It was a question of finding the right imbalance, was how Irene had put it. At the time I worked as a decorative painter, marbleizing foyers and stenciling nurseries, but only as much as I needed to pay the rent. Otherwise I holed up with my canvases. Irene made 16-millimeter films and worked at a photo lab. When we got stir-crazy we went to the bar. Irene and I spoke contemptuously of some of the other bar denizens who wore painter's clothes and had not made a thing in years, or the ones who hid out in graduate school rather than face the difficulty of earning a living and figuring out how to build a life as an artist. There used to be loads of people like us around, young and old, artists working without much thought for the business side or the academic side (there hardly was an academic side,) people like Meredith Davies. But I did not know them anymore and I felt, thinking of Michael's extravagant Manhattan studio where I painted five days a week, that I was missing out. Not the drinking in the dank

bar, but the sensation that I was in the thick of creating
and that I was alive with it.

I walked to the back of the apartment, raised a window,
and lit a cigarette, feeling flattened out and ordinary, Also
guilty, caught. A man pushed a coffee cart up the street,
alongside the noisy traffic, he was bundled against the cold,
his breath shot out of his mouth in bursts as he pushed. I
wished I could speak to Irene alone. When the man stopped
his coffee cart to rest and glanced up, I waved to him but he
did not see me leaning on the sill. I went back to the table.

"You and Idris need to hire a producer," said Hideki.
"And get married for the tax benefit."

"Why aren't you eating?" Irene asked Idris.

"I have no appetite. It must be all the assumptions you
guys are making." Idris looked at Hideki and me and then
he took Irene's flower and stuffed it into one of the arrangements. "I have a show in February and the Armory Show is
in March." He shook his head. "I'm sorry, but I'm a little
weary." Idris studied the wall of pictures behind me as
though they had just appeared. Two dingy oil paintings of
sailboats on gray seas Irene had bought at a stoop sale in
Brooklyn Heights; an old watercolor I had done of an eagle
perched high above a gray lake; a poster from the 1999
Banff Film Festival where Irene's nineteen-minute film
about an elderly alpinist had screened; a big geometric pattern of multicolored squares Idris and I had cut from sheets
of Color-aid; a rodeo poster from Frontier Days in
Cheyenne, Wyoming, and in the center a large black-and-
white photograph Idris had taken of Irene and me walking

along the water at Coney Island. "I am not going to drift along, growing old and sour. I never wanted to work for anyone, hide behind anyone, and I never wanted to marry a white woman."

I am sure Irene flinched.

"Ouch. You're a monster." Hideki's mouth was full of pork. "I can't believe you said that. How much wine have you had?"

No one spoke. Idris looked completely sober.

I chewed a piece of meat until the air had emptied of Idris's voice; each clatter of the knives and forks made me blink. We had never been delicate with each other, but my throat burned. I could not look at Irene yet.

"What's that sound?" said Hideki. "Do you hear someone in the hallway?"

"It's the landlord's Dobermans," said Irene. "He leaves them here to terrorize me."

"Us," said Idris.

"Who cares about you?" Irene spat the words.

Passionate, wet sniffing came from behind the door and long nails clicked on the wood floor. We were still, listening to the animals. I used to climb up and down the fire escape when the dogs were left in the hallway overnight until Irene discovered they were puppies that loved cheese and buttered toast and to be walked around the block without leashes. Once we brought them over to the handball courts and threw sticks for them in the snow.

Irene gathered two pork bones from the table. "I'm coming, guys."

Idris stared into his wineglass.

Irene stood in the doorway petting the dogs' hungry heads. They whined when she told them to give her a paw and then their heavy bodies collapsed onto the dusty floor and the chomping began.

TWO

SOMEONE BUZZED ME into Philip Cleary's West Side compound. The wet metal staircase smelled of bleach. Black surveillance cameras were mounted in the corner of each landing. I had an idea that touching any surface, the red-painted banister, the robin's-egg blue walls, would set off an alarm. I climbed four or five flights until I reached a door that was propped open with a brick. No sign of any cloying architect or interior designer meddling, thankfully. Infatuation with a man who heeded feng shui principles or hired someone to select throw pillows was out of the question.

"Anyone home?" My question ended in a nervous upward inflection and reminded me of the trepidation with which I still entered my parents' house in Baltimore. Years of being

told to be quiet so my mother could concentrate on her
reading combined with Philip Cleary's cleaning products
and another edifying adolescent experience, a strange
instance of parental encouragement. My father took me,
aged sixteen, to visit the studio of a family friend, a "talented" portraitist who received most of his commissions to
paint cherubic blond children through the Catholic
Church. We got cleaned up, drove over, and found no one
home. The great artist had forgotten his appointment with
us. These memories coursed through me as I fought back
giddiness and double-checked my fly.

I stepped over the threshold into the delicious smell of oil
inks. Opposite, two lithography presses and a rack holding
printing screens were evenly placed along the window wall.
On either side of the door meticulously organized shelves
held jars and bottles of chemicals for making mechanical
prints and a library of manuals and catalogues. I took a few
more steps. A clipping of a photograph of coyotes surround-
ing a buffalo was taped to the wall above a metal flat file,
and beyond it, a white porcelain slop sink and an etching
press. In the north corner two doors leading to built-in
rooms suggested a darkroom for exposing photo plates on a
light table and, perhaps, a room for acid baths to etch steel
or zinc plates. Some of Philip Cleary's earlier paintings
began with screen-printed patterns forming a complex field
for a seated subject.

When I write the word "portrait" in this sketchbook it
sounds static and stodgy, for me it fails to convey the emotions portrayed in art inspired by a person. Or an animal.

Unless I'm talking about someone major like Velázquez or Rubens, or Philip Cleary, who captures profound moments best, he seizes the look or impression that has been missing in the world and gets it in his picture. He can make a feeling live forever in oil paint.

Somewhere on the premises Philip Cleary might be painting and perhaps I could watch him for a minute. But I had to find him first.

I rapped my knuckles on a square table, an island in the center of the room. Beneath the tabletop, which was deeply scored and thoroughly cleaned, there were racks holding thick slabs of limestone and cabinets affixed with small keyed locks. I cleared my throat.

Nothing happened, no one appeared.

I had spent a couple of semesters making lithographs and etchings. I loved the machinery and the chemicals and the slowness of etching images on hulking Bavarian lithography stones and steel plates, but not the way one had to proceed step by particular step or else nothing worked. I had made my parents a four-color print of their old cat Clementine asleep on a dining room chair. I have no idea what became of that one. The paltry few pieces I had made and given away vanished into one black hole or another, as opposed to the work I made in Michael's name was heavily insured, prominently displayed, photographed, and reproduced ad infinitum. I would call this a hang-up.

I stopped looking for surveillance cameras and returned to the shelves of mineral spirits and mineral oil and tins of ink and rolls of paper towels and brown butcher paper. The

spines of a book of Barnett Newman lithographs, an Edition
Schellmann catalogue, and a Tamarind Lithography Workshop catalogue raisonné, 1960–1970, caught my eye from
among the alphabetized shelves. Only a paid assistant kept
a seldom-used studio so clean and well maintained. The
room betrayed very little about how Philip Cleary worked.
When was the last time he printed? Twenty years ago or yesterday? I ran my hand over the surface of a metal desk,
opened the center drawer, and found a black stapler, a new
package of double-A batteries, and a rosewood box. I lifted
the lid, removed a film canister, and spilled a small amount
of pot into my palm. I closed up the drawer and brushed the
pot into the inside pocket of my overcoat.

Back in the silent hallway I climbed another flight of
stairs and pushed open the final door. "Are they there yet?
Ask her if they've arrived yet. It's been over an hour," said
Philip Cleary.

He shouted. He was angry. This I did not anticipate. No
exit plan presented itself. It would be worse to be caught on
the surveillance tape sneaking out than to walk into his
maelstrom. I moved slowly, trying not to feel foiled.

A woman calmly answered. I could not make out her
words but recognized the same smoky Brazilian accent that
had wafted from the studio answering machine, beckoning
me to pick up the mask Philip Cleary had made for
Michael's benefit auction.

"Come on! Did those guys stop for coffee?"

Unsure of what to do, I stopped moving and surveyed the
scene. On either side of the enormous painting room two

unfinished canvases hung on opposite walls, mammoth and red-stained, awash in midmorning light. I made a little clicking sound with my tongue, a reflex, and that was enough to alert Philip to my presence. Somehow he came up behind me. He wore a dazzling gray suit and his hair was slightly wet. Definitely not dressed for work.

"Emma Dial!" He reached for me.

"Hello, Philip." It was the first time I called him by his name and it came out a little too breathy.

"Wait till you see what I made. I can't wait to show you." He slid his hands along my shoulders.

Philip Cleary literally gave me the shivers.

"That's a great print studio you have downstairs." I gestured lamely behind me and felt instantly stupid. I might as well tell him that I stole his drugs.

"You walked up? Why didn't you take the elevator?"

"I didn't see one."

He walked ahead of me, past the new paintings, toward the office where a woman in a brown leotard-catsuit covered with copper-colored zippers stood between two messy desks. She was on the phone and held a notebook and pen and a mug of steaming coffee. I smiled and she half smiled.

"That's Yessenia, my assistant."

He beckoned me to a round table piled with paper and photographs in clear plastic sleeves. A framed photograph of Isabelle's face hung between two windows. Still there was no evidence of pesky design professionals. The décor was ugly-ish and utilitarian in a midtown-waiting-room style.

"Have you seen this catalogue from the Pompidou show?

Michael and I are both in here." Philip Cleary's painting of a sickly-looking young man in a dingy sweater sitting in a green straight-backed chair faced Michael's picture of parents and grandparents on a lonely beach picnicking beneath a threatening sky, three young children running along the edge of the dirty surf. I had put a fine finish on that one.

"What do you think?"

"I like yours. I remember seeing it in your show."

"That's you and me side by side," said Philip.

I stood openmouthed. He could ruin my composure in seconds and I was growing to enjoy it. Yet I craved more control. I wanted to affect him equally. But the painting he attributed to me was not my own, nor would I ever have made anything like it.

"You are supposed to be at the restaurant, like, now," said Yessenia.

Philip ignored her.

"Okay, let me show you this mask. I hope I don't have a heart attack. The damn art movers have vanished with my paintings. It's going to be a good show if they ever turn up again. They wouldn't steal my paintings, would they?"

"If they're smart they would." I smiled at him and it made me blush.

Yessenia was still on hold. She looked as though her patience had been seriously tried.

He laid out the mask on the round table, but before I could get a look he snatched it up again and held it a few inches from his face.

"Do you like it?"

On linen torn to a shape no larger than a human face, he had painted hard, glassy greens and blacks. What was I seeing? Maybe bamboo shoots. Some type of leaves. I tried to apprehend what the colors composed but Philip dropped the mask on the table carelessly and grabbed the sleeve of my coat, helping me take it off.

"Yessenia, take Emma's coat. She has to try on my mask."

"Aren't you late for lunch?"

"I insist." He shoved my coat into Yessenia's arms. Then he stood behind me, bringing the mask down in front of my face. He tied it too tight. "It's black bamboo, eucalyptus, figs, and lavender. Perfect with your silver hair." He led me by the shoulders through the cavernous studio and along a narrow corridor to a bathroom where we stopped before a mirror. I peered through the eye slits at him, smiling behind me. Again I had the sensation of all my desires welling up, as I had on New Year's Eve: the need to feel myself equal to him as an artist, and a force. He made me feel competitive and agitated. My attraction to him was sexual but there was something else mixed in. I had become aware that I was not doing enough with my life. I did not want to pale next to anyone.

Still holding my shoulders, he asked, "What will Michael think?" He made his voice low and quiet. "What do you think?"

"I want it." It was such a peculiar thing for him to make. I could feel his breath on my cheek. "I want it."

The things I wanted grew exponentially in Philip Cleary's presence. I wanted to learn or co-opt or steal this way of his—beyond charisma, good looks, wealth, and success, which I had seen a hundred times before—the embodiment of immense desire in his paintings, even in a stupid mask, and his physical self.

"I'll make something for you. These are desert plants. Have you ever spent time in the desert?"

We were hiding from Yessenia in the bathroom.

"I'm going to miss that charity party, though. I'll be in Miami until I come back next month to hang my show. I work there every winter, since Isabelle was born. Did you know I'm fifty-three years old?"

I watched him in the mirror. The pull chain from the ceiling light grazed the top of his head. His teeth actually gleamed.

"I don't always enjoy the parties, you know. Not like when I was younger, when I was married and especially before I was married. I still have a hard time controlling my appetites for food and alcohol and nicotine. I have no willpower." He pushed his hair, now nearly dry, from his forehead. "That's not true exactly; I have a very specific brand of willpower. You smoke, don't you?"

"Yes." I reached to untie the blindfold.

He moved my hands aside to untie it himself.

"I can smell it on your hair."

Yessenia called out to him and he paused to listen.

"I think she said my paintings made it to the gallery." He stroked the back of my head once, an unconscious touch. "But you swim. When you first went to work for Michael you were an avid swimmer."

"Not so much anymore." I wondered how he knew about my swimming, was it something he remembered hearing a long time ago?

"It's hard to do everything. I swim a little in Miami. Sometimes I run a few miles in the morning, before I go in the studio, but there's never a good time. It's hot, it's dark, it's time for a meal. I'm always hungry. I'm starved right now." He pressed down on my thumbnails with his thumb, first one and then the other.

The bathroom was small and the scent of inevitability was in the air. Why else would he submit us to this strangeness? Standing with Philip Cleary beside an open toilet had to be funny. I was determined not to be the first to leave.

"I miss swimming in the ocean. It's been a long time since I swam outside, even in a pool."

Yessenia yelled his name again.

"I have to go. Will you be at my show?"

Yessenia appeared with my coat before I could answer and led us single file out of the bathroom and through the hall.

"Thanks for coming over," he said, falling behind me. "I'll see you soon, Emma Dial, won't I?"

"I would have liked this to last longer."

"Me too."

Yessenia walked me to the elevator, which was large enough to park a bus in, and handed me the mask in a brown box. The heavy door slid between us and I rode swiftly down.

2

I LEFT A MESSAGE for Michael at the Waldhaus in the morning to tell him I was not going to work for the rest of the week. Maybe longer. Normally he did not care when I worked as long as he could always reach me and the paintings were done by the dates I agreed to. Since he arrived in Switzerland I had been avoiding his calls. So far he had made no mention of the exhibition date being moved forward, so why not let him worry while he was on the slopes?

I read and napped on the living room floor until the late evening and then I ate half of a wheel of Brie. I did not know where Irene was. Idris had probably retreated to his studio full-time; if I was him I would. They wanted privacy, I figured.

Car doors slammed on Elizabeth Street. My neighbors were on their way to dinner. In the three years since I moved in I had grown to hate the apartment. At first I had been intrigued by how different it was from First and First but I never considered the place much. The street was tree-lined, I could afford it, and it was close to work, to Michael. He stopped by easily in the night. Each of the five stories originally had front and rear one-bedrooms but they had been gutted and turned into four "loft-style" apartments, Sheetrocked and painted a thin blue-white. I made semiannual attempts to unpack and settle in. The painting Michael had given me for my thirtieth birthday dominated the living room. I had opened the crate with great anticipation and found a black and green tornado he had painted in Greece when he and Therese took their honeymoon. The picture had been exhibited a few times and reproduced in catalogues, way before my time. Michael's new paintings sold in the neighborhood of a million dollars and even a curiosity like this could fetch half a million dollars on the secondary market. Living with it was a torment because it was a horrible-looking thing, the kind of painting an undergraduate made the day before a critique and then got bombastic about because he was proud to have thought to paint a tornado, a genius macho subject. To add insult to injury it's a ten-square-foot tornado, so anyone who came over mentioned it, reminding me afresh that one day I would sell it and when Michael found out he would be insulted, or at least pretend to be. Recently I had unrolled my red and brown kilim. But the apartment was hopeless, really. Elizabeth Street was an in-between place, transitory, and I felt like a visitor there.

I WENT ONLINE to check my email and read a message from the Modern advertising an upcoming exhibition, *Travelling*, which would include some of Philip Cleary's paintings from Florida. I clicked a link and found reproductions of four paintings: *Hermione Says "Portico," H (Alone for a Change), H Remembers Dover, Hermione and Isabelle,* all from 1985 to 1986, cast in the lavender light of Miami.

One painting of my grandmother's hung above the washing machine in the kitchen, the only painting of hers I have. She did it from a photo my mother took of us standing together in front of her station wagon in the driveway. My grandmother is a sinewy eighty-year-old and I am a skinny teenager. We are barefoot and, along with my mother, about to clean all the windows using the old newspapers stacked on the porch. I remember enjoying the day with both of them. This painting was a weakness for me, usually I hated when people had images of themselves around the house. I hid this one in a corner. I needed the daily sensation of my grandmother looking at me, otherwise I existed less.

Michael had visited Philip Cleary a few winters ago and said it was no wonder he did such good work at his Miami studio because more beautiful women populate Florida than any other state east of the Mississippi. There had been no adequate response for me to make.

I flipped through a book of William Eggleston photographs searching for images of West Texas, or a place that resembled my idea of it (flat, brown, menacing), something that could be a reminder, an idea, a connection to Philip Cleary, something new and undiscovered. I looked for a sign of him, one that only I could decode, in reproductions of paintings by Velázquez, Goya, Manet, Bacon, and Freud, and a catalogue of his work from 1994. When I sensed something close to what Philip Cleary seemed to be when we were alone (the gleam, the speculative desire), I memorized each aspect I could discern—the color or contour or volume, an expression, an arrangement, the light admitted to a picture. The search left me with a cooped-up feeling. I returned to idle dreams of the remote vistas on the Föhn website, which now featured a photograph of Joshua trees and agaves in the Mojave Desert. I wanted a new picture of Philip Cleary in my mind, a vivid picture of him sitting with me in the sand. Someone made a painting called *Camels Crossing* that I tried to pull from the recesses of my memory. I looked at photographs of Titian and Rubens paintings, and then I switched to a Bonnard book and then to Peter Doig's *Daytime Astronomy, Red Boat (Imaginary Boys), Music of the Future, Pelican,* and *Lapeyrouse Wall* and smoked until 4:30 a.m. and then turned off the lamps and went to bed.

In the morning I mixed the pot I stole with tobacco and smoked it while I played two Benny Moré songs over and over, "Pachito E-Che" and "El Cañonero," music from Michael and Gerda's collection. I played the CD on the deck in the kitchen while I made coffee and then put it on the living room stereo with the volume turned all the way up. I sat on the floor drinking espresso and imagined myself in Miami: I meet Philip Cleary in a nightclub where an orchestra plays these songs and we dance. It is 1952. Or when he arrives I am dancing with someone, the club owner, maybe the bandleader. The air is thick with tobacco smoke, Benny Moré's voice and the four trumpets playing together. Or it is 1959 and we have drinks at a table overlooking the stage and I dance with one of the friends, a dead ringer for Che Guevara. Philip Cleary smiles at me; he likes to be out late at night, watching me move in someone else's arms. I started the music over for each new story. I wore headphones so the neighbors would not hear me play the same two songs for hours.

Could I learn to mambo? I wondered as I lay on the couch, a blanket pulled up to my chin. I closed my eyes, trying to imagine the paintings I would work on in my studio—slow and precise marks rendered in loud, high-pitched color, like the trumpets—but I was interrupted by a fantasy of walking outdoors with Philip Cleary, his arm across my lower back, our feet kicking up dust.

I SPENT FOUR DAYS that way: listening to the mambo songs and lying on the couch looking at photographs of Philip's paintings. When it grew dark I lit some candles and found more images of his paintings online. I imagined drawing the mesquite amid the contours of knobby ground; highways and hawks crossing Texas; the sprawling quiet of his studio overlooking the Hudson. My mind wandered the immense distances between what I knew and what I imagined about Philip Cleary.

I kept this sketchbook nearby, ostensibly to draw but in fact to continue assembling notes about my days, such as my impression of the two framed watercolors of roses and oranges that had hung above the light switch in Philip's bathroom. Isabelle's, I decided. Standing so near Philip Cleary, I had smelled his black curls. Salty? Had there been a moment to kiss that I had failed to recognize?

Whatever was next for me would be a new challenge, an experiment that cast aside all the habits of efficiency and cleanliness that I developed painting for Michael. I longed for unruliness but was unsure where to find it, what form it would take, what color it would be. So far it was a faint harmony that played on the back of my eyes and it was inconsistent, when I looked for it, it was gone.

3

I CAUGHT UP TO HIDEKI and Therese walking laps around the Police Building, Therese's preferred track for sorting things out. They wore black leather sneakers and layers of thin, luxurious black fabrics. Therese's freshly blonded hair was covered with a jaunty cap that became her. She was fifty-four years old and had two grown daughters with her second husband, a teacher at the Cooper Union. Therese pushed the pace, Hideki looked wan.

"We're getting ready to go up to Therese's place in the country," said Hideki.

"We've already done eleven laps," she said.

"Therese doesn't know what she wants to do for the Armory Show," said Hideki.

"Don't you have anything lying around the studio?"

"I wish." Therese puffed up her cheeks and exhaled. "We couldn't get away with that."

"She wants to make something new and special, to mark the changing of the seasons."

Hideki assumed a patronizing tone with Therese that came from being close to her, running her life, being in charge of her finances and all the details of her career and her home. He might spend the entire night sitting with her while she worked, giving collectors tours of the studio and talking to them about her work, keeping Frederich at bay, and the next day picking up her dry cleaning and buying a birthday present for her daughter. Not always a rewarding occupation, especially for someone who had paintings of his own to make.

"How're Irene and Idris? Back from the brink?" said Hideki.

"I haven't seen them."

"What an awful night that was."

"Idris was on a mission, I saw it in his eyes. He's jealous of her."

"I thought they were fairly balanced," said Hideki.

"People like to give Irene money."

"Good for her," said Therese. "We're doing forty laps today." Therese stretched her arms over her head.

"You're insane." Hideki had told me on the telephone that Therese was overwhelmed with projects and she went out walking for half of every day instead of getting her work done. "I'm done when we get to twenty. I've got to go pack."

"Quitter," Therese taunted him.

"I have a blister!"

"He's a wimp. Come on." Therese gave Hideki a light push to make room for me between them. "You may work for our nemesis but you can still help us think, can't you?"

"I think my contract with Michael will permit that, as long as I don't come up with anything good."

We continued three abreast, turning left to head west on Broome for the short block before Centre Street. Half a dozen double-parked Town Cars lined the block.

"What's he giving Frederich for the Armory booth?" said Therese.

"A set of four aquatints." I would tell her anything.

Therese worked tirelessly on darkly lyrical paintings in her East Village studio. Her artistic influence had exceeded the narrow bounds of the art world. Various pop stars had paid handsomely for the right to use her work on their CD covers. Usually that only happened to men, but Therese made pictures that interested the larger culture.

"We haven't decided what we want to do yet." Therese said "we," referring to herself and Hideki as a team. Sometimes "we" meant her alone, but when things went badly, "we" meant him.

"We're scared because we heard from our spy that the Guggenheim was not over the moon about the studio visit we had last week," said Hideki, doing his American accent. He was devoted to Therese but in general he was short on empathy.

"You don't paint for the Guggenheim."

"No. Of course not." Therese smiled.

I loved the way Therese triumphed, despite the continuous criticism she received from men in every powerful corner of the art world. Critics were hard on her and accused her of making cold and aloof paintings. If a male artist made the same work I think he would be lauded for his daring and deftness, of course they would probably also be twice as large. Therese and Michael continued to influence each other and no one complained about the remoteness in his work.

"Does anyone actually live here?" The entrance to the Police Building, a Beaux Arts landmark that had been turned into condominiums in the early nineties, was quiet. "I only see delivery people when I pass by. And fat pigeons."

"Maybe all the prisoners are still inside," said Therese.

"Five minutes ago she confessed a desire to project romantic optimism," said Hideki.

"I didn't confess, I stated my strategy with ambivalence, like an authentic solitary artist-hero." Therese shoved him toward the gutter with her hip.

"Just don't actively de-skill your painterly craft. Or employ any de-essentializing moves."

We all laughed. Lifted from the pages of art magazines and exhibition catalogues, we made the lingo sound absurd on our lips.

"Don't you think it would be cool if Therese did a suite of lithographs? She could revisit an old work. A seminal piece like *Sugar Free* would make a great centerpiece for a triptych. *Heart and Lung Sound Sensor, Sugar Free,* and *Control Unit*."

"That's a fantastic threesome. People would be happy to see a print edition."

"But it would feel boring. It's the same as saying, I don't care, or, I'm out of ideas—which happens to be the case for today." Therese puffed her cheeks again.

"That's not true! You haven't done any multiples or prints in a few years. It would welcome younger collectors into your market, the ones who can't afford an original piece," said Hideki.

"I know. I know all that." Therese marched on, her hands on her hips, ignoring him. "It's impossible to keep up with all these shows." She measured her words, her gaze focused on something in the middle distance. A few people walked ahead of us, but the sidewalks were mostly empty. "I've got two big paintings I'm working on. These extra projects drive me nuts. I'm ready to disconnect the phone so no one asks me for anything for a couple of months. You can't say no without seeming miserly."

"What do you think of a triptych?" Hideki turned to me for reinforcement.

"It could be interesting. Are you kicking anything else around?"

"I thought I would make something new. I mean, really new. But maybe a triptych could be fun."

"A departure." I tried to let my mind drift toward an alternative.

"Sure. Whatever. How about an edition of one hundred? Easy money." Hideki rubbed his gloved hands together. This sort of plotting was his forte. Therese would be back in high gear within the hour.

"I want something that will be a good prologue to my show in the fall." Therese took a roll of mints from a pocket somewhere at her waist and offered them to us but we smoked instead. The three of us were quiet along Grand Street before turning back onto Centre Market Place.

"The prints could be sold as a set for fifteen thousand dollars and some sets could be split up. Or a smaller edition, say thirty-five, or fifty, at twenty-five thousand a set. Big bucks," said Hideki.

"You could go as low as twenty-five and really crank up the price. Why not?" I should support Hideki's idea, though he was plainly trying to make his life easier instead of getting Therese to push herself.

"Not impossible," he said, still calculating the numbers.

Therese let out a deep groan.

"Do you have any time to do some work at the studio? Even a few hours a week would really help us out. I'm completely overextended."

I was shocked. The artists who used assistants frequently tried to poach the best people, but Therese made all her own paintings. She did not need me. I was flattered to be asked and curious how it would be to paint with her. Would we work together or would I end up doing everything alone? Maybe working for Therese would be gratifying.

"We're really busy preparing for the show at Frederich's." I had a fleeting image of myself, after Michael discovered that I had painted for Therese and gone berserk, locked in a dungeon. Frederich would deliver bowls of canned soup and oversteeped tea gone cold.

"Think about it. It would be great to have you around. Wouldn't it, Hideki?"

"We'd love it."

He might have told Therese that I would be tempted by the offer and I felt guilty not saying yes.

Hideki called Irene while we waited for Therese to stretch but there was no answer.

"Maybe we could make a triptych from some of the drawings I did this winter." Therese touched her toes and then began moving again with new resolution.

"Now we're in business," said Hideki.

We kept on, quiet again. Hideki and I imitated Therese for one lap, swinging our arms exaggeratedly and taking long, weaving strides.

"Okay, back to work," said Therese at twenty-five laps. "We've got to talk to the printers and see if there's even time to do lithos." She chewed her thumbnail.

"They'll make time for you."

"They better," said Hideki.

He reached behind her and tugged on the tail of my coat. We dropped behind Therese a few paces and watched her speed toward her studio. By the time she was back at her desk she would have narrowed her selection down to three drawings. Hideki would have the printers pick them up and their trip to her house in the Berkshires would only be delayed by four or five hours.

WHEN I CAME IN the bath was running. Michael walked across my living room in his pants, bare-chested, looking for something to read. His face was sunburned around the outline of ski goggles.

"Emma, where is the newspaper?"

"I left it at the studio."

"I haven't set foot in there yet."

He shook three aspirin tablets into his palm and ate them without water.

"Join me for a bath?"

I knelt on the counter to search the upper cabinets for something sweet and discovered a package of fairly ancient chocolate chip cookies that I brought into the bathroom and set on the edge of the tub.

"And you wonder why I don't cook for you." He raised his nose in mock disdain.

"I don't wonder that." I clicked off the overhead light, leaving only the dim light on the mirror. "Did the phone ring? I'm waiting for Irene."

Michael shook his head and dipped underwater for a second. He wiped his eyes with the backs of his hands.

"How was your trip?"

"Did you miss me?"

"Not at all." I kissed him. "I'm worried about Irene. I haven't spoken to her." I stuffed a cookie in my mouth.

"I don't know how you can eat that crap."

I held one to his mouth and he took it, like me, in one bite.

"Aren't you going to join me?" He slapped the surface of the water with his palms.

"Don't splash."

Michael went underwater again.

"She hasn't called. Nothing."

"Stop talking and get in."

I left my clothes in a pile on the floor and stepped into the tub.

"It's too hot."

He ran his hand down my leg.

"No, it's nice. Sit down."

We faced each other and I knocked the cookies in the water.

"Are you trying to ruin my bath?"

I fished the soaked package out and tossed some big crumbs toward the sink.

"I'm worried about Irene."

Michael rubbed his eyes and wiped his nose. He paid nocturnal visits after being gone for a while and I looked forward to them.

"Irene's fine, she's gallivanting." He reached to pull the clip out of my hair. "Get your head wet."

He could not see how I relied on her. I slid down to my shoulders and leaned back.

"Who do you think is the greatest living painter?"

"Besides me?" he said.

"Yes, besides you."

"Phil or Therese. Richter has things pretty well figured out. Phil in the long run, I think."

"No one younger?"

"I don't think so. Maybe there will be a few. There are too many things working against young painters."

"Such as?"

"It's too expensive to live in New York and you have to paint for a long time to get really good at it. Anyone can make a few nice paintings when they're young, but to want to do it for your whole life—and plenty of artists do it for life but don't have the financial success—is riskier. When I moved to New York there was a painting establishment and it was our job, my generation of painters, to push those artists, challenge them, and ultimately dethrone them."

"I'm worried about my future." A hazy memory of assuring my parents that I would go to graduate school and study something normal returned to me but I blocked it out.

Michael gripped my calves under the water.

"You're just tired. Stop thinking about Irene."

4

MICHAEL HUNCHED OVER a new drawing—a nude of a woman resting her hip against an undrawn object—when I arrived at eleven. From the doorway I could see that it was something he bought in Europe. He was back in his daily work attire: jeans, sneakers, a gray sweatshirt, and he looked great, albeit disgruntled. All the pictures and advertisements and invitations were cleared from his desk and dumped on the floor behind his chair. He would forget about what was in them, lose things, fail to show up where he was expected, to call people who were waiting to hear from him. I recognized his effort to move on without looking back. When his obligations caught up with him he would blame Frederich, then me, then Gerda.

He did not look up from the nude. My role in this routine was to pretend I was not disturbing him even though he waited to be disturbed. My parents played this stupid game. The cause could be anything from jet lag to loneliness to rage—that I did not work enough while he was away, the success of another painter's show, the creation of a great style by an artist in a previous century, memories of Therese, alcohol-induced self-doubt from the night before, the drawing I had not admired. Eventually he would say. I left my coat on the back of the desk chair and wrote the date in my book, February 6. Michael had doodled some numbers in the margins. I hated when he did that; seeing our handwriting on the same page pissed me off.

I flipped through the stack of exhibition invitations beside the telephone. Most of them were addressed to Michael with a few duplicates for me. I examined the paintings that were reproduced on the cards. Artists still made plenty of the minimal, depthless paintings I had once tried to do, the flat, airless, lonely interiors, poetic-looking figures in three-quarter profile. Nothing on the cards appealed to me, but it was difficult to tell from little two-dimensional reproductions. Irene had told me about a convention of quantum physicists in Mumbai discussing the twelfth dimension. "I had no idea we were so far beyond five," she had said.

Still no talking. The nude, it occurred to me, was by Balthus, an early one, from the teens or twenties, and was meant to be an affront to my artistic judgment, a presentiment of what was to come.

I checked out a *Munsell Book of Color* that Michael left beneath the mail. He was fascinated by logical color systems and he liked the little coded paint chips and the idea of analyzing color in terms of Munsell's three-dimensional color space: hue, value, and chroma. But he had no aptitude for it. The notations he had made next to a swatch of canvas with paint marks made no sense. I doubted he understood the way it worked.

"Aren't you going to say hello to me?" he said.

"You look like you're concentrating." I went to the window.

"I didn't know you weren't going to work while I was away."

"I was here yesterday, I'm here now." I turned toward the painting studio. It would speed things up if he thought I might leave before he got to be sufficiently shitty to me.

"I made some lists before you got here. I have the order of the paintings worked out."

"That's great." And unnecessary. *Stand of Evergreens* was nearly done, so there were only three to finish, *Substitution, Phu Quoc,* and *Interstices.*

I fingered the edge of the page he had written on. He had doodled his own name a few times, some numbers, probably profits from sales, a series of odd shapes that resembled ham bones, or islands. He could not control his handwriting, it sunk below the line and pushed above. He did not form letters consistently, mixed capitals with lowercase, cursive with print. Irene did it too. A simple lack of physical control. This was not a characteristic that would normally bother me but I detested it this morning.

"I spoke to Frederich and the show is going to be in May. The second week of May, the eighth."

"Why?

"You know why."

I appreciated him admitting that he had a pathological need to beat Therese out of the gate.

"How's it going to happen?"

"We're going to work double-time."

Double time ensured I would not see the inside of my studio until spring. I opened the desk drawer with the toe of my sneaker and tapped the spines of all the diaries I had kept, the record of all my labor, dozens of paintings, and the lists of words and events, of colors, of materials and dimensions, of names and dates and cities, all in relation to Michael's career, like the one beside the phone on his desk that he was working and reworking until the figures satisfied him:

> 10 paintings = 10 million
> fabrication
> overhead including materials to May
> personal to May
> profit
> overall cost
> overall sales
> overall profit

"What's in it for me?"

"I'll give you a bonus." No longer angry. He had to get a new commitment out of me and he did not anticipate any difficulty. "You know I always think of you, Emma."

"What's the bonus? I'm curious what you have in mind."
I had always been easy. Now I wanted more.

"I hadn't thought of it yet."

"Think about it now. Before I go to work."

He continued to benefit from my work long after I finished a painting. But once I put his check in the bank, it was over for me.

"Emma, it's a lot to accomplish, but I know you can do it."

"Okay. But let's talk about my bonus."

Michael thought sighing gained him sympathy but it hardened my will. Gerda was upstairs planning for their annual trip to the Caribbean.

"One of the paintings. *Sea-shadow*."

"No way." He looked at me as though I were a pig.

"Which one?"

"Emma, don't be greedy."

He had worked out all the possibilities of this conversation before I arrived, certain that he would get what he wanted without having to part with anything. He would not even offer me the stupid Balthus drawing.

"Emma, didn't we have a good time last night? You're so tough."

"Pick one for me and put it in writing."

"I have to talk to Frederich, find out what's spoken for. I don't know if he's been talking to people."

"He hasn't placed anything." We both knew Frederich hated pre-sale, he thought it signaled desperation. "Pre-sale is a strategy for people who are negotiating from a position of weakness."

"Not so. Lots of people do it to good effect."

"Immature artists whose careers will tank after a season or two."

"Frederich says it doesn't work that way any longer. Not for me."

"Whatever. Which picture are you going to give me?"

He still ran the possibilities; estimating the least expensive way to pacify me. He might try to add one to the series but not include it in the show.

"I've been working on some new collages."

"Choose from these ten."

I could feel him caving in. He had to.

"Fine." He paused. *"Interstices."*

I restrained myself. This was a coup.

"Great. Write it down."

Interstices is a giant architectural painting that straddles two centuries. Nestled below a series of imposing rocky hills, a strange city—roads and buildings but no sign of people, animals, or cars—on a beautiful empty river. Maybe the Danube. One could only guess.

"That's a good one for you, Emma," he said, really livid now. "You should be happy."

5

ANOTHER FIVE DAYS passed before I made a stealth visit to
First and First to retrieve my giant Philip Cleary mono-
graph. Irene and Idris were still away and I wanted my book
and also to avoid either of them making fun of me for own-
ing it, which they would if they knew.

In one of the essays Philip mentioned all the different
places he had worked on paintings over the years, Odessa,
London, New York, Los Angeles, Berlin, Miami. The apartments and houses where he lived and painted, studios in
garages, places where he lived for a short time and how he
seldom drew when he traveled. He took photographs to
help him remember.

The same lamp was lit beside the couch, the one Irene left

on when they stayed out all night or left town. The red light on the message machine blinked, the computer was cold, the coffee machine was cold, the ceiling fan was off. All the cut flowers had wilted and lost their petals. The damp wood smell and creaky floor made me homesick.

I found the book tucked under the chair where I had left it. I peeked into my old room, now Irene's office, but more of a closet or museum: papers and clothes had been dumped on the floor, the shelves crammed with china teapots and porcelain espresso cups Irene collected, boxes of her photographs stacked on milk crates full of letters and cards. On the wall over the desk, left of the window and drowned in shadow, three of my old drawings were tacked in a row: Irene in the front seat of my parents' car with Clementine the cat beside her; Idris watching television on the couch; Irene on the street with a Nikon around her neck and pigeons at her feet. The human subject is primary and everything else is incidental.

A tiny reproduction of an etching that led to a painting called *Mark in the Desert* showed a man standing in an open, light-filled doorway. On the same page was a quote of Philip Cleary saying that where he made a picture was important to him though he did not try to get the place into the painting anymore. "I've been around the block a few times now and I can release a lot of narrative elements. Timelessness is what I'm after. Nailing the location works against that objective."

The landlord shuffled along the sidewalk carrying a stack of letters. I checked that the door locked behind me.

"Oh no, you can't be living here again. Everybody is moving out before the spring."

"How are you, Mr. Fontana? Have you seen Irene?"

"No." He walked away.

Irene had not said they had to leave.

6

MICHAEL'S SISTER SUSAN, a trial lawyer in St. Paul, was an ardent Smith College alum. She lorded over an administrative assistant and two associates who managed her good works, charities, and pro bono cases, and kept her in touch with former classmates and law professors, as well as Smith grads with whom her four years in Northampton, 1969–73, did not coincide, via email, telephone, and a monthly personal newsletter that detailed the highs and lows of being a partner in a major Minnesota firm that counted among its clients a large manufacturer of snowmobiles and the Catholic Church. Michael and I were included in Susan's extensive mailing list and indulged in a hearty laugh at her expense when we read aloud from articles titled

"Changing the Face and Place of Due Diligence" and "Passport to Success."

Once a year Susan hit Michael up for a print edition or drawing to donate to one of her worthy and well-considered causes. She left detailed messages on the studio answering machine, knowing that other people would hear them, asking rhetorical questions to the effect of: "Why don't you do something for someone else for a change?"

Susan's freshman-year roommate, Rachel Cannon, was founder and president of a group of tristate-area businesswomen known as the AIDS Action Alliance that produced an annual event to raise money for women living with HIV and AIDS. The organization had enormous support from the Smith community and its proceeds were spent on housing and health care. Rachel figured prominently in Susan's monthly newsletter, two- and three-paragraph updates about the Alliance and Rachel's to-ing and fro-ing on Wall Street were frequent. It was not uncommon for these articles to be accompanied by a photograph of the two women together at a conference or luncheon, perhaps joined by other Smith professionals, to the degree that I speculated aloud that Susan and Rachel were still sometimes lovers. Michael laughed uncomfortably. It "tickled" him to "admit" that he found lesbianism "hot" and could not associate his "very own sister" with "such an activity." Also, Michael had slept with Rachel on a visit to the Smith campus in the spring of 1970, and still waxed sentimental about that trip and the green campus in the early morning, fresh from Rachel's twin bed. "All that wet hair," he said, remembering the women hurrying to classes, "many of them virgins."

Last autumn, in a one-two punch, Susan and Rachel convinced Michael to chair a benefit for the Alliance in the Waldorf-Astoria ballroom. They arrived at the studio wearing nearly identical gabardine suits and armed with a laptop with files of projected costs and photographs of mostly non-white women suffering from poverty and terminal illness. I hunched over my desk ordering canvas while Michael told them he would be honored to invite nine artists of a stature on a par with his own to create masks the Alliance's members and supporters could bid on in a live auction at the hotel, and that he would work with his friends and colleagues to sell as many high-priced tickets as was humanly possible.

"It'll be a cinch to fill that ballroom," were his exact words.

Susan and Rachel beamed at each other.

Michael and I did not discuss the benefit. He put in calls to Yoko Ono and David Hockney and to modeling agencies to find women who would wear the masks. It was a bottomless favor.

THE DAY BEFORE the event, Michael informed me by Post-it note that I would be "delegated the fun job" of making a mask. Over a slice of pesto pizza I painted William Westmoreland on a piece of balsa wood that Patrice Awofeso cut.

"It's too in-your-face for the Murray Hill crowd," said Michael.

Murray Hill was his damning catchall for people who had no aesthetic interest or what he considered poor taste. They bought Monet mugs in museum gift shops.

"Emma, I have to be beyond reproach for these people." He returned to the ham and cheese croissant and cappuccino at his desk and continued to seethe over *Interstices*.

Patrice cut more balsa wood.

"I saw you in Brooklyn." He turned the saw off and handed me the cut piece and then picked up another square to cut out the shape I had drawn on the surface.

"A few weeks ago. Where were you?"

"Driving by. You were walking by yourself. You working there or living there?"

"I bought a big cake at Fortunato Brothers."

"You know, I moved to South Eleventh Street. I am sharing a place with my sister. She came from Lagos in the summer. Come see my studio next time you are around."

I enjoyed a spectacular dalliance with Patrice years ago. He was married then but he was not married anymore, which he reminded me of from time to time.

"What's your sister doing in New York?"

"She's going to Baruch, she will be an engineer. One day."

"Does she like it here?"

"Sure, she likes it. Come and meet my sister. I'll give you my telephone number."

Patrice was irresistibly suave and gallant, a sublime lover and a meticulous designer of wooden objects, the statues he built in his studio, boxes and crates he built for artists. I was curious what a sister of his could be like.

"I have your number."

Michael approached. Patrice winked at me and turned on the band saw, I picked up a brush and painted a middle-aged Vietnamese man's face in black and white, vaguely based on a grainy image of Võ Nguyên Giáp, which Michael decided was perfect and signed while it was still wet. Patrice built a tiny crate for it and, when it was dry, attached a wide piece of elastic to the back with a toxic silicone he carried in his tool bag. He placed it alongside Philip Cleary's brushy black bamboo blindfold that had been stored on a shelf above Michael's desk.

The participating artists' addresses had not been released to the AIDS Action Alliance in order to protect them from a flood of humanitarian mail from Susan and her cohorts, all ruthless mailing-list plunderers. Patrice had been entrusted with the safe delivery of the remaining eight masks to Michael's studio where Rachel's administrative assistant picked them up without a trace of curiosity about what they were or who had created them. After the administrative assistant took all the masks downstairs to her station wagon using Tony's hand truck, Michael came over to where we were working.

"Do you guys think she's a lesbian?"

"I don't know." I tried not to laugh.

Patrice did not voice an opinion. We exchanged a dead-pan look and he winked again.

VINCENT BENCIVENGA, a newly prominent young art dealer in a purple velvet jacket, was leaving the Waldorf as I arrived. Known for matching up new collectors with emerging artists, I took it as a bad sign that he had no coterie. We had not met before, though thanks to Hideki, I knew that he dated Lucy Trost, a Londoner whose photographs he showed in his Chelsea gallery. Lucy had cut her mask from an iris print of herself.

"Look at the size of that flower arrangement." Behind him towered an overflowing vase. "I can't tell if it's real or not."

"I can't parse this crowd," said Vincent. "I'm going to skip the dinner and try to make it back for the auction. Maybe pick up something good. I don't know who is going to bid on these masks."

"I hope I don't end up having to buying one. Or more than one."

"I'll let you go." Vincent buttoned his top button. He had no intention of returning.

My eyes adjusted to the dimly lit ballroom, which was heated like a nursing home. I downed a glass of red wine at a temporary bar set up in a remote corner. Five hundred or more people in full-length gowns and tuxedos milled around like sheep but the room was so immense that it looked as though the party had not begun. It was an eerily sedate group. I was underdressed in a turtleneck Irene had brought me from Paris and black Föhn trousers. I carried my coat over my arm. It was far too warm.

At the edge of the dance floor Michael introduced Lucy Trost to Susan, Rachel, and another woman. Lucy was wearing leather pants and a very tight purple T-shirt. Just behind them, Gerda and a friend held their cigarettes under the table, the smoke billowed up to the chandeliers. Michael's eyes darted back and forth between his sister, who was laying out how the evening would proceed, and Lucy's breasts.

Tinny recorded music with a whiny, breathy vocalist of indeterminate gender played softly. The dry air carried the scent of cleaning fluids and salmon. Guests crossed the room by walking around the empty dance floor except for an occasional woman in a strapless dress who would glide across alone, smiling and squinting beneath the glimmering chandeliers.

I could not tell who these people were. They were not artists or people related to the business of art. If someone told me they were all from out of town, perhaps lawyers from the Twin Cities, I would have believed it. My attire garnered disapproving looks from bejeweled women returning from the restroom. I wondered about the masks, whether the guests would know who the artists were, and whether any of the artists, other than Lucy, who was about my age and just beginning to be invited to participate in events like this, had decided to attend. I kept seeing Philip Cleary in my peripheral vision, even though he had been in Miami for over a month. I wanted to talk to him about his studio and learn why he worked in Florida, perhaps he would tell me something I needed to know. The heat was brutal and I regretted not wearing something presentable under my sweater.

"There you are." Yessenia came up behind me. "I need

your help. A few of the masks got damaged in transit and need some touch-up." She wore another catsuit, gray with a sheen.

"I think Philip's is a little scratched. Would you look at it?" Yessenia stepped toward the exit. "They're in a room at the end of the corridor. Grab a drink and meet me, okay?"

"I'll be right there."

"I've got all the materials." She patted the gold leather bag that hung from her shoulder.

I needed water but there were deep lines at every bar. Say hello to Michael, reassure him that I would take care of his mask and any of the others that were damaged, drink water, find Yessenia. I wanted to get my hands on Philip Cleary's mask. I hoped it needed plenty of work and I would have the chance to do a perfect job restoring it.

A couple swayed on the dance floor. He kissed her ear and ran his hand across her bony back. She tucked her head against his. More strangers from Murray Hill.

Susan and Rachel's voices were elevated to a troubleshooting pitch. They pointed at various employees who nodded emphatically. Michael tried to follow along and bobbed his knees to emphasize Susan's directions. Clearly a bad time to interrupt. There would be water where Yessenia was, or nearby, likely without a wait. Yessenia might have a bottle of spring water in her gold bag. More fur coats entered the ballroom. Just outside the doors, the corridor was quieter and brighter but not cooler. Which way had Yessenia gone? A pair of women in minks approached, scrutinizing me, I was sure. They parted to pass on either side of another flower arrangement the size of a VW Bug, and then paired again, making no eye contact when they were about to pass by. Why did they look at me and then pretend I did not exist? Lesbians, Michael would pronounce. The flowers should be wilting because it was an airless place. Plastic flowers? Silk flowers? When had I last seen a window? I thought of sick buildings, tiny interior rooms, lavender light, labyrinthine hotels. Then I fainted.

A WOMAN SAT on her haunches looking down at me. Behind her was a wooden desk with brass pulls. In a row above the desk hung a calendar covered with notations made in pen, an engraved plaque, and an overlit color snapshot of two little girls in matching red sweaters holding seashells on a beach, seagulls tiptoeing on the sand behind them, hunting for snacks. The unconscious tableaux people created fascinated me. Calendar-plaque-family photograph was probably a common one, but it had its beauty. The door at my right was shut and something rustled behind it. I imagined rabbits, white and fat, and had to keep from smiling. I lay on the carpeted floor.

The woman had dark eyes and olive skin and a lightly lined forehead. Her thick black hair was loose.

"How do you feel?" she said.

I looked away, thinking of what to say. Perhaps Philip Cleary paced up and down the hall outside the door, waiting for me to emerge.

"Fine." I should sit up. "Thirsty."

She handed me a bottle of water.

"Do you faint?"

"Excuse me?" I drank. "No. I have to work. It won't take
me long." It took a few moments to correctly apprehend the
question. "Oh no. I'm not a fainter." I got to my feet.

Once Irene had fainted at a Mekons show during the sup-
porting act's acoustic set. She said it happened because she
smoked a joint and then drank two pints of beer on an
empty stomach. She would find it funny that I fainted at the
Waldorf-Astoria.

The woman rose to her feet too.

"How do you feel now?

"I feel good." I could not have been unconscious for long.
People do not faint for long when there is nothing medically
wrong with them. "Where are we?"

"You fell just outside the door." The woman smiled but
her voice remained serious. She glanced around the room. "I
don't know whose office this is." She shrugged; it did not
matter to her.

"Thanks for looking out for me. I don't really know what
to say except I appreciate your help."

I patted the front of my clothes and touched the lacquer
clip that held my hair up. It was hard to act normal in a
stuffy room with a stranger.

"Did you drive here? How will you get home?" She held
her purse, a black suede box with a wooden handle, like a
miniature doctor's bag.

"I'm here for the AIDS Alliance benefit that my boss is
doing. I have to help him." I worried that I would not be
able to catch up with Yessenia, and that the auction would

be held up because I disappeared, for who knows how long. Michael would use me as a scapegoat if the auction prices were below par; he overreacted to anything I did that was unexpected. I needed to hurry but I was afraid to be rude to this severe woman.

"Go home. Who is your boss? I will tell him that you are unwell and had to leave. You must rest."

"Are you here for the benefit?"

"No. I'm staying at the hotel." She opened the door. "Let me walk you out."

What a wonderful idea—leaving—simple and luxurious, and as long as I focused on this new person, who had no understanding of my responsibilities, it made sense. We slowly walked down the hall.

"Are you on vacation?"

"I'm working. Do you live far?"

"Downtown. Not too far."

The immense lobby had emptied of hotel guests and their visitors.

"Do you have money for a taxi?" She caught the attention of one of the porters and mouthed the word "taxi."

"Yes, I do." It would be inappropriate to ask her to elaborate on her visit to New York, but I was extremely curious. "Thank you again. I think I will go home."

"Get some sleep and be well."

We said goodbye. I fought off the notion that Susan and Rachel would think ill of me. Normally I was reliable. I lingered beneath the art deco grille above the entrance, watching the traffic on Park Avenue. I remembered when I had only heard of the Waldorf-Astoria, somehow I had learned its name when I was a child, long before I had an image of the place.

A man in a fur-collared overcoat emerged from a black car and strode past me, ignoring the porters who greeted him and held the door open. I had not thought of the hotel in a long time and wondered for whom did it represent some pinnacle or other, who stayed there now? That had been my first visit.

AT MY DESK I READ a boring essay on Philip Cleary's work written by a curator at the Tate. "Yet rather than fall help-lessly under the influence of Rubens' virtuosity, Cleary reconfigures existing forms and imagery to assert his own artistic identity." The writer hemmed and hawed for quite a few pages without being able to come out and say that Philip Cleary was a master of composition and design. There was not a single sentence about his colors.

I shoved the keyboard aside to make room for my sketch-book. In an interview from 1987, Philip Cleary discussed the period of 1979–82, when he and Hermione spent the academic year in Los Angeles. She taught drawing to archi-tecture students at UCLA and he painted in a single-car garage that served as his studio. He said he tried to incorpo-rate elements of the landscape and climate in his work at the time—proximity to the ocean, trails in Elysian Park and Topanga Canyon, coyotes, lizards, ants, dehydration, kid-nappings, mud slides, and fire—despite how little time he spent outdoors and how infrequently his paintings were

located in nature. "I didn't go anywhere," he told the inter-
viewer. "My experience of the city and its inhabitants was
culled from the *L.A. Times,* which I bought every morning
at the Mayfair around the corner from where I lived."

I drew rapidly: a figure falling through the air, a pale limb
tensed and waiting in the dark, hidden men disguised as
their prey, the full concentration of listening to the night.
Each drawing filled a small page. My single uncorrected line
reminded me of Philip Cleary's transcribed voice, plain and
certain, but with a measure of flamboyance, showiness. The
strange figures were foreigners in my imagination, someone
else's pictures. They frustrated my hand. They were false
starts and I angrily scratched them all out and gave up at my
desk for the night.

I SLID FROM BENEATH the gray quilt and hurried out of the bedroom, hungry, thirsty, restless. Blue lights of a police car flickered across Michael's tornado painting. The phone rang three times before I reached the receiver on the kitchen counter.

"What are you doing?" said Irene.

I looked down at a car accident on the corner of Elizabeth and Spring where, in addition to the police car, an ambulance had parked diagonally at the northwest curb. I curled into the couch and fiddled with the elastic at the leg of my underwear.

"Waiting until it's time to be awake and worrying about

the future." My voice sounded calm and alert considering it was quarter to four and I had not heard from Irene in weeks.

"Why?"

"How come I never go anywhere? You're always the one who calls from a different time zone."

When we were in his bathroom Philip Cleary had punctuated a sentence by pressing on my thumbnails, first one and then the other.

"My life is spinning out of control."

"No it's not," said Irene. "You have a nice life, it runs so smoothly."

"I know that's not a compliment from you."

"What are you talking about? What happened?"

"Everyone I know is out of town. I don't know if I have any good art ideas. And, as if that weren't bad enough, I'm getting old."

"We're not old. Sorry to disappear. I meant to call."

"It's okay."

We had been friends since the day we arrived at The School of Visual Arts in 1992, roommates from the time we were sophomores until Idris crowded me out and I found Elizabeth Street. Leaving had to be okay, I just never got used to it.

"Where are you?"

"Standing in the middle of the street, Guerrero, where I'm staying." Irene called away from the receiver in a honeyed tone, "I'm not talking to you, I'm on the phone."

"Who's there?" Not Idris.

"Cinematographer. I'm using his phone. He's a doll but he grinds his teeth."

"Michael grinds his teeth. It's a disgusting sound."

"Are they his real teeth?"

"Shut up. How's it going with the film? With you?"

"I think I'm going to cut these guys loose and head out on my own," Irene whispered. "It's so great here. The people, the sun, the jungle. One day you have to come down with me."

"We should do that." I whispered too. I pictured myself behind the wheel of a VW Beetle, grinding the gears as I merged onto an empty highway.

"What have you been up to?"

"Painting, forty hours a week, at least." I ripped a piece of dry, callused skin from the back of my heel. I felt sorry not to have something interesting to tell her. When we lived together First and First was never dark, never sleeping. We cooked up late night meals, projects got under way, and visitors dropped in and crashed for days. We had not kept regular hours and everything was makeshift. Now Idris was gone but it was too late for me to move back.

I went to my computer. Today the Föhn site pictured a street of houses in Colombo. A man in a sarong and sandals walked away from the camera and an inset photograph showed a crimson sitting room with a flamboyant mural of Buddhas and elephants which reminded me of all the wall paintings I had designed for art lovers who fancied their West Village lofts in Tangiers or Paris. Camels and slate roofs. "I don't have time to paint.

Michael moved the date of his show to May so I have to work double-time."

"Really." Irene lit a cigarette with a match and inhaled. She blew the smoke into the receiver, underlining her lack of interest in my work troubles. "I see a dead horse across the street."

"It's been a long time since I've seen anything dead." I recalled a flattened retriever on Eighth Avenue and Nineteenth Street. "Was it killed or did it die on its own?"

"I don't know. It was there when I got up this morning."

"Can you smell it?"

"I think so. Maybe I'm imagining it."

I heard Irene shuffling indoors and her body settling in a chair. Her gold rings clanked when she flipped the pages of a book.

"Now what are you doing?"

"Reading a Spanish dictionary, conjugating some useful verbs in the present tense. My Spanish is getting pretty good."

"Should you call someone about the horse? Someone in Chiapas?"

We both laughed.

"Was it old?"

"How would I know? Maybe I'll go take a picture of it for you."

I pulled on the clothes I had left in the bathroom, splashed warm water on my face, and gathered my hair back with a barrette. I would go to Michael's early and, if I was there alone, take a midmorning nap. The ambulance drove off sounding its siren. I took a swig of orange juice from a container in the fridge, locked the door behind me, and ran down to the street.

"YOU STOOD ME UP!" Michael called across the room. "I was in black tie and you didn't even get to see how fantastic I looked."

I had a surge of affection for him. He caught me off guard when he joked about something that once had dire consequences.

"I did go but a weird thing happened." I laughed, relieved that I would not spend the morning making excuses for myself. "I fainted."

His laughter sputtered and ended in a confused smile. "I can't tell if you're joking, Emma. What happened to you?"

"I fainted in the hallway outside the ballroom."

"Fainted! What did the doctor say?"

"I don't have much time left."

"Emma, you're fucking with me. Be serious."

"I saw you in the ballroom. I drank a glass of wine and then keeled over before I could meet Yessenia."

"Who's Yessenia? What did the doctor say?"

"I didn't see a doctor."

"We should go to the emergency room right now!" Ready to blow the whole thing out of proportion.

"I just got overheated. All the excitement."

"Ha! I was braced for a fiasco but it turned out fine. But please, please, please remind me to say no to them next year."

"You always say yes before I can get to you. Who bought your mask? Anyone we know?"

"Some Wall Street guy, a friend of Susan's. It could have been worse. She did her best. But those people don't care about art. You can see it in their eyes. The dull, empty stares. Of course they want masks. They live and breathe functionality."

"What about Philip Cleary's?"

"Eleven thousand. Just a little more than mine. I think the woman who bought it was a friend of his." He waved his hand dismissively and started dialing the telephone.

"I'm going to work."

I left him to make a series of phone calls, beginning with Gerda, to relay my misadventures and solicit medical anecdotes about migraine, eating disorders, and lung disease which he passed on to me when he demanded, two hours later, that I join him for coffee. He even went to the deli himself. I could tell by the smile on his face that he wanted something in return.

"You have to relax." He lit a match.

"I don't want to relax." I took the cigarette he handed me. "*Substitution* is not relaxing." I had been tangling with the painting's dense network of thin vertical and horizontal lines.

"I like this girl who tends bar on Bleecker Street."

"Uh-huh." This happened so often I was inured to his infatuations. Mostly.

She had written her number on a matchbook.

"Emma, let's just go have one cocktail after work."

"It's not even eleven o'clock in the morning. Besides, I may be admitted to the hospital. I'm sick, remember?"

"You're the picture of health." Michael plugged his laptop in and searched for fresh news about himself online. "Maybe there are photos from the Waldorf." He needed to know that he had more mentions on the Web than his peers.

"Nothing new." He snuffed. "I've seen all this before."

He found a photo of himself on a paparazzi website, standing beside Therese Oller at a party in Berlin.

"Have you been to this bar before? I think it's new." He tossed the matchbook onto my desk.

A loud noise from out front startled me; metal on metal. A car crash. Michael did not blink.

"I like this picture of me," he said. Therese wore a scarlet gown, her shoulder and hip were cropped out.

"I think it opened last year." I threw the matches back and he caught them.

At the window I saw the drivers, both men, emerge from their crunched cars.

"Ouch. T-bone."

"Did I tell you this girl is a painter?"

"Nope. Are you going to see her work?"

"Sure I will. Why not? She's like a flower. She's a lily." Michael continued to admire himself on screen.

"Does she like Balthus?"

"What?"

"Nothing." I walked back to the painting studio feeling sulky and jealous.

WE ATE CHEESEBURGERS for lunch and drank fountain sodas with crushed ice, our feet propped on our desks. Michael stayed extra chummy to get me in the mood for the bar. Cocktails with Michael at the end of the workday meant marathon beer-drinking. In an effort to disguise his return to the bartender-painter in less than twenty-four hours, he suggested we recruit Irene.

"*Substitution* is halfway there and we could all celebrate."

"I hate getting drunk on beer."

"We haven't been out together for so long, Emma. Don't be a drag."

Alcohol made him self-conscious, though he was usually able to shake it off in a day. He never drank at his own opening parties and Gerda got mad when he came home stumbling, especially when he wanted to fuck drunk. I, on the other hand, enjoyed it, particularly if I had been drinking with him.

"I'm going to some galleries. I'll come get you in a few hours."

"I could be dead by then, remember?"

"Contractually, you can't die until after my show."

HE ORDERED ME off the scaffolding at five sharp. I practically had to run to keep up with him when he marched up Christie Street.

"You go in first and act like you've been here before. I want it to seem like it was your idea to come." He opened the door and pushed me inside. "Play along, Emma."

"Yeah, right. My idea."

Even when we were up to something stupid his cheer was irresistible, especially when he was in one of his conquistador moods. No one was behind the bar. We took stools in front of the window and Michael scanned the empty room.

"It's pretty early."

"I know." He quickly became unself-conscious and wanted to have a good time. "Hello? Hello, hello, hello! I'm here!" he called out. "She's going to be surprised I'm back, right?"

"One way or another, you will surprise her." I felt in my pocket for money. "Do you have cash? I'm going to get cigarettes."

"Get some chips too. Sour cream and onion." He gave me twenty dollars.

On my way back from the deli on Bowery I walked behind the woman with the shillelagh whom I first saw at Michael's exhibition in 2001. Even though we did not look alike, I thought of her as my doppelgänger, someone whose lead I followed and who knew what she was doing at times when I felt lost. I tailed her down to Houston Street, where she continued south and I looped around Elizabeth to Bleecker.

Michael had two pints and two whiskies in front of him. A skinny girl in a tank top pushed the buttons of the cash register.

"That's her."

The girl behind the bar had straight hair to her shoulders, green eyes, and a narrow body, all like me. A lot like me.

"How old do you think?"

"Thirty."

"Younger! She's much younger than you! You have to introduce yourself. No, no. I'll introduce you. Shake hands so she has to say her name. I'm not sure I have it right: Alicia, Alysia, Elisa. I don't remember."

"What did you do with your matchbook?"

"I gave it to you, Emma. Is Irene coming?"

"She's out of town."

"Liar." Michael slapped the side of my leg. "Who can cheer you up besides me?" He squeezed my knee and let his hand rest on the inside of my thigh.

"Don't." He felt good and he knew it.

"Where is she?"

"Mexico."

He rubbed my hip.

"Get off."

"I don't know why you're at sea. You have a good life. And now you own one of my original oil paintings."

Michael refused service from the second bartender who arrived after we had already had a few rounds. He had enough drinks to spoil his remote chances with the painter-bartender, who was quickly distracted by various younger men.

"She's popular."

Michael waved an arm to get her attention.

"Not as popular as me."

He bought more whiskies, which she charged him for, thereby killing his interest in her. He told me about moving

to the city in the late sixties and sleeping on top of a scaffold on Astor Place for a few spring nights. We shared a
romantic view of old New York.

"I miss those days," he said. "When we struggled, Therese
and Phil and me. We didn't even have chairs in our apartment. We ate our meals on the floor. Phil would come over
and make linguine with clam sauce and then we'd sit around
drawing. We had nothing to lose. No one cared what we
did. It was the best way to work."

"I remember that feeling. Part of it is being really young
and not knowing history and the art world."

"We made our own scene and Frederich wanted to be
part of it and he brought the money people and museum
people to us. My theory has always been that you have to
keep up the hard, lonely work for five years after you leave
school, and if you can stick with the art, while all your
friends are buying houses and all that, getting married, having kids and second mortgages and careers with a title, associate manager of conference calls, then you might be a lifer.
Hard not to choose the easy identity."

"Easy fucking peasy." Tipsy.

"I'll tell you who surprised me. Philip Cleary. I thought
he'd be the first to quit. No desperate need to succeed, no
family to escape or overcome. His parents adore him and
they are oil-rich. He had a lot to lose. Phil could have skated
through life but he moved to New York and has kept on.
Beautiful paintings. They move me to tears, practically."

I pictured tears falling down Michael's face, caught in the
lines around his eyes and mouth.

"Your Irene is like that. She pretends she's not up to anything. Miss Innocent. But she keeps going, pushing it, getting better."

He might know Irene used his darkroom. He looked soused.

"What about me? Where do I fit into your theory?" I sipped my whiskey as though I was without a care.

"The problem with you is you don't have the balls to let nature complete the picture. You're a shrinking violet. You can't hear the fucking tweet-tweet-tweet, the little helpless animal screaming that nature doesn't care about humans. Even the larger mammals, the big dogs, the horses, put their needs first. Like me, I'm fucking Leo Tolstoy fighting Napoleon in the snow. You make the picture happen, Emma. Some people get lucky, the rest of us have to come up with the goods and say 'me first.' "

"You're shouting."

"Of course I am, Emma. I'm telling you the truth, Emma. As your lover and boss and as an artist."

"Stop shouting and stop saying my name like that."

"Like what, Emma?" He finished his whiskey. "Don't be upset. Emma, Emma, Emma. I can't hear myself anymore. Let's get out of here. I'm sick of looking at that girl."

WE LAY DOWN in the mess of quilts and sheets and Michael rolled onto the bed beside me, running his hand from my knee to my waist, kissing my neck. I turned to him, flung my leg over his, brushed his chilly foot with my chilly foot.

"I like all this." His hand lay flat on my stomach. "I like that I get to have this."

I did not think of Philip Cleary exactly, but of sex with strangers or someone I did not know well, someone who would not act as though I belonged to him. I lifted Michael's T-shirt over his head and concentrated on not resisting his touch. He would go home to Gerda soon and they would load the car and drive upstate for a little get-away. I traced his spine with my fingertip when he sat up to unbutton his jeans. I remember thinking: I should really go out to Brooklyn and visit my studio.

8

I PUNCHED IN my alarm code and flipped the light switches. The air smelled cold and dead. A mouse rotted somewhere but I was not going to look because it might be a rat. I unlocked the painting room, turned the radio to the news channel Tony listened to in the elevator, dropped my coat on the floor, and drank my coffee on a wooden stool in front of the painting. Everything looked like a problem, beginning with the color separation of two shades of brown; I had prepared them wrong, a careless mistake. I hardly remembered mixing them. There was not enough of a difference between the hues and now a four-square-inch passage in the upper right of *Substitution* was murky and did not read. I was seized with fear that someone might know. I snatched a section of the *Times* off the radiator and held it in my lap. The article on the cover of the Friday arts section was about a woman who had once been Michael's assistant for about two weeks before he fired her. He called her "the Feminist." She had made mistakes all the time and was unremorseful, she did not dote on him, and most unforgivably, she did not put his work before her own. Now the Feminist had a serious career and Michael Kimmelman, the chief art critic for the *Times,* spent multiple afternoons over the course of a week in her spacious studio in Brooklyn watching her work. She was also married and had two young sons.

I had to get out from under these paintings.

Instead of facing the color problem, which worsened the longer I sat in front of it, I drank one of Michael's diet sodas and reread the article about the Feminist. I ought to telephone the gallery to confirm Frederich's visit later in the morning but I was stricken with envy. The Feminist's studio was in Sunset Park near Bay Ridge, not a trendy neighborhood with expensive loft buildings like Williamsburg or Dumbo. Six photographs accompanied the article: two color pictures on the front page showed a shoebox-shaped room with windows at the deep end and a skylight, a long table in the middle of the floor, finished paintings in racks and hanging on the wall behind her painting chair. The Feminist sat before a wall of newly gessoed and sanded canvases.

I buzzed Tony to bring the elevator up to the second floor. The sound of his radio rose from the basement, announcing targets in Iraq being hit every day. We rode down to the street and Tony exhaled smoke disdainfully when the president was quoted. He held the elevator on the ground floor while I ran to the deli where I bought soda and cigarettes and two coffees. Tony waited for his—light with half half-and-half and half milk—smoking on the sidewalk.

A solution for the colors began to take form but I reread the continuation of the Kimmelman article instead, showing four black-and-white photos of a painting in progress. The Feminist had two full pages of the *Times,* two museum shows up until spring. I had three enormous canvases to finish. I ignored *Substitution* until noon, then remixed the colors. I sighed repeatedly, as though I were working at some new altitude. The photographs on the front page of the Kimmelman article showed salsa jars of green and pink acrylic paints on a messy card table. Provided I worked slowly I could avoid the panicky feeling in my chest that paralyzed me when faced with the truth that even though I could paint anything, my mind was not leading me to paintings, was not thinking in terms of paintings. What was I afraid of? That maybe my mother was right? That I was not a real artist? I looked at the transparency of Michael's maquette through the loupe. A new assistant called from Frederich's to set up a late afternoon appointment with a Houston collector who visited every year. Last winter he brought his new art advisor with him, a rangy man in a red sports coat who spoke in an adenoidal voice, calling me Emmie.

I tossed my empty soda can towards the garbage bin and

remixed three shades of brown. Mud colors, shit colors, tobacco colors. I made a test on a swatch of canvas, chose my round brush, and hopped up to my perch. My hand sailed across the canvas, marking the rolling curves.

Michael called from the Adirondacks at four.

"Did you run to the phone? You sound out of breath."

"I didn't run. How's the hiking? I mean the diving. I mean the service."

In the background Gerda hurried him in Dutch.

"I want you to send me some pictures of *Substitution* so I can see how it's going."

"Sure. Call me back when you're alone."

"We have to hustle, Emma. Email me some photos so I can give you notes," said Michael.

"Are there wolves in the Adirondacks?"

"Yes, and they have long skinny legs, like you. I almost ran one over this morning."

I knelt under the warm lights, repairing the intricate brown maze, the edges moving out of focus into slashes of pure paint.

9

SOON AFTER DARK on Saturday night Irene strolled down Spring Street from the Bowery and jaywalked through the Elizabeth Street intersection, exhaling a gust of cigarette smoke. Over jeans and a black sweater she wore a three-quarter-length white mink coat. She pressed the buzzer, then stepped back to the curb and looked up at my living room windows. I watched her through the glass. Every passerby noticed her waiting; her black hair fell to the middle of her back, the coat glowed under the streetlight. I closed the Royal Society for the Protection of Birds website and raised the window, but before I could stick my head outside she called up to me.

"Let me in."

AFTER SHOOTING FOR three weeks Irene had decided the fifty-thousand-dollar budget was not going to cover the cost of the production. Then the cinematographer got into a fight with the boom operator, a local volunteer. Both men walked off the set. The cinematographer took off in one of the rental cars and got busted smoking a joint in the park.

"He got cocky with the police. It took me two days to find him in jail and then bail him out." Her face was tanned and luminous. "So good to be home."

I would wait for her to bring up Idris.

She said she did not care about the film, she already knew of two documentaries about Chiapas and she had an idea for a screenplay, a caper film with a romantic subplot.

"I could sell this one to Hollywood."

Irene had never mentioned Hollywood, ever.

"Where's the crew now?"

She looked embarrassed and brushed at the arm of the coat. Even her fingers were suntanned.

"Don't ask me anything else yet. I have to get my story straight."

"I won't hold you to anything."

She took a handful of wooden spoons and a spatula from a ceramic crock and laid them out in a row on the butcher block and then covered the arrangement with a tea towel. She had visited me at Elizabeth Street so seldom; it was funny to see her there, touching everyday objects as though they were new. She might be changed now, without Idris, and looked for signs of a new Irene.

"I drove from San Cristóbal to Mexico City over three days."

Last night she was in Puebla, drinking beer at a café with the guitar player in a band she heard perform a set of cover songs in English.

"He did 'My Sharona'!"

She smiled lasciviously to make me laugh. In the early morning she returned the rental car and got listed to fly standby on all the flights to New York. The man at the gate bumped her up to first class and she slept the entire way home.

"So the guys are down there still."

"As far as I know. I don't want to think about them anymore."

"What did you do all afternoon?"

"I had to get out of the apartment so I went shopping," said Irene.

"Did you buy anything?"

She still wore the coat.

"I walked up and down Madison looking for a shop I'd seen before I left town. The window display had changed. Eventually I found it. Now there's a mannequin dressed like Geraldine Chaplin in *Doctor Zhivago*."

"It looks warm."

"I'm used to the tropics. I had to buy it. It was on sale, too."

"You practically made money."

"Exactly. I knew you would understand."

"Is there anything left of the budget?"

"Enough for a couple of months. I want to do something else now. Don't you?"

"You bet."

Snow fell on my face and caught in my eyelashes. I jammed my bare hands into my coat pockets and felt a matchbook and an eraser. In a few hours I would go home and look at Philip Cleary's paintings, but for now I wanted to cook up plans with Irene.

My downstairs neighbors got out of a cab on the corner looking dour. She was pregnant and had recently quit her job administrating a private fund that gave grants to independent filmmakers; he directed television commercials. I called them the Peppers because I frequently saw them carry cases of Dr Pepper soda upstairs and blue recycling bags filled with the empty cans out to the garbage.

"Look how miserable they are," said Irene under her breath.

"Something happened while you were away."

"You're mumbling," said Irene.

Before I could speak, Dr. Pepper said, "What a gorgeous coat." His voice was far too enthusiastic and Mrs. Pepper put a hand on her big stomach and winced. Irene could start fights with her mink.

"Some packages came for you today." I walked backward and tripped in the gutter, nearly falling on my ass. Of course they would notice the boxes in the foyer; the Peppers were avid online shoppers. "See you." I turned to cross without looking at the traffic. "They give me the creeps. Don't put the whammy on him, he's about to have a kid."

Irene jogged a few steps to get in pace with me.

"Not my fault," she said. "They were already in a fight."

"I don't know how you do it." But I did know. I had witnessed Irene effortlessly captivate men and women from every corner of the tristate area, and beyond, for well over a decade and had learned to inhabit the invisibility her spectacular appearance afforded me. "It's a gift, I guess. Do you have cigarettes? I forgot mine."

"I got hooked on these cheap filterless ones. Delicados."

She stroked the front of her coat and folded her arms across her chest. The white fur made her hair look blacker, her eyes browner. Jennifer used to say she felt ugly when she was with Irene. She could leave her house feeling attractive and when she saw Irene she wanted to go home, take a shower, and change her clothes. Or go home and stay inside. Jennifer could not tell when Irene felt bad, as she did tonight, hiding under her new mink. Her film had been a disaster, another one, and she had come home alone to a cold, empty apartment.

We bent our heads against the wind. It was difficult to hear without raising our voices so we stopped speaking before we crossed Houston Street, saving everything until we could sit down and be warm. At the end of First Street Irene's dark windows topped the corner building. Neither of us mentioned Idris's absence.

REMIZ WAS FULL and three couples were waiting at the bar to be seated. I told Stuart we were not in a hurry but he seated us at the next open table.

"Can I hang this for you downstairs?" He helped Irene out of the mink.

"I prefer to keep it close." She hugged the coat to her chest.

"Right then. I'll be back, ladies."

"Has he slept with all of the women who work here, or none of them?" said Irene.

"I've often wondered. He has a penetrating look that I find nauseating."

Stuart brought martinis and told us the specials.

"I wasn't listening," said Irene when he left us to decide. "I'm distracted. I think I recognize everyone but it's just because I am so excited to be back."

She spread a napkin on her lap and rested her elbows on the table. Her face became expressionless and inscrutable. When I looked at her closely, I saw that she had been crying. She had probably cried from Mexico City to the Yucatán and back again. I would be miserable too if I had lost Idris and then sabotaged the first project I undertook without him.

"Have you ever seen *The Wages of Fear*?"

"Not all the way through." Michael and I had fallen asleep in my bed before arriving at the oil field.

"Let's rent it. I've got a taste for Yves Montand."

Neither of us was hungry but we ordered what Stuart recommended: lolla rossa with aged chèvre, yellow beets, blood oranges, and poached Blue Island oysters to start; New Zealand snapper sautéed with red wine and marrow for Irene; loin of lamb with green olives, cumin, and cilantro for me.

"I've got a Lebanese Cabernet especially for you two," said Stuart.

"I've had tacos every day for a month."

"I've been living on macaroni and cheese from a box."

Tables of angular brunette women wearing pale silk blouses and diamond stud earrings flanked us. I pegged them all as gallery assistants and entry-level museum curators. Between bites they turned their pale pinched faces to study Irene.

"So what happened while I was away?" Irene sipped her drink.

"I did a strange thing. Not that strange, really. But it reminded me of you."

"You quit your job?" Irene liked to guess.

"No."

Irene cast her eyes along the bar; she had a graceful way of absorbing the glances she commanded without showing off or seeming coy.

"Don't tell me. I'm thinking."

I was curious what Irene thought I could get up to without her.

"Hint?"

Irene shook her head no and absently tapped the toe of her boot against the table leg.

"Not your parents. Money, maybe. Did you blow a bunch

of money?" She turned in her chair to pet the mink on the shoulder.

We were especially dissimilar in this way: I was frugal and ruthlessly discarded keepsakes. Irene was compulsively frivolous, a spendthrift, who kept every handwritten note, ticket stub, and champagne cork. She could while away hours arranging mementos and souvenirs into tableaux on any flat surface.

"You're having an additional affair with someone you shouldn't?" Irene tipped her glass to her lips. "I'm drinking this much too fast." She pushed the glass away from her and then pulled it back again and finished it in a gulp.

The quiet in that vast painting room haunted me, when I did not know where Philip Cleary was or how he would act. I tried to recall his face and voice but it was the empty sound of the studio and the sticky red canvases that grew in my mind.

"You stole something."

"I stole pot from Philip Cleary's studio." Saying his name aloud felt like diving into cold water.

"That was easy."

We agreed that I had given her too much information to start.

"What the hell were you doing at Philip Cleary's?"

The gallery assistants to Irene's left turned to her fully. They had been discussing some very explicit Lee Friedlander nudes. "They're really weird. I don't know if we would be able to ship them for an exhibition," one of them said.

Irene met their glances.

"Hello," she said, startling them. She pointed to the chocolate-caramel hazelnut-crusted tart they were sharing. "I want one of those." She turned back to me. "Philip Cleary must have an awesome place."

"A cross between a hacienda and a minimum-security prison." I was thrilled to talk about him. The gallery assistants listened to every word.

"Perfect place for a little innocent nosing around."

"I ended up making a beeline for his stash."

"I thought only potheads could do that. Then what happened?" Impatient. "Did you get busted?"

"He showed me a catalogue from a show that's up in Cologne now."

"Uh-huh." Irene twirled the ends of her hair.

Aware that Irene construed my anecdote as a prelude to sex, I pressed on.

"A painting he did of a frail, tubercular-looking guy with a sunken chest and hollow cheeks. Stellar job on the skin and eyes." I drank. "I mean, the whole picture is completely amazing. On the opposite page is Michael's painting of a family on this ugly industrial beach."

"I don't get it."

"Get what? You saw the one I made: these people are eating and playing, oblivious to their toxic surroundings, and you have to think: What foolishness."

"What did Philip Cleary say and then what did you say and then what did he do?"

I could not choose my words carefully enough.

"He said that's our work in the same book. Me and him."

I grabbed a piece of lamb with my fingers and jammed it in my mouth. "He's pretty complimentary about the stuff I've made for Michael."

Irene did not respond, she watched me.

"It's not like that." But I felt as though I had been caught at something. I looked around the restaurant to check that no one was in earshot. Stuart was at the bar helping a new server with drink orders. Sitting across from Irene, who remained dubious of my laissez-faire attachment to Michael, I saw it was an obvious mistake to go careening down the path of longing for Philip Cleary, who was, by some estimates, the biggest fish of all.

"So what happened next?"

"I picked up a thing he made for a charity auction and then I left and went back to work."

"What did he make?"

"A mask." It sounded idiotic.

"So the strange thing that happened while I was away is that for no apparent reason, or no reason that is apparent to you, you stole drugs from one of the most celebrated living artists and then he showed you pictures you both made that someone else had paired up and he told you how great you are, but only in relation to how great he is. But there was no actual kissing."

"I guess it's not that strange." I had wanted to talk about Philip Cleary more but I had set up the whole story wrong, it came out too fast and too neutral, and now I was too self-conscious to be openly enthralled.

"It's too soon to tell." She fiddled with her watch, Idris's old Timex. "Is he married?"

"Divorced."

"Kids?"

"Everyone has kids."

"Funny how that happened. Let's hear it: How many and how old?"

"One daughter. She's twenty. I wonder what it's like to be that good. He's so sure of himself."

"He should be: he's being pursued by Michael Freiburg's right hand—you know they must be competitive with each other—and he already lives in a state of total success. He should be feeling pretty fine. Does he know about you and Michael?"

"I don't know. I'd say no."

When the gallery assistants left a pair of middle-aged men took their table and discussed the pros and cons of sleeper sofas.

"Do you think Philip Cleary has ulterior motives? Don't be defensive. I just wonder." The idea of Philip Cleary excited Irene.

"He has no reason to lie to me."

"Ha. People always have reasons to lie. Let's go drink champagne at my place. I'm sad about my film. I wasted all that money."

"You're all cried out, aren't you?"

"I think so. It's just us now, baby bird."

THREE

1

THE CIGARETTE SMOKERS stood packed together on the sidewalk in front of Susanna Mackie's Gallery on West Twenty-fourth. The approach of Irene in her mink registered from half a block away.

Most of the faces outside were familiar from other openings and parties. I sensed people recognizing me too and that made me bold. I waved to a couple of Hideki's friends, So and Yuko, both painters, who were at the center of an all-Japanese satellite forming beside a fire hydrant.

"Here." Irene offered me a cigarette from her open pack.

The crowd streamed in and out of the gallery.

"I forgot to bring a camera," said Irene.

Helicopters crossed the Hudson, their rotors menacingly

loud. Despite sharing a couple of innuendo-laden exchanges, I was braced for Philip Cleary to be indifferent, unfriendly, or blasé. An opening was not the place to look forward to intimate communication. People would talk business, eavesdrop, and overinterpret every observable detail, especially Philip Cleary's. The helicopters hovered over the water.

"It is impossible to breathe in there!" A woman in a velvet dress unbuttoned to the end of her sternum stepped onto the sidewalk. She pranced on reckless high heels, holding everyone's attention except the Japanese as she cast her eyes about. A man with long sideburns and a white shirt open to the middle of his chest lingered in the doorway, preparing to make a dramatic exit. He was a video artist from Los Angeles. A few years earlier I saw him outside a gallery on Fifteenth Street where he showed two videos of avalanches in Andorra. He had berated another man for mistreating his car: "Only an ass drives all the way from Cerro Gordo with the parking brake on." He touched the woman on the bare skin above her breasts and dove into a tan Chevy Caprice that idled at the curb. He left the door open. She scrambled into the car and slammed the door.

THE GALLERY WAS MOBBED. Only the edges of the canvases were visible above the crowd. Frederich Hecht spoke to a couple of collectors from Santa Monica who had once watched me paint while they sat on the floor eating tuna salad sandwiches and asked me where I grew up, what my parents' professions were, whether I had siblings. They thought they were being friendly and democratic but I found their questions silly and it was humiliating to talk about myself in front of Michael and especially Frederich.

We all scanned the room for people we knew. Hordes of young art professionals with advanced degrees in curatorial studies and arts administration swiveled their heads looking for the stars: Michael and Philip's peers, the ones who got successful thirty years ago, the big dealers, collectors, and curators, and a whole subset of photogenic art lovers: film directors, actors, musicians, and their model girlfriends. One museum director kept his hand proprietarily on Therese Oller's naked shoulder. Anyone who was not famous was someone's assistant.

I lost Irene. A man in a leopard-print suit explained the process of making crème fraîche to Michael and Gerda, refrigerating it and bringing it to room temperature over a twenty-four hour period. I pushed through the bodies searching for Philip Cleary and met Hideki and Shiro in the center of the room. They were posing with their friend Maya, a performance artist who worked at the Studio Museum, while a girl in a short leather jacket snapped photos of them.

"We're not going to the after-party," said Hideki. "Come for dinner at the Japanese barbecue place on Ninth Street."

Shiro made a disappointed face because he wanted to have drinks with Philip Cleary.

"Sometimes it's better to be missing from a good party," said Hideki. "The Modern reserved two of the paintings and the rest were sold before the opening. I don't know if it's true."

"I can't see them in this crowd. Are they any good?"

"Same old fake grandiosity. He should get rid of the assistants who paint for him."

"He doesn't use assistants."

"Then he should hire some."

When I turned from Hideki, Philip Cleary was staring me down. His daughter Isabelle and another young woman stood at his sides. Except for a few black curls that fell across his tanned forehead, his hair was combed back and he wore a lumpy gray suit and tie that lent him an old-fashioned air, like a painter from the 1950s. That was probably why he had chosen it.

"Are you going over to say hello to him?" said Hideki.

"Nope. I think he's going to come to me."

I wanted everyone in the room to forget about Philip Cleary so I could have him all to myself.

"Let's see if he can make it over without being waylaid." Hideki rejoined Shiro and Maya, leaving me alone. "Good luck."

A pack of women, including three who had broken from the Japanese satellite outside, milled around Philip Cleary. He did not engage another person. Isabelle and her friend's laughter and conversation continued until they were no longer speaking to him. He began to cross the room and it seemed that no one noticed, he was invisible, even though he was the source of all the energy at the gallery. Then he was in front of me, the side of his shoe touching mine.

"When will you come stay with me in Florida?"

When I glanced down at my feet I felt his breath on my forehead. I could not gather a coherent thought.

"I am dying to see you in a . . ." He frowned. "Um. What are those things called?" He shook his head, waiting for a word to come to mind. "Those things women wear at the beach." He brushed his hands together toward my hips as though gathering fabric.

"A sarong?"

"Maybe. But that's not the word I was thinking of."

"Pareo."

"Yes! Yes, I want that." He placed his index finger firmly on my collarbone and then lifted it away. "What's the difference?"

"Polynesian and Malaysian, I think. I'm not completely certain." I had never worn either.

"Mmm." He pressed his lips together and returned his finger to my collarbone, pushing his luck, considering the proximity of Isabelle, Michael, Frederich Hecht, everyone who had remembered to bring a camera. We had another second or two of this semiprivacy before someone noticed us or came too close. "Not that I don't like what you're wearing tonight," he said. "You should come down and work with me. Think of the paintings you could make in Florida, Emma Dial. It's a crime not to come."

"Hey, Phil, you have to meet Gerda's cousin from Brussels," said Michael.

His face muscles twitched from pretending to ignore me. He wanted to be photographed with Philip Cleary and recount conversations he had had with de Kooning back in the day. Without fail he trotted out the de Kooning anecdotes at big openings. He took Philip Cleary's arm and led him away from me.

TWO YEARS AFTER I started to work for Michael, I brought Irene to the opening of the first exhibition of paintings I made for him: four 11-by-25 foot canvases of gnarled winter trees. The images were taken from photos and sketches Michael's brother made in West Germany, where he was posted in the late 1950s, before he went to Vietnam.

I gave the gallery Irene's name so an invitation to the initial viewing could be sent to her. In anticipation of the occasion we spent an afternoon going through the racks at our favorite secondhand stores looking for the men's suit trousers we wore with our linty sweaters. Irene found nearly matching pairs at the Salvation Army on Eighth Avenue. We feasted on cheeseburgers and strawberry milkshakes at Joe Junior's coffee shop. For days everything was a celebration.

On the night of the show we drank neat whiskey at First Street and walked in a cold rain to Frederich's gallery. Flushed faces crowded the room. Michael, surrounded by fans, posed before one of the canvases, shaking hands and having his picture taken by friends and journalists. Flashes sputtered when Philip Cleary and Michael embraced. Irene and I observed from the front of the room, beside the windows overlooking the wet street, watching people stream out of the elevator.

"I can't believe you did all this painting," said Irene. Then she found a guy she knew and went down to the street to smoke a joint with him.

Michael introduced me to his dealers and collectors. With each handshake I felt I was joining the real art world. People made inane remarks about my silver hair, how Michael must work me too hard. Everyone raved about the show. I felt those people knew things about art that I needed to know.

Frederich Hecht told a couple of men that all four of the paintings had been placed, which was not true. It was my first glimpse of how he controlled who collected Michael's work. Those men did not have a collection Frederich considered useful for Michael's market.

The woman with the shillelagh separated from the thick crowd and made room for herself in front of my favorite painting, a forest outside Hannover charged with an eerie atmosphere of viciousness and lassitude, gracefully masked by Michael's stylistic restraint. I would have preferred less restraint, or much more. Michael's London dealer had called it a "million-dollar painting" and bought it for $200,000 for his own collection before the show opened, before it was even varnished. The woman examined the painting for several minutes, ignoring the people nearby talking about their own shows and where they were going for drinks later. It impressed me how at ease she looked when I felt so out of place. The excitement other people were caught in was unavailable to me. The woman eventually turned to me, lifted her shillelagh off the ground, a nod or a wave, and then rejoined the crowd.

THEN IRENE STOOD in front of one of Philip Cleary's paintings with a boy.

"This is Bart from Rotterdam." She was amused with herself. "He paints."

"That's great."

We made our way outside.

In the dark Bart looked too young. When we passed under a streetlight I could see that he was at least old enough to buy his own cigarettes.

"I'm still studying but I'm going to drop out," said Bart. "It's bullshit."

"He's going to SVA. We went there a million years ago," she told him.

Bart beamed at her. He was tall and broad-shouldered and had flawless skin and full wet lips, which he did not shut all the way. Another remarkable feature was his hairdo: the fair, silky locks had been shaved into a combination mohawk/mullet, a skillful gradation of sticky hair which was about six inches at its longest, a tall stripe down the center of his head, ending at the nape of his smooth neck. He wore tight jeans and oxblood Doc Martens and various chunks of metal dangled from his leather jacket, zippers and chains and buttons celebrating bands from thirty years ago. Bart did not have much to say for himself right off the bat. He walked in silence, dragging his boots and smoking cigarettes.

"Crawling with critics," said Irene.

"Every last one of them." I was still reeling from my exchange with Philip Cleary.

"Fuck that shit," said Bart.

"Indeed, sweetie." Always a good sport, Irene laughed at whatever Bart could manage.

No sooner had we stepped off the elevator into Mark and Mary Bertram's loft on Twenty-sixth Street than Philip Cleary sailed past us, surrounded by a fresh group of terrific-looking women. He made a funny face at me, raising his hands to the side of his head and wriggling his fingers as he dropped his jaw and flashed his eyelids. I had no clue how to react.

Two of his paintings hung behind the sprawling sectional. In one a heavyset man in a jacket and tie sits in the corner of a long sofa beside a woman in a navy dress, they fiddle with their hands anxiously. The other picture is an elderly mother standing behind her daughter in their dining room. There is flowered wallpaper and the women wear frowsy flowered dresses. Behind them is an arrangement of framed photographs, cut flowers, and a pale blue china tea set on a mahogany sideboard.

Bart looked at these pictures for a long time and his face grew sullen. An older couple on the threshold of the room marveled at his hair. When Irene returned holding three glasses of red wine he kissed her on the mouth and grumbled that the people in the paintings looked like his relatives, the ones he left Rotterdam to escape. He gracefully settled their drinks on the coffee table and apologized for not fetching them himself. He helped Irene out of the mink and then kissed her again. His practiced manners were entrancing.

Mark Bertram pecked my cheek.

"You look like a million bucks," he practically shouted. Michael called him Mr. Loud. He was a real estate developer who punctuated his sentences with a booming laugh. "How are you tonight?"

A man in a white shirt approached with a platter of tiny meatballs stuck with toothpicks. He offered the hors d'oeuvres to us and Mark Bertram nestled four of them in a cocktail napkin.

"Don't you want something to eat?" he hollered.

Bart removed his own jacket to reveal a fairly stunning torso in a George Jones T-shirt. I tried not to be transfixed. I told Mark Bertram it was a wonderful party, that they had a lovely home, and that I had had a fine afternoon when he and Mary stopped by with coffee and pastries to visit with Michael and see *Spring Field with Police,* a painting they aimed to purchase.

Irene and Bart would not be able to remain on the couch for long. Irene was wearing a moth-eaten Föhn V-neck sweater of mine, without a bra, and Bart was beside himself. If I wanted them to stay they needed to be relocated to a less cozy place.

Gerda and her cousin from Brussels appeared from behind a walnut screen. Word of Bart had traveled.

"He looks just like my nephew," said Gerda. "Marie's boy."

"Yes, like Sebastiaan," said her cousin. "Cute!"

I strolled to the kitchen in search of another drink. Isabelle leaned against the fridge with her plump arm draped over Michael's shoulder. Not wanting to be introduced to Philip's daughter by my boss, I turned on my heel before he noticed me.

I hoped to find people to talk to whom Philip Cleary would approach. In the right company I could get another turn with him. A bar had been set up in a study off the dining area, where Yessenia nodded to Susanna Mackie. They both looked exhausted.

Yessenia called out to me and Susanna tried to place me.

"She's Michael Freiburg's studio assistant," said Yessenia.

Then Susanna explained that she was in the throes of renovating her apartment on the Upper East Side and had foolishly decided to stay in the apartment while the improvements were being made but staying there had quickly become impossible: too noisy, too dirty, too slow.

"My cat is miserable, too, and has taken to shitting on my bed whenever I go out."

"I think she should take the cat to live at the gallery," said Yessenia.

"What are you doing to your place?"

"A new kitchen and repairs to the floor in the living room and a new bathroom with tiny Italian marble tiles in a glorious shade of gold."

"Nice."

I sensed Philip's approach. This time a woman in her stocking feet and carrying a bottle of tequila led him from one of the bedrooms across the dining room. He let go of her hand and made the clown face at me again, twinkling his fingers beside his red cheeks for what felt like an eternity.

"Philip," said Susanna wearily.

"Who is that?" I could not help but wonder aloud.

"Who knows," said Yessenia.

I had to leave before Philip could make that face again. I joined Irene on the couch and we reclined until we were nearly horizontal.

"Bart's peeing," said Irene. "I want to make a documentary about an art patron. One of the younger ones, like that patent lawyer who collects Hideki's paintings."

"Hideki says he's dull as ditchwater. I'm going to head out." I sat up, looking for Philip.

"Shall we share a taxi?"

"You guys go on your own."

In the hallway a throng of teenagers, the Bertrams' kids and their friends, hugged the walls and passed a joint around. I loved the smell of marijuana in cold air. It reminded me of when I came to New York and people smoked on the streets all the time, or perhaps I just noticed it more then.

2

I DREW *PHU QUOC* on a 108-by-84-inch canvas. The image was an aerial view of a river delta. Michael had found a satellite photograph taken from an altitude of over five hundred miles. On the computer he changed the palette from the infrared wavelengths measured by the satellite's sensors to a spare selection of blues and browns, whites, and two sumptuous reds. He also recropped it. In 1966, Michael's brother was killed on this island south of the Mekong Delta.

Michael telephoned from upstairs right away; somehow he knew exactly what I was doing.

"How's my pretty little island?"

"Populated by flying squirrels."

"Emma, Tigers."

"Sloth monkeys."

"Why do you come up with these strange animals?"

"I can't help it. It's an old habit, exacerbated by the Internet."

"How's the drawing? Have you started painting yet?"

"Good. Nope."

"No? I might change the colors so don't start painting."

I could get into a rhythm where I forgot about the people who fueled my labor—Michael and Frederich Hecht, the Breslauers. Beginning a new picture made me confident, my doubt or affirmation was not required.

Then he called to see how the painting was going.

"Come down and speak to me in person."

"I'm with Gerda."

"I'm batching colors now."

When I had been working for long hours and the studio was quiet and the work went steadily, making and solving problems, adjusting mediums and seeing the maquettes clearly, not being expected anywhere else, it could be a pleasure.

He called me once more, when he knew I would be gaining momentum.

"I don't know if I want to do that painting at all. It's too upsetting."

I kept working. Then it was quiet except for the pigeons and the cars. Every concern receded. When I caught myself considering an adjustment to the reds—zapping some of the orange out—that signaled the end of the workday. Pretending I had free rein meant it was time to get out.

PEARL PAINT on Canal and Broadway brimmed with art students buying supplies for a new project. I spent twenty minutes in front of a rack of brushes, slipping protective covers off the sable hairs and snapping them against my wrist. A young clerk with a pierced face asked if I needed help locating materials.

"No." I glared at him.

He shot down another aisle.

The kids near me were in the same painting class. They read brush numbers off a syllabus and searched the shelves. I watched them go back and forth between different displays of hair and synthetic bristles, comparing prices, complaining about the expense, picking up the brushes carefully and then putting them back in the wrong compartments. I selected one large round brush after another, dropping the plastic covers on the floor and flicking the hairs to loosen the protective glue. The students were planning the paintings they had to make for their studio classes. One girl said she was going to make a copy of Seurat's *Bathers at Asniè res*. Building light from color. I wondered if Meredith Davies remembered me and if I would ever see her again. I wanted to choose something for myself, not another sketchbook, not an expensive tool to charge on Michael's account. The serious Seurat girl paid at the counter. I jammed another brush back into the rack, rattling the lacquered wood handles. I pushed past the kids on the stairs and out to the street, empty-handed.

3

PARALYZED ON THE SOUTHEAST corner of Broadway and West Houston, I struggled to decide which direction would yield the best bacon, egg, and cheese sandwich on a roll. It was nine-thirty on Saturday morning and I was on my way to see Philip Cleary's paintings, alone. If I arrived at the gallery at ten sharp, hardly anyone would be out yet. Perhaps I would have a chance to speak to Susanna Mackie, or someone else who had heard from Philip Cleary since he returned to Florida. According to my computer, it rained in Miami and it would rain for days. Maybe Philip Cleary read a newspaper and drank coffee in his studio, the rain pouring down the windowpanes. Föhn's website pictured three zebras, two lying down asleep, the third eating leaves off a young tree.

Someone called out to me when I settled on heading north and the light to cross Houston was mine. Hearing my full name shouted by an unfamiliar voice disoriented me at first. The man looked like a stranger. I focused on his face, ordinary in every way, his skin, eyes, lips all pale and washed out, muddy, chubby features; an orange and black knit cap with some straight sandy hair sticking out. He wore a navy down coat with jeans and sneakers and carried a brown leather satchel, slung across his chest, from which the *Post* stuck out.

"Emma! It's Chris Cagnasola. From school. I haven't seen you since junior year!"

"Holy shit, Chris."

We embraced, a more intimate gesture than our acquaintance warranted, but so much time had passed.

"I can't believe it," said Chris Cagnasola. "I'm surprised I recognized you."

He examined my hair. I could no longer explain in a convincing way that there was nothing wrong with me. My brown hair had been gone for more than ten years and talking about it now felt like more of an intrusion than when it first happened. Irene and I had watched my brown hair turn lighter every day. She once suggested that I see a physician, even a psychiatrist. I insisted I was my usual self except that I was not painting anymore. I only painted for someone else. But I was no longer as gloomy as my hair made me appear.

"How have you been? Have you been in the city all this time?"

I remembered that Chris Cagnasola had transferred to Tisch.

"Yes, I have. You too?" he said.

"The whole time."

My curiosity grew as hazy recollections of teenage Chris Cagnasola returned to me: he had been a star early in our freshman year, adept with oils and cursed with a freakish memory for pictures he studied. Irene named him "the Compulsive Historian" and had a tryst with his roommate Kip during our second semester. Now Chris lived in Carroll Gardens with his wife, a translator he had met in a German-language class at NYU, and they had a six-year-old daughter.

"Tell me, tell me everything." He spoke with genuine friendliness. "I don't know anyone from school anymore."

My mind sped along, not making a lot of sense, because an opportunity revealed itself. The only friend I kept from my earliest days in New York was Irene. And Jennifer, but we never saw her. I had spent most of my time in the city with Michael, in his studio, which I did not want to explain either. It would be a cinch not to see Chris Cagnasola again.

"Painting's going really well these days. Really well."

What an exhilarating lie! I wished I had told it a long time ago. I had no bad feelings for Chris, but it was more important to tell this story, try it on, see what happened if I acted like I was the person who had kept working, steadily, year after year. Before I could begin to elaborate Chris confessed that he had quit painting right after college. He had finished his degree at NYU, in art history, gotten his doctorate at Columbia, and had been working as an archivist for a collector ever since.

"A photo collector. He produces Hollywood movies."

His voice had the tone of a confession, inferring that because he was not working with paintings at all he had failed his auspicious beginnings more than one might immediately realize.

"Of course you are still painting, probably one of the few," he said. "I used to only know painters. Now I don't know any."

The more distant Chris became from any art scene, the more I wanted to talk to him. I leaned against the building corner, where someone sold three-dollar umbrellas whenever it rained, and let the lies pour from my lips.

"I have a studio in Brooklyn, that's where I'm going now. Slowly. I was just looking for a place to pick up breakfast so that I could eat on the way and not waste work time. I hate the smell of food in the studio."

"I remember you never ate in class."

I had forgotten. I ate at Michael's all the time and was a slob about it too.

"I am working on two pictures now. They are tacked to the wall, staring me down."

"Haunting you."

"Exactly. One is kind of a family—four frozen figures—but they are shouting or howling in the darkness. Goya-like. Disaster-like. The other is more static, from a vision I have of seeing a gang of kids on the bridge years ago. On the Brooklyn side. I'm doing them from memory. Figures on the bridge at night. No moonlight. Nothing romantic and cheesy. Just really dark." I had no idea these pictures existed in my imagination.

"Do you still have people sit for you?"

"Memory, life, photos—I like to use all three for a painting if I can."

The lies melted in my mouth. I had not said a single word about exhibitions yet!

"Painting from life is so hard," he said.

"Really rendering. Yeah. But it changes what you see. Photos always need a lot of editing, there is too much. You have to leave a lot of it out of the picture."

He nodded emphatically. "I remember those portraits you did of your friends."

"I don't know where a lot of the early stuff is anymore. You know, once they are out of the studio they have their own life. Hopefully."

I was on the verge of cracking myself up, pronouncing you as "ya," like Philip Cleary did, but aware of how fragile this pleasure was going to be. Chris was being honest and I, mean as ever, revealed nothing truthful.

"You're going to work now?"

"I was going to go talk to Susanna Mackie but I don't want to lose the day." I knew exactly what that sounded like to Chris. "I'm going to grab a sandwich and hop on the train."

"I'm really happy to hear your work is going so well. The

attrition rate is so high. But you were making great pictures even then. Way ahead of the rest of us."

We both knew that it was he who had been outstanding.

"I don't know what happened to me. I couldn't face those canvases, they made me so fucking anxious. Even looking at paintings now can bring it back. It's still a relief not to have to do it."

He described many of my feelings—the loneliness and insecurity and isolation—but my capacity for empathy was completely absent. My heart raced along. For an instant I considered how convincing I really sounded but decided I was doing an excellent job playing the role of myself as I would like to be. I hit all the right notes.

"What about Meredith Davies? Is she still at SVA?"

The sound of Meredith's name brought my rushing adrenaline to a screeching halt. Wherever Meredith was now she knew that Emma Dial was standing on a street corner lying her ass off.

"She left a long time ago. I actually have her old studio."

"Wow," said Chris, impressed. "She was awesome. When I think of her I am ashamed that I gave it up."

"She did." Now I was a traitor, taking out my bad faith on Meredith Davies.

"Meredith Davies? She would never stop. She was the real deal. I am sure she still makes pictures, wherever she is. 'Nothing is as sexy as a well-drawn line.' Remember her saying that?"

"Yeah." I had automatically assumed that leaving New

York meant quitting. I had no clue what Meredith Davies was doing now.

"I remember Meredith saying something . . ." He trailed off.

"Saying what?"

"I have to pick up my daughter. She had a sleepover on King Street."

"What did Meredith say?" I was as insistent as I could reasonably be.

"She really liked your work. Don't you remember? During a crit she said she thought your struggle was going to be deciding what you wanted to invest yourself in, what subject, what style."

Meredith Davies had said I would have to find a way to commit to my paintings, be possessive of them, particularize my subject rather than merely render it. I could copy anything but I had to decide to give the picture weight. Keep them from going sentimental. This was a long, long time ago but it made me shiver now. I had not been able to let Meredith's words reach me when I was her student; I had been ruled by a superficial sense of competition.

We said goodbye. My kiss landed beside Chris's mouth. I started backtracking east.

In the depths of the Delancey Street JMZ station, I jumped down the last four stairs and ran across the platform. A man thrust his walking stick in the doors to keep them from shutting. The car rose swiftly out of the tunnel and crossed the Williamsburg Bridge. I loved being up high, above the cold water of the East River, at that hour clogged with garbage barges. I could be in Chelsea surrounded by other escapees rather than facing a vast array of my own shortcomings in Brooklyn. A man with paint-covered shoes caught my eye. He was going to his studio, too.

In the deli on the corner of Broadway and Marcy Avenue I picked up Windex, paper towels, chocolate milk, and two candy bars. The life-size wood carving of an Indian chief in the window of the Santeria botanica and florist, the liquor store a few doors in from the corner on Havemeyer, the run-down brownstones along South Eighth Street and the already decrepit prefabricated houses that were put up around the time I moved to New York, were still the same. I recognized some of the cars and even some of the kids who milled around. Twin brothers who came from the Dominican Republic after I got the studio were now teenaged. They ambled to a black station wagon parked at a hydrant, each with a white girl holding his arm.

The building was as neglected as ever. The ring I carried in my pocket held the two brass keys. Inside the front door, a pile of unclaimed phone books, broken umbrellas, and a pair of muddy rain boots stood in the corner. A shoebox full of junk mail for former tenants, catalogues and menus over-flowed on top of the tall radiator cover. The stairs were still filthy and listed away from the wall where they curved up to the second floor.

Only the paintings I described to Chris Cagnasola were missing. If two incomplete canvases waited on the wall, I could choose between them and start in. I had blank walls and empty easels and rooms full of ancient supplies and references.

I sat on the floor of the living room, ate both chocolate bars, and vowed to stay until dark. What reality had I been in when I invited the Breslauers to come over anytime? Irene had saved me from myself. Dust covered everything. It took an entire roll of paper towels to clean the windows that overlooked the bridge and the yard. I vacuumed, drank chocolate milk, and sat down again, picking my toenails with a palette knife. Looking back, I could see how I let the glamour and emergency of Michael's life overtake me. He lent me importance at a time I felt I had none. When I had no grandmother or teacher to shepherd me as an artist, Michael came along and needed everything about me: my youth, my body, my talent, my commitment to painting. Now I wanted it all back.

I had never gone to the studio solely to do maintenance work before.

Once I had found a sketch that fell between the floorboards of a big cat swatting playfully at a dead rat. I went to my shelves to search for the picture but forced myself to stop. I did not need to see the sketch to feel small and foolish about the time I had wasted or to remember the beauty of Meredith's drawing.

I ran down to the corner bodega for cigarettes, more paper towels, and Cheez Doodles. Idling outside the building when I returned was a blue Honda Civic with Joyce Barnes in the driver's seat, wrapped in an overcoat and wearing black leather gloves. Through the steamed windows she appeared to be either reading the newspaper or taking a nap. Joyce had taken over the garden apartment from a painter named Maria Ostrovsky who moved to Los Angeles in the early nineties and became popular. According to a photograph I had found among Meredith's belongings, the two artists used to drink bottles of Ballantine Ale on the stoop in the summertime. Maria Ostrovsky lived with two smelly old shepherd mutts that destroyed all the molding around the doors and windows. Years after she was gone, the dogs probably long dead, Joyce still complained about their smell and Maria Ostrovsky's disregard for other people's property.

Absorbed in her newspaper, Joyce drank coffee from a stainless travel mug, a pack of cigarettes and a lighter balanced on the dashboard. Talk radio and heat seeped out of the window, which was cracked a quarter of an inch. I tapped on the glass. Joyce started and unlocked the car door when she registered my face. I hopped in the passenger side.

"Where have you been, young lady?" said Joyce.

"Home. Work. I don't know. What are you doing in here?"

"It's cheaper to be warm in here than in that damn apartment. Drafts come at me from every which way. You know Ralph has been out here exactly zero times this winter to replace my broken panes and repair the destruction that Russian racked and ruined."

The building was owned by Ralph and Susan of Montclair, New Jersey, which is where they waited for the real estate market to peak again so they could sell the place for more than 2 million. Ralph had confided in Joyce that he could get 1.5 from the Hasidim who wanted to turn the building into a synagogue. Meanwhile, Joyce's apartment fell apart.

"How is everything? How are your daughters?"

"They're good girls. Too busy to see me most of the time. Jeanne had a baby in November. They're doing fine."

"A boy or a girl?"

"Sweet little girl. Would you like a cigarette, honey? You still smoke, don't you?"

"I'm very dedicated to my smoking."

"You know, everyone is always trying to quit." She chuckled. "But not me."

She showed me photographs of her older daughter and her husband with their new daughter, Joyce's first grandchild. She also carried a snapshot of her younger daughter, who lived in Newburgh where she worked as a bank teller. For sixteen years Joyce had assisted a partner at a Park Avenue law firm.

"How are you, honey? How's your family in Baltimore?"

"Everyone's fine."

"Do you ever go see them? You know, I'm starting to get a cramp in my leg. My coffee is cold. Let's go inside. I'm going to cozy up with my newspaper and my TV."

I tried to help Joyce gather her belongings but she did not need any help.

"You come and visit me when you're out here, allright? Don't be a stranger for so long."

"You're always at work."

Joyce stood behind the iron gate outside her front windows. She had a separate entrance under the stoop.

"Do what I say, young lady."

Upstairs I diluted the Windex with water and finished cleaning the windows, all of them black with soot. I filled two black plastic contractor bags with paper garbage without checking a single table of contents or reading one opening line.

I found a tarp and buried the painting racks, making a hulking floor-to-ceiling ghost of them that ran along an entire wall. That was a project for another day.

I dragged four metal folding chairs and a card table that were jammed into the bathtub out to the street and scrubbed the entire bathroom down. I eyed the couch but it would be impossible for me to navigate the narrow and curved staircase alone. Patrice Awofeso and I had spent a day and a half on that couch ravishing each other, memories of which I could not entertain without trembling.

I vacuumed the wall in the front room, cut canvas and tacked up two pieces, 24 by 18 inches and 29 by 20 inches. Then I sat on the floor and smoked eight cigarettes. I had to get used to being in my own place again. Everyone went through this, I knew. I debated calling Irene, Hideki, Jennifer. I considered calling my parents to say hello. It would be dark in another hour and a half. I mixed up gesso, smoked two more cigarettes, took a brush from a can, and applied thin coats. It only took minutes. The difficulty was never about how long any task took to do. Though time was an obstacle, facing and enduring it, letting myself get tossed around in the waves. The bad decision that lurked behind every corner could stop me in my tracks. I was supposed to be beyond that kind of thinking. Some people accumulated knowledge that safeguarded them, like Michael. He learned from his mistakes. My mistakes came flooding back to me if I held my own brush. The scratching out, the painting over, the remixing, the erasing, crumbling up, the contractor bags of paper garbage to be taken away. Chris Cagnasola believed Meredith Davies would never give up making art. Who would ever say that about me? I envied Meredith Davies anew.

I killed time designing ambitious plans: I would come in the morning before work—begin one of these paintings before Wednesday—come back tomorrow and begin painting—immediately return to painting in my studio every night after work—not even go home after I left Michael's—finish both pictures before my birthday in May.

Car headlights crossed the bridge into Brooklyn. Joyce Barnes was in her apartment downstairs, alone, following the news. This day was the first step away from being a quitter toward figuring out what sort of artist I was going to be.

At ten past five I stuffed my candy bar wrappers in my coat pockets, locked the door, folded my empty chocolate milk container flat, and tossed it in one of the cans outside the building. Someone had already taken away the metal chairs and table. Blue light from Joyce's television flickered in the front windows. The streets were busier than they used to be. New station wagons and trucks with supercabs sped along Broadway when I walked back to the JMZ station. People worked happily on their careers now, making rush hour later. No one like Meredith Davies was around, no one walking alone, cold and tired. Except for Joyce, all those women had gone somewhere else.

4

A HOLLOW METAL DOOR opened directly into the tiny bedroom Hideki and Shiro shared. Behind their messy bed, piled with folded laundry, was a window that led to an air shaft where two bicycles stood on their rear wheels, looped with a heavy steel chain. The windows in the 14-by-9 foot front room, where they kept computers and a sound system, were covered with wooden blinds drawn against the busy block of East Ninth Street. The walls were lined with towers of books and records and CDs, including four copies of Andy Warhol's *Index.*

Somehow they had managed to paint all the walls since my last visit. The front room and the bedroom crimson, the bathroom was newly gilded with Rust-Oleum, the kitchen and a narrow hall beside the bedroom, chartreuse.

"Three coats," said Shiro. "It's called Guava Green."

The entire apartment was less than 400 square feet. It amazed me that they could share such a miniature space.

"I tried Irene a bunch of times," said Hideki, annoyed. "They aren't answering the phone anymore."

"Idris is back in Chicago."

I handed Shiro the three bottles of Burgundy.

"One for each of us. I'll get the corkscrew."

They had given each other jagged haircuts and turned in front of me to show off their choppy heads, laughing at the spots where they nicked their scalps with the clippers. Their black hair shined.

"Can we cut your hair off? You always wear it the same way."

Shiro grabbed the scissors off the desk behind him and snapped them close to my head. Hideki examined my face.

"Just a trim."

I took the clip out of my hair.

"Okay, cut."

"I can't."

"We love your silver hair," said Hideki.

Hideki ordered Burmese food from a restaurant on Second Avenue and put on a new LP he won in an online auction, a German band called the 39 Clocks, singing "I saw Nixon in a bomber plane, drinking Cuba Libre." He kept

the album sleeve on his lap and propped his glass on it. He
already knew all the lyrics.

"Great song, right?"

They always had new things to show me, music I had not
heard before, things they had made, things they had started
making together. Pictures, clothes, home improvements,
they were always up to something.

"We're building a bike rack over the bed so we can use the
air shaft for a yard. I want to put a chair out there. And a
grill. And a dog," said Hideki.

"A dog?"

"A small one."

Shiro poured the wine when the buzzer sounded. We
watched Hideki try to calculate a tip for the comely deliv-
eryman. Therese called from her house in the Catskills.

"I don't know why they didn't use 'Coming Up' on the
cover," said Hideki. "I know they promised." He unpacked
the food. "I'll call the editor in the morning without seeming
like it's you who cares. Like I'm just curious. I'll say I want to
get the transparencies back from the photo department."

"I thought it would be Irene," Shiro whispered. "Therese
can't get through the weekend without calling here ten
times."

"That's why she pays him so well."

Hideki put the phone down.

"Tell him how Michael is much worse. Once he tracked
you down here because he'd seen us walking up Second
Avenue. He wanted you to leave and go meet him at the studio. Remember that?"

"They pay us for friendship, it's like being part of Elvis's entourage."

"Bloated Elvis," said Hideki. "I don't think I'm going to last much longer. Do you think I should quit?"

He made this lament every six months.

"Yes."

"You always say yes."

"I mean it."

"We can never leave them. Therese and Michael left each other but they can't function without us. But Shiro and I do fantasize about moving to Kuala Lumpur and opening a Burmese restaurant. He'll cook and I'll be the delivery guy."

They had been to Malaysia in the autumn to visit Shiro's family.

"Where is Emma's present?" said Shiro. "We keep forgetting to give it to you."

They brought something home for me whenever they left New York. Hideki passed me a thin white parcel. I turned the careful wrapping in my hand and laid the gift on my lap.

"Open it so we can eat," said Shiro.

"I'm nervous." I tore the paper apart. Inside was a square of pink and gold fabric. I began to unfold it.

"It's a songket," said Shiro. "Made in Malaysia."

"Like a skirt. Guys wear them also. Gimme, I'll show you how to put it on," said Hideki.

I pressed the bright material to my chest; an intricate pattern of gold thread was woven into the pink silk brocade. Hideki got up and held the songket above his waist and it fell to his ankles. He wrapped it close around his body, and folded over the top four or five inches so it stayed up. A pattern of gold vines floated over the rose background. The distance between the pareo and me might be closing!

"Perfect for the studio, right? Michael will like to watch you climb the ladder when you wear this."

"He has complained about my appearance. Let me try it on."

"I'll do it, Hideki doesn't know how to wrap it right."

I ate my tea leaf salad wearing the songket over my trousers. At midnight I wore it to run to the deli on the corner to buy cigarettes. Irene never called. We chain-smoked and looked at slides of Hideki's new paintings, projected on the wall over the bed. He had made two big abstract pictures since I was at his studio, bright confusions of pinks and oranges settling over green.

"How's my color, maestra?"

"Fantastic. Fantastic." I could hardly get it together to compliment his liquidy shapes at all.

WHEN I GOT HOME the door was unlocked and I found Michael asleep on the couch with my laptop balanced on his stomach. The remains of his takeout dinner were spread out on the table beside him. He looked extremely peaceful unconscious, which I resented, so I woke him up on the pretense of having a beer.

"This couch is so comfortable for napping. Did you and Hideki have a good time?"

Even awake he was in a serene mood.

"I tried to watch a movie but it wasn't very good. I'm distracted because Frederich ate dinner with people from the Met tonight. He said they discussed my work at length. At length, Emma." He licked his lips. "This exhibition at Frederich's is going to be fantastic." He knew the work would be done in time, he had nothing to worry about. "How's Hideki? What did you do?"

"We ate dinner."

"What did you have?"

"Stop it. What do you care what I ate? You know I'm in a bad mood and that's why you're being so nice to me."

"I'm always nice to you, Emma."

We sat beneath his tornado painting while he drank his beer and I tried to pick a fight with him.

"You wouldn't mind if I sold that painting, would you?"

"Why would you do that, Emma?"

"For the money."

"Then wait for the market to go up. Frederich says it's going to get even better."

"So you wouldn't mind."

"Not if you got a good price for it. Sell it to Frederich. Or I'll buy it. No. Sell it to Frederich."

Even when I tried to insult him he found a fucking bright side. If I sold his painting he would probably end up in the newspaper because Frederich would get an astronomical sum for it. I could not win with these people. The universe gave Michael a little more of what he wanted every day.

"Are you going to drink that?" he said.

"You can have it."

So he drank my beer too. Any feeling of competence eluded me. His guzzling brought me to tears.

"You know I'm not an artist anymore? You are not looking at an artist." I cried, shutting my eyes hard.

Michael should say something wise and reassuring, we should be able to have a genuine discussion about my goals. He poured brandies. I would have to take the lead if I wanted to get anywhere with this harebrained late-night idea of forcing Michael to take an extended, meaning longer than momentary, interest in someone beside himself, namely me. I wiped my eyes on a paper napkin.

"I can't imagine making my own work." The two new canvases at the studio were blank. Michael's colleagues referred to me as his right-hand man. That was the problem: they were not my colleagues.

"Everyone knows how talented you are, Emma."

"Why are you so quick to make excuses for me?"

"I don't get your meaning." He picked up a magazine from the floor and paged through, purposely, I think, not reading an article on the economics of art in which he and Philip Cleary featured prominently in the section on auction prices. $800,000 for a 1970 in 1991. $900,000 for a 1985 in 1995. Philip Cleary fetched $3 million for a 1979 in 2003. Michael refilled his glass. It was as if he never expected anything more of me.

5

EMMA:

Continue with topography, if you get to coastlines, just do the land, not the water, then paint interior water, in north, go ahead on all except center of island and everything south of airstrip, this before Gulf of Thailand.

Watch color breakdowns.

A little more yellow than transparency but make sure the coast doesn't get too yellow, watch curved lines.

Do mountains, do not paint around major arteries, finish backgrounds where redrawing is *not* going to be redone, can start northwest coast, do up to tributaries at top, entire central valley should be left until I get back.

Continue redrawing, as we discussed.

Do second coats.

6

ALL I HAD TO DO was pick up the studio phone and speak to Billy Lerner's new wife Liz. They owned all the parking garages in Dade County, as well as two of Michael's paintings, *Avalanche* and *Description Without Place*. Liz told the answering machine that they had planned to move the paintings from their townhouse on East Sixty-fourth Street to what they referred to as "the Cabin," a pink stucco six-bedroom in Bal Harbour, for their Art Basel Miami Beach socializing, but Liz had been too disorganized to get the paintings shipped and insured in time.

"Billy makes me do everything myself."

Liz also needed someone to supervise the rehanging.

I calculated how long I would be away and imagined how to tell Michael I was leaving town without him.

"I'll do it," I practically yelled into the phone.

Liz offered me a place to stay but I looked forward to a hotel, cable TV, room service. Maybe a swim.

"We should have a little party while you're here. Wouldn't that be fun?"

"I don't know anyone." The words shot out of my mouth. "Except Philip Cleary." A throwaway comment.

"We saw Philip at the shooting range this morning and all of us agreed it was time to get together for a meal. *Parfait.*"

"Yes, it is." I felt pleasantly devious. "I'll talk to Patrice about the crating and shipping and then get back to you. Is there someone at Sixty-fourth Street to let him in?"

"Of course."

Simple. Three days, two nights. A three-hour flight.

I FOUND A WEBSITE that listed all the hotels in South Beach. The ones with good names I looked up—Astor, Brazil, Crest, Greenview, La Flora, San Juan. I could not decide how long to stay, a weekend or a week. I counted the days until I could be sure that my period would be over. I reserved a ticket to Miami and a room at the Hotel Astor for three nights. According to the website, each of the hotel's forty rooms had custom French-milled furniture, halogen lighting, and a 25-inch color television mounted on a swivel stand for 180-degree viewing. The man who took my reservation over the phone felt compelled to add that the mattresses and cushions were uncommonly thick and the walls were double-insulated. When he asked how many guests, one or two, I said I would not know until I arrived.

I FINISHED *Phu Quoc* alone and started my painting, *Interstices,* drawing the false map of truncated paths from Michael's maquette. *Interstices* began on the bank of the river and headed north, across the water, up to the main street of the town, following a series of narrow golden roads to the gray stones that rise above the buildings, patched with green. One day I would live with this picture and I meant for it to be the best of them all.

7

HIDEKI SURVEYED Berry Street through a cracked pane. A group of high-school-aged boys surrounded a blue '67 Cutlass, the hood was popped so the motor could be admired.

"What are you going to do in Miami?"

My intentions were twofold: to practice my story on Hideki and to coax him into talking about Philip Cleary without letting on that he was the reason I wanted to go to Florida. Hideki must know a thing or two about him.

"I'm going to hang some paintings for Michael. Hang Michael's paintings, I mean."

I already sounded like a liar.

"In South Beach?"

"I'm staying there, but the people are in Bal Harbour."

"Nice. Who?"

"The Lerners. I haven't been. I'm the only one who hasn't been to Miami."

"The Lerners are good friends with the Lambs, the sisters who collect Therese."

Hideki tucked himself into the deep windowsill, his knees under his chin. The number of colored glass bottles in the floor arrangement had doubled and so had the plastic owls. Now there were two of them on the bookshelf, their gold bodies covered in melted and hardened candle wax.

"Camilla and Cornelia Lamb. They live in a castle outside London."

It was an obvious opening for Philip Cleary to be inserted in the conversation, considering all the paintings of Hermione, who was the daughter of an earl. Perhaps her family had a castle too.

"They keep their boat in Connecticut."

"That's right, it's called *Black Rooster*. What's going on with your studio?" he said.

"*Black Rooster* is an ugly name. Nothing is up with my studio. Why?"

I felt the keys to South Eighth Street in my pocket.

"Why don't you get rid of it if you don't use it. I know it bugs you."

"I feel obligated to step across the threshold every now and then." I hated to have this conversation in Hideki's studio, surrounded by his blazing bright paintings.

"Why? That's stupid. Stupid torture."

"Because my old painting teacher gave it to me."

"You mean the one who got married and left the city? Why are you burning candles for her?"

"I'm not burning candles. What's wrong with leaving New York?"

"Nothing. Unless you're a painter."

So I was not the only one who associated leaving New York with quitting.

"We could strike a deal if you wanted to part with the lease."

"A love nest for you and Shiro."

"It would be my studio, in case I lose this place. I don't want to live in Brooklyn, despite how wonderful everyone thinks it is."

"I used to think I would live on South Eighth Street one day."

Among the things Meredith Davies abandoned was a pair of ivory-colored silk sheets. They were sloppily folded and shared a shelf with a cracked bicycle helmet and a 1500 piece jigsaw puzzle of Manet's *Le Déjeuner sur l'herbe*. It impressed me both that Meredith owned silk sheets and that she did not want to keep them, they did not even merit throwing away. A gift from a lover who did not last long, I figured.

MEREDITH DAVIES used to stride across Twenty-third Street, flicking her cigarette butt into the traffic. I watched her from my "Survey of World Art" class on the third floor. She had the appearance of a person I would like to paint: wiry and standoffish, sleek and catlike, independent of everyone and everything. When I saw Meredith's paintings in a storefront gallery in the East Village I became determined to work with her. Little square canvases with a dark figure in the ocean at night, a rangy woman in the yard with her dogs and daughters; the same woman with a mouse on her head. I did research, beginning with Meredith's faculty bio in the School of Visual Arts bulletin. She had lived in Spain and Argentina after graduating from the Cooper Union. I pursued Meredith beginning the first session of the first class, "Painting Workshop," a six-hour studio, for second-year students.

Meredith was in her late thirties then, but she had not seemed old to me, the way other SVA instructors the same age did. She was a demanding painting teacher, not a cheerleader who met students for drinks and swapped woes and lamented lost ambitions. She flunked people. She told her studio classes that she was not interested in discussing anything except making art. Meredith Davies did not have students copy old masters paintings so I never got to show off the Vermeer copies I made during my foundation year. She did not divorce the study of materials and techniques from ideas. She had stood behind my shoulder and watched me work on a Masonite panel propped on the metal easel. I painted my grandmother's deaf dog asleep in the driveway and Irene and Jennifer huddled in the back of a car.

"Who are they?" said Meredith. "Is that one you?" She spoke without inflection.

"They're my friends." The images gushed out of me; I aestheticized whatever I loved.

Then she made a clicking sound with her tongue and moved on to the next student. I became addicted to that little sound of approval.

Sometimes I glimpsed a book in Meredith's satchel, or she talked about what she was reading. She sent the class to see exhibitions at the Drawing Center and White Columns. Any detail was a gift. As soon as Meredith left the school building I was anticipating her again, working hard all week to present new work the following Wednesday morning.

I learned she was insomniac. All night she painted or read books on painting and the political and art histories of her favorite cities, Madrid, Mexico City, Santiago de Cuba, the places she had lived or visited before she started teaching. She practiced her Spanish using flash cards. I mimicked her habits: I read what Meredith read, I painted in my bedroom on First Street while Irene shut herself in the bathroom printing, then we stayed out all night. Irene found parties so we could eat and drink for free.

After my junior year, Meredith got me a summer job as half of a two-man crew painting liquor billboards on the state highways in Maryland.

"It's the best way to learn to work on a large scale, to be effective and not overly precious about technique," Meredith said. "Good things to know, even if you don't use them in your own work. Just practice."

I had arrived each dawn to find my partner Frank drinking a tallboy, waiting for me, expecting me to have quit. It was a backbreaking, low-paying job and common for new hires not to last more than a few weeks. Meredith had once worked alongside Frank too.

When I drove up on the third consecutive Monday morning Frank yelled to me: "I thought for sure you were a no-show."

Frank was the company's best and fastest worker. He painted perfect ice cubes, the hard rim of a rock glass, pouring liquids. He could rig any scaffold, drunk or sober, and never misstepped.

I photographed Frank in front of a nightclub sign I painted across the exterior wall of a house in southwest Baltimore, a side gig Frank had lined up for me. One of his shirttails tucked in, one sleeve rolled, exposing a meaty elbow, the words LADIES INVITED loomed over him.

"It's important to practice letters," Frank said. "They're easy, but not as easy as they look."

Over ham and cheese sandwiches I told him about school, making paintings of Irene and her sisters, a group show I submitted slides for and hoped to be in, Meredith's brutal final critiques.

"Meredith's the nicest gal you'll ever want to meet," said Frank. "A real artist's personality, always thinking and working. I've been painting billboards for over thirty years and no one ever called me an artist. But I sucked one dick and they never stopped calling me a cocksucker."

"Where am I in the artist-cocksucker spectrum?"

"You'll be off the charts when I'm done with you, hon."

I missed working while Meredith circled the studio, mumbling a few words each time she stopped. "What is that color? How did you make that color?" Then the clicking before she walked away, but Frank was right. When I left him at the end of the summer I was a crackerjack, I could paint anything.

Senior year, I found the courage to ask Meredith if I could see how she worked and was granted an entire Saturday with her. We met at school and walked down to Third Avenue to go to Central Art Supply. Meredith wanted new brushes. She ran her fingers over everything and then bought a Kolinsky red sable #24 round for two hundred and fifteen dollars. We walked south along the Bowery, to Pearl Paint. Meredith did not want to stop in any galleries; she only went during the week, when fewer art students and tourists were out. We looked at brushes and canvas, found that she had gotten a good price at Central. We took the J train out to Brooklyn. I had wanted to walk, to draw the afternoon out, but I was too shy to protest. It was an overcast spring day, finally warm. People were outside and there were a lot of bicycles suddenly.

The subway car was empty but we stood holding the overhead bar, looking out the window, down at the Lower East Side, the river, the end of Meredith's street. The train ran along the bridge's pedestrian walkway where couples walked to and from Brooklyn holding hands. A girl facing the train kissed her boyfriend, her eyes open. He lifted her denim skirt and pressed his hand against the side of her thigh. She blew smoke rings in his face. I remembered every detail of that day.

The year after I graduated Meredith left New York with a

new husband, a scenic painter in the film union. She had
called and offered me the lease on the South Eighth Street
studio. It was overly generous of her, considering how brief
our connection had been. I found stacks of flash cards
tucked into corners, windowsills, in cupboards over the
stove. Spanish vocabulary words written in Meredith's tidy
all-caps with a black Sharpie. I never tried to reach her
because she also left behind her painting supplies and I
thought this meant she gave up.

ON THE STREET Hideki lit my cigarette. My bare fingers
were pale and my nails were bitten down and had spots of
dried blood around the cuticles.

"You have ugly hands," said Hideki.

"You should see my feet."

"Why so stressed?"

"Too much time under the studio lights, I guess."

I did not enjoy conversation with Hideki that day. When
I let my mind wander, it was my studio I thought of and the
empty canvases waiting for me on the wall. What would
become of them? Maybe I would paint Hideki's creepy plastic owls and colored bottles.

"What are you thinking?" said Hideki.

"About later." I was about to walk away from my empty
canvases again. I had to remember to bring the mambo CDs
to Brooklyn so the songs were ready for me next time. I
needed the trumpets to start painting again.

"How are the paintings going?"

For a moment I thought he had read my mind.

"Beautiful. Michael's paintings are fucking beautiful."

"I can't wait to see them. What are you going to do for him next?"

The idea of more paintings gave me a sinking feeling.

I said goodbye and headed for the bridge. A long, damp walk could lead to a nice nap, or maybe an afternoon movie. Sitting in the dark while it stormed outside appealed.

Three helmeted cyclists passed as I approached the entrance to the walkway. Their gears clicked as they climbed the incline without standing up. Then they disappeared, single file in their red and purple and gray rain jackets, around the corner and over the river, like a team. The walkway, still new to me since its renovation, rose over the eastbound traffic and then made a short jog to the right where it leveled out and the structure became a suspension bridge. I used to look down through the cracks at my feet, through the junky old tiles at the two lanes that ran into Manhattan. Car horns and squeaky brakes grew louder. A ferry emerged from beneath the bridge, heading north.

Since I described those paintings to Chris Cagnasola I felt obligated to make them but I knew there was no way in hell I would do it. I still could not see my paintings. I tried to let the pictures come to my mind but instead I saw old pickle jars filled with Irene's fading lilacs.

Despite the wet weather three Hasidic families, parents with young children, walked to Brooklyn. After they passed I was alone in what was becoming a downpour, the noise of frustrated and impatient drivers below. The floor vibrated

Samantha Peale

beneath me. I began to hurry along, head lowered, watching my boots get soaked.

Fifty feet ahead four men squatted across the span of the walkway, equidistant from one another. Fear shot through me. I had heard countless stories about people being mugged and variously attacked, wallets, ATM cards, bicycles stolen and vicious wounds inflicted. I had seen all manner of mischief perpetrated on the old bridge, fights, drug deals, tricks, clouds of marijuana smoke wafting above a huddled group of bicycle messengers, bottles and epithets hurled, junkies nodding and dozing. I had heard about a gang of kids holding a taut wire across the bridge at chest level, which sent any cyclist who pedaled in the dark flying when they crashed into it. On one of my first solo walks I had come across a man lying in a growing pool of blood, his head beaten.

Now it was my turn to be unhorsed. I slowed to a near stop and lost track of the sounds around me. Crossing the bridge used to make me feel invincible; I never pictured myself as someone who could be toppled. I repeated to myself something along the lines of: Things should be different for me, starting now. Obviously, I should have gone to my studio. Starting now. Now. Until I realized that the men were painting. Each one held a spray can. My sense of threat came from an earlier time; the bridge was no longer the eerie and dangerous place it had once been. Two of them traded colors, and I could hear the rattle of the marble inside the cans when they shook them. Crimson, black, and silver, rich and wet colors for the personal insignias they repeated all over the city. I passed between them, invisible. A Rottweiler puppy slept curled in a ball, a heavy chain attached to the dog's collar was wrapped around the ankle of a painter who slashed huge proud letters across the bridge. I was sick of being unnoticed.

FOUR

1

IN THE LATE AFTERNOON SUN, the taxi passed two golf courses and mown lawns that could be golf courses. The buildings under construction were not skyscrapers. Nothing covered the sky; the entire city complemented the sky and the Atlantic. Palm trees and pink sidewalks lined streets of art deco buildings. It was seventy degrees.

Women wore light skirts and high heels that showed off their tanned calves and red toenails. The men had black hair and drove big American cars, Cadillacs and Lincolns.

The hotel lobby was a long, high-ceilinged room. A tall concierge in a perfect narrow black suit spoke gracefully accented English. Chrome chairs were tucked under café tables on a terrazzo porch. The mezzanine smelled of

Casablanca lilies. Each window overlooked the ocean, the sunset, or the turquoise pool. A silent mirrored elevator led to carpeted hallways with heavy doors. Everything in my room was smooth and white and smelled of citrus and sugar.

I pressed my cheek to the air-conditioned glass. All the hotels were the color of the beach. Boys in windbreakers raked the sand around green and blue shade tents, chaise lounges with pastel umbrellas, and the wooden lifeguard stand, an empty purple tower. No one was in the ocean. On the horizon one white ship sailed south.

2

LIZ LERNER WAITED at the front door. Brilliant light drenched her from a skylight above her eggy blond head.

"It's been forever," she said.

We kissed hello and crossed the soft bamboo floor in the foyer to the sunken living room. Liz kicked off her heels before stepping onto the shimmery white carpet.

"You don't have to take your shoes off," said Liz. "I love the way this carpet feels on my bare feet. Try it."

"You don't want to see my feet."

A pitcher of lemonade and two tumblers had been set out on a glass table. The walls were freshly painted the smoothest turquoise, pale and silky. The room held so much light it was as though we were sitting in a swimming pool.

This was the kind of modern home that was a mess the moment you tossed a jacket on the back of a chair.

The last time I had seen Liz Lerner was about two years earlier, at a bar on Wooster Street. I was tucked into a booth with Irene, Jennifer, Hideki, and Shiro, and Liz teetered over to say hello, unmarried and brunette then. She used to be an artist and then she assisted David Salle for a while and that was how she met Billy.

Liz had all the art magazines laid out on the lower tier of the glass table. A spectacular painting of a boy leading a pony hung behind her, a contemporary homage to Picasso with its own intrigue and raciness. I could not take my eyes off it.

"Did you hear about that woman who was visiting from New York?"

Clutching her glass of sweet lemonade, Liz reached out but stopped short of touching me. The ice cubes clinked against the glass and a drop spilled on her knee.

"She was renting a house nearby. She left a party last night and she got hijacked in her own rental car. A man locked her in the trunk and drove her all the way to Marathon Key. That's over one hundred miles! The poor woman had her cell phone so she called the police but she didn't know where she was. Eventually they found the car in the parking lot of a Publix. I can't believe you haven't heard this."

"I don't think the hotel staff discusses this sort of thing with guests."

"You have to be careful here. It's not like New York."

"Don't try to scare me. Tell me about life in Miami."

"It's so fucking boring, but it's beautiful and warm and it beats waiting for the N and R."

"Right on."

We raised our lemonade glasses. She should tell me about the boy with pony painting. Maybe they bought it before I met them or it could be new.

"I miss my friends. People visit but it's not the same." Liz ripped the end off her pinkie nail, removed it from between her teeth, and wiped it on the rim of a crystal ashtray. "Sorry to be gross." The edge of her finger bled. "Do you want to see the paintings? You've seen them plenty; I mean I'll show you where they are. You are so nice to do this. I promise you a great dinner later. Promise."

The library overlooked a garden on the side of the house where cast-iron lawn furniture was arranged around a dirty stone birdbath. The room smelled of oil-based paint and was completely white and empty except for the two crates Patrice had built that leaned against the window frames. I took a measuring tape, hammer and nails, and white gloves from my knapsack and pried the crates open. Billy Lerner had left a drawn diagram of where he wanted the paintings—side by side on the wall to the right of the new built-in shelves with twenty inches between them. This was the first time I had ever been alone with any of Michael's paintings after I had finished them and they left the studio. Even the ones I touched up at Frederich's before an opening, there was always someone else around. These two were made three years apart. *Avalanche* was from my third year with Michael and I found it tame, more romantic than I cared for now. *Description Without Place,* a mountain village buried under snow and ice, was rougher, confident and solitary. But they belonged together, like lovers. Michael could conceive of this smart pairing despite the years and distance between the two pictures. Hard not to be impressed.

I RETURNED TO THE HOTEL, where I forced myself to swim a mile in the rooftop pool, took a two-hour nap, and ran a hot bath. I tried to read the *Times* in the tub. A photograph in the front section showed two men and a woman walking on a sunny street. The caption said the people were Colombian citizens in Bogotá. The image had no relation to the story about American military advisors in Colombia. This disconnection reminded me of *Interstices,* which was still an empty canvas, and of the empty canvases in my studio. My body felt heavy in the water. I wanted to look at the Lerners' boy with pony painting again. Why had Liz not said anything about it? Who made it? I should have made it. I dropped the folded paper on the floor and slid deeper into the bath until the water covered my shoulders and my legs were submerged and my toes touched the tile wall in front of me. I ran my palm across my stomach and between my breasts. I was hungry and sunburned. My legs looked lean and slick in the water. Would Philip Cleary ever see so much of me and would he like how I looked?

THE ELEVATOR DOOR OPENED one floor below and two women pulled a green plastic laundry bin into the car. We all smiled at each other. I got out at the mezzanine and walked to the low railing from where I could see the entire lobby and the crowded bar at the far end of the room. A DJ set up turntables and chatted with girls in satiny dresses. The doorman stood on the threshold, with one foot outside, as he greeted a couple and their young son. This was the kind of place where I might have a great time at a party but later dislike for being overdetermined, to use Philip Cleary's parlance. I mourned the days when every public space was not pictured in the portfolio of an architect and an interior designer. There should be visual highs and lows, some places ought to remain nondescript or even ugly. I turned back to the elevator; it was too late to address my concerns about being overdressed and not knowing what to talk about at dinner. I could not recall any information from the article about Bogotá, or even whether or not I had read it.

I heard loud voices before the elevator door slid open. Two attractive couples wearing evening clothes smiled as they stepped aside for me to pass. New Yorkers. A man Philip Cleary's age, bald with wire-rim glasses, shook hands with the doorman. The timbre of their voices was distinctive but I could not make out any words, even as I passed between them. The Lerners' car idled across the street. The driver dozed, his head resting on the steering wheel.

BILLY LERNER LAY on the floor in the living room with a sofa cushion under his head, his hand stuffed down the front of his jeans, watching CNN on a flat-screen television and eating goat cheese and olives from ceramic bowls on the table beside him. The way he sprawled on the carpet made me think that he and Liz must have sex there regularly. It had been a long time since I had seen a man so comfortable on the floor.

Liz peered across the foyer from the edge of the kitchen.

"I hate that thing mounted on the wall," she said, loud enough for Billy to hear her.

"I love my beautiful plasma-screen TV!" Billy baited her.

"I know: you love it more than you love me. You're so fucking funny."

Liz poured wine for me and for Corina, her sister who was visiting from Los Angeles. Corina was at the six-burner stove sautéing tomatoes with caramelized onions and garlic in one pan and browning minced beef and pork in another. I admired her moves with the two cast-iron pans. She looked like a pro.

"Can I help? Shall I set the table?"

"Oh shit. I forgot the table. Let's sit on the floor in the living room. It's much nicer," said Liz.

"That sounds perfect. Corina, what can I do?" I felt uncharacteristically eager, and happy.

"Honey, you're a guest," said Corina. "How long are you here?"

"I fly out early Monday. I wish I had another day, at least."

"Quick trip. Means you have to come back."

"Here." Liz handed me a wooden bowl. "Make a salad."

I rooted around in the refrigerator until I found some

good stuff, surprised by how much fun I was having passing a night in Liz Lerner's kitchen.

"Can I brown these a little?" I held up a package of figs.

"Plenty of room. Here's a pan. Here's a burner." Corina stepped to the right to make space for me.

I combined the arugula and quartered figs and squeezed two Meyer lemons over the bowl, sprinkling it with sea salt and a drizzle of olive oil.

"You cook?" said Corina.

"No." Michael used to make this salad all the time.

Corina had opened her own restaurant on Melrose last year, a bistro called Pavia, named after a great-uncle who immigrated to Paris in the 1930s.

"He was a poet." Liz took a full garbage bag from the bin beneath the sink. "Philip and Isabelle will never get here before nine."

"Oh really?" I sounded stupid.

"They went out on someone's boat today." She began washing bowls and knives that Corina was finished using. "Water bugs, those two."

AT TEN THE FRONT DOOR opened and Isabelle and Philip Cleary strolled in, salty and sleepy. Isabelle's hair was combed back, still wet from a shower. Philip had buzzed his hair since his opening and now had a crew cut that revealed the shape of his head and his face. I liked how he looked. They each carried a gold box, like the ones Michael and I received from the Breslauers.

Isabelle lightly kicked Billy's leg by way of greeting. She took the box from her father's hand on her way into the kitchen and deposited the champagne on the butcher-block counter.

"Isa, you got a lot of sun today!" Liz hung a saucepan on the rack over the stove. "You have to be careful."

"I'm Isabelle." She extended her hand to me.

She had Philip Cleary's black hair and brown eyes and a thick, compact body, wrapped in a baby blue bateau-neck T-shirt and camel cords, both slightly too small. She was direct and self-possessed with an easy smile with lots of big white teeth. I liked her right away.

Philip Cleary called out from the living room.

"Where is she? Where is Emma Dial?"

"He's been talking about you all day," said Isabelle. She winked, a friendly confidence. She probably understood her father's passions, perhaps better than anyone else. She poured herself a drink.

I returned the wink. Philip appeared in the kitchen and put his arms around me.

"Nicely done, Emma Dial. Now I've captured you!"

"Are you loaded already?" Liz handed him a glass of red wine.

Close up he seemed like a different person, as though he had grown physically larger in the weeks since I had last seen him. He stepped back to look at me, up and down, up and down.

"I'm happy you made it out of New York." He raised his glass to me. "What a funny glass." They were thin graceful globes without stems. He turned one in his hand. "You can see all the fingerprints right away."

"Complaints? Already?" said Liz.

"How was your day on the water?"

"Nice," said Isabelle. "Long." She turned to her father.

"We only make friends with people who have boats," he said between gulps. "I don't know why we spend so much time over here."

"For the food," said Liz.

"Because you're freeloaders," Billy yelled from the living room.

He was still watching the news with the glass Corina brought him balanced on his chest.

"Yachts," said Isabelle. "That's my credo." She looked around for a reaction. "Just kidding."

"I hate boats. They make me feel trapped. Or I have felt trapped on the few boats I've been on," said Corina. She plated the Bolognese, serving me first.

"Me too." I waited for someone else to take a plate and move into the living room ahead of me. "Loads of things will give you a fast ride but just make you feel imprisoned. Horses, for example."

"I don't like horses." Philip Cleary smiled conspiratorially.

Liz and Corina agreed that horses were overrated; Isabelle loved horses, even the smell of manure; Billy called out that he liked betting on horses and was an astute handicapper.

"You are?" said Liz. "Get in here if you want dinner."

Isabelle took a plate to the living room. Billy chucked her chin when they passed at the foot of the staircase. He had turned off the television and all the lamps and lit candles on the mantel over the gas fireplace and tea candles in a glass chandelier over the dining table.

Isabelle and I sat beside one another on the carpet, our laps covered with linen napkins. Again I admired the painting of the boy and his horse. I wanted to be alone with it, maybe grab it off the wall and hold it, stare at it for a while. The artist had loaded it with eerie cold lavenders that crept toward blue and gray. I could imagine painting it, adding the distinct short and narrow brushstrokes, and was annoyed that I had not thought of this image myself. The possessiveness of the boy and the liveliness of the pony were perfect to me.

"I really like this painting. Despite what I just said about horses."

"Me too. It's fucking awesome." Isabelle popped a noodle in her mouth. "So delicious."

"She put whole chiles arbol in the sauce."

I took one of the candles from the mantel and placed it between our plates. Over the sideboard behind the dining table was a modest square painting of two figures walking on the beach. In the candlelight the image appeared brushy and dense with paint in shades of gold. The figures were Isabelle and Philip Cleary.

"Is that yours?"

"It's old." Isabelle swallowed another noodle. "High school work." She shrugged.

High school work was the right way to describe it but it had something special too, something in the closeness of the figures. I could see what Philip Cleary meant when he said Isabelle would be a good painter if she stuck with it.

"So what's next for you?" said Isabelle.

"Good question." What a surprise. "No one has ever asked me that before."

"Well, everyone around you benefits from you staying exactly where you are. It's pretty fucking profitable if you don't do something next. Right?"

"Sure. But I can be replaced." Not easily.

"That's not what my dad says."

"That's nice. It's nice of him." I wondered if he said that on the boat this afternoon, when he knew he was going to see me later, or if they had talked about me earlier, on a different day.

"He's got a killer instinct, though. I mean, he didn't get where he is by putting other people before him. Know what I mean?" Isabelle picked up another noodle with her fingers.

"I don't know him personally. I don't know how he is."

"He's great, I'm not saying he's not great. He saved me from my mean mom. Major rescue."

"I have a mean mom too." It would be stingy not to be open with Isabelle.

"Sorry to hear it. Screamer?"

"Silence and the occasional lobbed grenade."

"My mean mom used to yell at me all day long and when she got tired of screaming she would smack me. I couldn't do anything right with her. My dad put an end to that. She hates that I am painting, it's like the worst betrayal. She tries to pretend it isn't happening."

"I stopped showing my parents what I made a long time ago. Too much of a letdown. I steer clear of them."

"It's the only way." Isabelle's voice trailed off. She looked away, toward the picture she had made of her and her father.

"I'm sorry." This was more than I should know. "I don't know her."

"Mean and angry. Though if you met her you would never know," said Isabelle.

"That's the secret of all mean moms, I think. They don't let on that they're embattled and have no control over their feelings." I picked a noodle from my plate.

"You were saying what you are going to do next."

"I'm going to quit my job and move to Miami and try to be an artist." I spoke without thinking.

Isabelle laughed and clapped me on the shoulder. She had a high-pitched laugh, a surprising sound coming from her because it was the laugh of a much younger person.

"I have the same plan! First, I am going to finish school, which is crushing me with boredom, but you-know-who is forcing me to finish, otherwise no boat trips and no allowance and nothing good. Then I want to live down here full-time, set up my own studio, and hang out with Liz and Billy."

"You really like it here?"

"New York is all business and people live and die by the *Times*. I get sick of it. Don't you?"

"Yes. I hadn't thought of it that way but I think I agree with you."

"When will you move here?"

"Oh, I don't know." Dismissing the idea. I was enjoying Isabelle but Philip Cleary, and likely the Lerners, would hear about all of this. "I have a lot of work to do for Michael."

Isabelle pushed her plate away and unfolded her legs so that her feet were under the glass table. The art magazines that had been laid out earlier in the day were gone.

"Are you married?"

"No." I could not gauge the nature of Isabelle's interest, whether she inquired on her own behalf or was this about my rapport with her father.

"What are you two talking about?" Philip interrupted.

He sat beside me on the floor.

"The meaning of art," said Isabelle, her mouth full. She looked at me as though we shared a secret.

Liz and Corina and came in with plates and Billy made several trips back and forth to the kitchen to bring bottles of wine, grated Parmesan cheese, and my salad, which I had forgotten about.

"Straight to the heart of things," Philip Cleary said to Isabelle.

"Why not? Why fuck around with small talk?"

"I am ravenous," said Billy.

"Good. *Bon appétit.*" Corina raised her glass first.

"Bottoms up," said Liz.

The Bolognese tasted so good that no one spoke until the plates were nearly clear, then Billy asked Isabelle what the meaning of art was and she became embarrassed and looked to me for help. We were connected now.

"The more you make paintings, the more you can under-

stand what is humanly possible if you make an effort. Painting is a way to increase experience."

"Over a period of time," said Philip.

"It can inspire thought, and thought can develop into
considered ideas." I avoided his eyes. "It can represent a person's awareness of the potential and the dynamic."

"Change. I agree with you." Isabelle drank out of my glass.

"Sounds good to me," said Billy as he picked at a wine
cork. "What do I know? I build parking garages." He
laughed, I thought, because it was clear that he had an idea
of his own about art. He sat under the luminous boy leading the pony picture, his hand on Liz's thigh.

"Whose painting is that?" My voice came out too loud.
"I've never seen it before."

Liz hesitated.

"It's new," she said.

"It's kind of perfect, isn't it? I can't stop looking at it."

A telephone rang somewhere in the house but no one did
anything about it.

"I think so too," said Billy.

Philip laughed uncomfortably but neither Isabelle nor the
Lerners reacted.

"It's yours?"

"I just finished it when I got down here. You like it?"

I had responded quickly and strongly to the picture and
knew that it would figure in my future. Maybe I would
repaint it or reconstruct it in a drawing, try to figure it out
for myself. I did not know yet. The telephone continued to
ring or rang again.

"Yeah. Yeah, I do."

"I feel like I'm in a Raymond Chandler story," said Corina.

"Carver," said Liz. "I don't. That's a morbid thing to say."

"We're all being nice to each other," said Billy.

"So far," said Isabelle.

I asked where the bathroom was and Billy pointed to the staircase.

"Be nice to each other while I'm gone."

Philip followed me into the foyer, took my wrist, and turned me around. I leaned against the banister and looked at him boldly.

He climbed the first step, pushing me up one higher; his breath was warm against my cheek and neck. It was thrilling to be so near him. I studied the broad planes of his face. I resisted touching his hair.

"Your hair."

He ran his hand back and forth over his head.

I had no way to convey how disarmed I was by the evening, by him, his daughter, and their friends, and by how essential yet everyday making paintings and living with art was for them. Alone and barefoot in the dark foyer, neither of us knew what to say. I reached out and ran my palm over his hair and down the side of his face. He was as surprised as me.

I WATCHED MTV Tr3s and ate peanuts and cashews from the minibar. I could imagine everyone else leaving. Michael ran late for the lunch meeting, the premiere, the private viewing. Gerda waited in the car downstairs, in the airport bar, the hotel lobby. Irene perpetually came and went and risked being thrown out. Hideki left for Long Island weekends, Kyoto to visit his family, Europe in the spring. Philip Cleary had already lived all over the world. I turned off the television and lay in the dark hotel room. Everyone moved easily except for me. I had no picture of myself. I trained my eye on a scene of Michael sitting on a leather banquette before a table heaped with wineglasses covered with greasy fingerprints and plates of half-eaten food. I stood by like a server and told him: I don't want to paint your pictures. I won't smooth any more transitions. I need to be replaced.

3

THE PHONE BESIDE the bed rang at quarter to eight.

"Good morning." It was Philip Cleary.

I had forgotten about his creamy voice while I slept.

"Where are you?"

"I'm two blocks away."

"Can you come up here?" My mouth was dry.

"You're in 202."

"302. Good thing you called."

"What?"

"Good thing you called or you would have gone to the wrong room."

"I'll see you in a minute."

I peed and brushed my teeth. I had slept restlessly and my

hair was knotted and dirty, the color of old nickels. Standing in a windowless hotel bathroom waiting for Philip Cleary, I felt sick.

I unlocked the door, got back into bed, and shut my eyes, the covers pulled up to my chin.

He tapped on the door and let himself into the dark room.

"How are you?"

He bent over me and kissed my mouth. He pushed the covers down a little, lifted my shirt, kissed my breast. I watched his lips move and close on me. He slid his mouth down my stomach and reached between my legs.

"How are you?"

He pulled my T-shirt over my head and threw it on the floor.

"You're not talking to me?"

"Not yet," he said.

He pulled my underwear down to just below my knees and I kicked it off. He put his finger inside me, found my clit with his tongue, and pressed hard but did not move his mouth at all for a long time. I felt his whiskers on my skin.

"Come here." I tugged at his shoulders.

He stood with his back to me and took his shirt off without unbuttoning it. He took his shoes and pants off and sat naked on the edge of the bed. He pulled my legs apart. He put his tongue inside me, his hands under my hips.

"Don't make me wait anymore."

He fucked me slow. When I moved my hips he said, "Good. Good. Good. Good." Close to my ear.

"I'm coming," he said.

I wrapped my arms tight across his back, slid my hands down to his ass, and pulled him into me. He kissed my mouth, my face, my neck.

"I've missed you, Emma Dial."

He must have decided that he was going to walk into the room and fuck me. It did not feel like a spontaneous decision, it was something that had worked for him in the past. He was not sexy to me until his tongue was between my legs and then I could not help it, he just knew how to touch. He had fucked a lot of women and he was great at it.

We lay close. He wiped his dick on the sheet, drew me to him, with his arm across my shoulders. We lay quiet. I watched his face: his eyes were shut, the skin at his temples was a little slack, his crew cut did not get messed up. I traced a long scar on his chest with my thumb. He pulled me closer.

"I've missed you," he said again.

I had hoped we would not talk about how we felt. I would be bored if I had to pretend to feel emotional in any usual way, beginning with gratefulness for sex.

"Make me hard," he said.

I took his dick in my mouth and he raised his hips to me.

"That's good," he said, over and over until he was ready to come. "Be on top."

So I fucked him for a long time until we both came.

HE TOOK A SHOWER alone. I listened to the running water and watched male reindeer mashing their antlers together on the muted television screen.

He lay with a towel around his waist and I pushed it aside. He talked about Isabelle and her friends visiting the night before and spilling soda on the living room rug. One of her friends had a toddler and had left a box of wipes and sippy cup behind. Something about this made him laugh. I put his hands on my stomach.

"I don't like a mess in my house, it's annoying. Especially someone else's mess."

He stroked my hip. I put his finger inside me and he made me come with his hands and he came in my mouth.

He had an easy gesture of pushing my hair away from my face, his fingers lightly crossing my skin. I let my hair get messed up so he would touch my forehead and cheek in this gentle way.

Philip began to dress when I walked into the damp bathroom. I heard him moving around, not lying in the dusk in a reverie anymore. I kept from hurrying under the water. I washed my bony feet thoroughly, noticed a new blue vein behind my left knee, shaved my armpits. I wiped the steam from the mirror: now I was a person who began an affair in a lonely hotel room.

Philip pulled the white towel off my hair and twisted a lock around his fingers.

"I'll meet you this afternoon."

MY HAIR WAS WET from the pool when he called a few hours later to say he could not get away from the studio. That was fine with me. I was ready to be alone, to eat something greasy and bad for me. I had dreaded making arrangements to meet him outside the hotel and having to endure any uneasiness, or fool around in his car or some other semi-public place.

"Come back and see me soon, Emma Dial."

I picked up McDonald's and brought it back to my room.

I LOOKED FOR HIM in the airport. I walked through the main terminal where I took a stool at a bright restaurant counter. The menu was in Spanish and English. I ordered chicken soup, a salad, and a large coffee. My book fell from my lap, and when I reached for it on the floor, one leg still straddling the stool, one extended toward the paperback spine, my neighbor at the counter looked at my ass, my body reaching. I felt his eyes on me, like a pressure on my skin. He ordered a café con leche and a chocolate croissant that the waitress warmed for him. Could he tell I had been having sex in a hotel room and that was why he surveyed me without caring if I noticed? He read a copy of *Newsweek* magazine that had been stolen from an airplane, still in its plastic cover. I frowned at him to express my lack of interest and he shrugged at me.

"Asshole." Just a whisper above mouthing the word.

He shrugged again.

I left money on the counter and went to sleep on a plum-colored chair in the windowless departure lounge. Planes boarded for Nassau and Tampa. No one spoke English any-more. It was warm and stuffy. I dreamt Philip Cleary was with me, that he was beside me in his own plum-colored chair. He wore exquisite Föhn clothing that made him appear as though he just arrived from somewhere fantastic and far away, where alone he had braved something elemental in himself. Around us passengers gathered, waited, watched television, talked on their phones, and boarded planes. He opened my shirt and held my breasts in his warm hands. Our tongues licked hard and slid into each other's wide mouths. My skin was smooth and pale beneath his callused hands. I shifted in my seat. At the first boarding announcement for my flight I hurried to the newsstand for mints, soda, and the *Times*.

4

ONE POST-IT NOTE stuck to the color table: *Emma, wait for me before you do anything.*

I had been settled on the scaffold all morning, concentrating on the riverbank of *Interstices* when Michael took his chair and started picking on me about the brush I was using.

"It's worn out, get a new one."

The brush was well cared for, not old.

"I told you to wait."

He smoked three of my cigarettes. He only smoked to make an impression, at a party or in front of people he could not communicate with directly. He sighed, he coughed, he let the phone ring without answering it, fidgeting in his

dirty yellow chair. He went to the window to tap the pane
and scare a pigeon off the sill.

"Fuck off, birdie," he said.

I needed to stay calm and not get flustered in advance of
the maelstrom. If I spoke first he would be worse, it would
last longer.

He tossed my unfinished cup of coffee in the garbage,
mumbling about how messy and careless I was. He turned
the radio off. He slumped back into his chair, scuffing his
shoes on the floor.

I put my brush down.

"I want to listen to the radio. I need the radio to paint."
This should have been obvious to him. He focused on the
painting, not on what I had to do to make it. Choosing not
to divide one's attention was a luxury, a perk of fame. I hated
him for it now.

He turned the radio on again. A commercial for car
insurance.

"Emma, our whole relationship is based on trust, right?"

I loaded the slim brush with a putty color. Perhaps he discovered traces of Irene in his darkroom. Given his attraction
to playing Lothario, I had calculated he would not mind too
much when he did find Irene in his building with a copy of
my key and alarm code.

"I wouldn't say the whole thing."

"All these years. If not trust, then what else? What could
keep us together for so long?"

His eyes were wild and unblinking. The conversation had
no safe direction, it was a minefield.

"I work for you for money."

He heaved his breath, dropped his shoulders, and scraped his feet on the floor like an angry bull.

"You are the most cynical fucking person I have ever known. I can't look at you another second."

He bolted from the room and slammed the door behind him. I lifted the brush to protect the canvas when the wall shook. His footsteps began to recede and then returned. He peeked in and saw I lifted the brush again. I know he appreciated my protectiveness. Maybe he would calm down.

"You got a call from Philip today. Don't you think that's interesting, that my old friend is calling you from Florida?"

It was a low moment. Philip Cleary called the studio to upset Michael, but I was not entirely displeased. Seeing Michael full of jealousy was exhilarating. I felt powerful in a trivial way, but powerful nevertheless. Philip ought to be calling me.

"He's been revisiting some of my work and following your history with me. 'Emma Dial is the one to watch,' he said. 'She's masterful with a brush. Hold on to her, hold on tight, so she doesn't get stolen.'" He spat on the floor. "What does that mean? Why is my friend taunting me?" Michael had lost control, not me.

"Because it's easy." Philip Cleary called me masterful. It was obnoxious that he said it to Michael, but he still said it.

"Can't you see what's going on, Emma?" His body went stiff, electrified with fresh anger.

"Tell me about what is going on."

I knew in a crystalline way that Michael believed he was

good enough to be making and showing paintings. The way
he did things worked. Even though I could draw and paint
in any style and he could not, I have not always had the con-
viction to make and show work. I chose to put Michael first.
But now I was done with that way of thinking.

"I didn't let you go to Florida so that you could horse
around with Phil. You work for me. You were supposed to
help the Lerners." He spewed saliva with each word.
"Legally, you can't do anything. You're my person. If you
work for him I'll have you thrown in jail. I can't even look
at you!"

"You're not needed in here."

He flung a piece of paper in the air and then left the
room. I watched the little scrap float to the floor beside the
scaffold. He had written a telephone number with a 305
area code. His insinuation that Philip Cleary was after my
skills hurt me. It might be true, it might not.

Michael and I used to yell at each other all the time, especially if he wanted me to redo something without saying
why. I could never abide that with him. He picked on me
when it seemed like I could go on without him, then he
made himself necessary. I asserted myself in some fairly
meaningless way. Then he would fire me. By the time I had
cleaned up, he rehired me. We never apologized. We favored
the dramatic sexual reunion, something fun and ridiculous
like fucking in the stairwell or the bathroom of a restaurant.

He would leave me alone for a while. Fighting with
Michael focused my mind. I worked perfectly all afternoon,

without distraction. No breaks for coffee or chocolate or to rest my eyes.

Once at the very beginning he had to make drawings for a print edition he had committed to doing with a Munich gallery. The gallerist was due to come and pick up the originals that would be made into a pair of lithographs. He spent the morning procrastinating, frustrated and uncomfortable. He complained about his teeth and sinuses and a sty he suspected was blossoming in the corner of his lower left eyelid. He ran back and forth to the bathroom to inspect his face. He talked about doing the drawings, how much he revered the gallerist, how honored he was to work with her since she was basically a living legend, her parents were German royalty. Her elegance, her braininess—these were words he reserved for women he would not fuck. (Seductive women were called something else—a fox, a lynx, a doll, a flower, and in my strange case, a matador.) His fear permeated the entire studio. About midmorning, I suggested that I go buy some nice paper for him to work on. He was enthusiastic. He would join me. We drank coffee on the walk down to Pearl Paint. Once inside he asked if I preferred any particular type of pencil, so I chose some and he bought those too. He carried paper, markers, pencils back to the studio. "We could be mistaken for a couple in the throes of a home improvement project," he said. I was in a panic the entire time, certain he was testing me. I wanted to be helpful but was actually afraid of failing him. I second-guessed every thought that passed through my mind and became catatonic. I tried to remember Meredith Davies' words: What did I have to lose? Exactly nothing. Back at the studio I sat at my desk with the new pencils. "What do you want the drawings to be like?" I took a few sheets of paper from my own notebook, so it was informal, potentially throw-away, and lit a cigarette. I began to draw what he described to me: two sleeping bodies on the deck of a small boat, no water in view, an arid sleep. I thought of Therese and Michael, peacefully entwined on their honeymoon. I thought of lions napping in a zoo.

"That's pretty good, Emma." Michael watched over my shoulder.

I made half a dozen different views of the sleepers until he settled on one. Then he told me about a calm sea over-looked by an ominous mountain.

"The kind of mountain that would be a volcano if only it could be. Not a pretty Cézanne kind of thing," he said.

"No Sainte-Victoire."

"Nothing against Cézanne."

I drew three versions of the mountain before he brought me two photographs of young Therese Oller trekking a steep rocky path, only more mountain ahead of her, and told me not to copy them.

"Just for tone."

"Let me get you some more paper," he said.

He delivered the new paper to me; we pretended nothing was happening. Assurance seeped into my hand, I wanted to help him and I could.

"I need the radio to draw."

He turned on NPR and adjusted the volume until it was loud enough. I settled down. The radio announcer introduced an author who had set her new novel in Kraków, London, and Madrid. I wrote down the title. At that time hearing the names of faraway cities made me excited about art and the future. I believed I would see the world and that belief was linked to my painting. Michael returned with a cup of coffee. He placed it before me on the desk and then left again. I made two versions of each picture. I chose the best two and laid them aside with the others nearby, also good, but slightly inferior, because they were too light and there was some hesitation in them. I felt proud for rescuing him. I considered leaving a note but there was nothing to add.

WHEN MICHAEL RETURNED his demeanor clearly expressed his feeling about me: he would rather I worked a seventeen-hour day than have any regard for him. In the intervening hours I had decided that all of his emotions were fabrications. A real Michael did not exist. His personality had long ago been subsumed by his art. He could not be genuine if he tried. Maybe he had to look down on me, patronize me, think of me as inferior to him so that he could compete to be the best.

"You're still at it." After lots to drink and coaching on how to deal with me from Gerda or Frederich or both, he made his voice soft and came close to me, raffish and flirty. He took one of my cigarettes.

"I'm leaving, though."

This is when I went into some kind of state, like a free fall. Earlier I wished he would calm down and stop overreacting, but now I could have predicted every word and gesture and finally the epithets he had for me, as though we had been through this before and I was remembering the battle or we had decided for some reason to relive it. This was the ramp up.

"Give me the brushes. I'll take care of them." He dragged deeply on the cigarette and reached toward me with both hands.

"That's all right." I climbed down, clutching my brushes possessively.

He held the pack of cigarettes up but I shook my head.

"You look tired. Why don't you take tomorrow off, or come in late."

"I have to finish here."

"You will. It's going great. Don't worry about the paintings."

"I am going to finish these. These are the last ones I can do." I opened the heavy metal door to the slop sink closet.

"What? Emma, what did you say?"

"I'm not making your paintings anymore." I half expected one of us to laugh in disbelief. I quit my job. I had only ever been fired by Michael. This time was real. There was no way for him to appease me.

"Emma. Don't be upset about Phil. I know he can't come between you and me." He sounded afraid. "I really don't care about that."

"I know you don't." I did not quite have control over my face and voice and a birdlike screech came out.

"You're so tired. Don't be unreasonable. We can talk about it tomorrow."

"Let's talk about it now."

"Don't do something you'll regret, Emma. This is where you belong."

"I used to feel that way but I don't anymore and that's good. It's time for me to paint my paintings."

Michael made his own birdlike screech for which I could have murdered him with my bare hands.

"That's great to see you have a sense of humor about this. It will serve you well when you interview new assistants. 'Likes to laugh a lot. Maintains a playful attitude in the workplace.' "

"Emma, you're being too serious. I'm not 'laughing' at you." "Laughing" in quotes. "You should make some paintings of your own. You should do exactly that."

"I don't have anything else to say about it, Michael. This has been a good job for me. But I have a studio in Brooklyn. Did you know that I have a studio?"

"No. You never mentioned it."

He was right. Why had I never mentioned it to him? He should have seen my place on South Eighth Street a long time ago. Except he hated Brooklyn and would have recommended that I move it to Manhattan or offered some other utterly senseless, useless piece of advice.

"I'd like to see it. I'll come and see what you're up to."

"Sure."

"Who's seen it? Has Phil seen it?"

"Oh yes, he's been there many times."

"What does he say?" I thought he might have a conniption.

"Masterful. Genius. The one to watch."

The only times my studio came up in conversation I lied. This was not lost on me. I felt pathetic but Michael was not in a fighting mood. He wanted to be conciliatory, which was boring. I had moved beyond the point of no return. The sound of his voice made me tired.

"Your work is important and here you are painting at the highest level."

"Don't talk anymore. You're not saying anything meaningful. Say good night."

"Emma. We'll talk in the morning, Emma."

I listened to him go out. I dialed Philip Cleary's number but there was no answer and I hung up on the machine. Nearly unemployed and unattached to Michael, I should feel more different. The relief, or whatever came next, should be more immediate. Instead I felt sleepy, achy, and disoriented from being alone too much. I turned off the lights and an image of saying goodbye to him slipped into my mind. Leaving him alone in the studio, in the office, in the stairwell outside the door, running away from him on the street. I slept fitfully in his chair, covered with my coat. He may have come down again when he did not hear the doors shut and lock. He may have looked in on me, put his hands on my arms and kissed me. My eyes fluttered in the dark, heavy with sleep. He may have asked me not to leave him but when I woke up I could not remember.

5

MICHAEL HAD CLEARED off my desk except for my note-book and a row of neon Post-it notes.

Emma, Can you eat dinner on either Thursday or Friday night?

Emma, Do you know where my photos of Spanish Wells are?

Emma, Can you be here for the interview I have on Friday afternoon at four? If you want to make it earlier in the day call the writer and tell her I have a doctor's appointment or something.

Philip Cleary called.

Emma, Call the gallery and tell them they can't bring any-one here on the weekend because I am working and we cannot be disturbed.

He seemed to be pretending nothing had happened except he was avoiding me, I was sure of it. He had filled the margins of my notebook with drawings of Swiss chalets and little mountain landscapes, surrounded by heavy blue cross-hatching. I tore the strips of Michael's doodles out and set fire to them in a coffee cup on the windowsill and dumped the ashes out onto Christie Street.

I unlocked the painting studio and found the color table was covered with more notes.

Emma, The reds and ochres look different. What have you done to the paint?

Emma, Let's get this one done fast! I'm tired of looking at it!

Emma, Don't let the dealers come over while I'm out of town. They can't come here whenever they want. I'll be home late on Sunday night. Don't answer the phone unless it's me calling.

I turned off the lights and fell asleep in Michael's chair until midday and then ordered two coffees, a cheeseburger, a liter of Coke, and cigarettes from a restaurant on Second Avenue that delivered quickly. I tossed the leftovers on the floor, amid my cigarette butts and coffee cups. At two-thirty I climbed the scaffold and worked on *Interstices* for fifteen hours, all the tiny windows and slate roofs, stopping to find a lighter and stretch my legs. At dawn I locked up and walked over to my apartment, napped fitfully for a few hours, and went back to work.

THEN I WAS ON a fucking roll with my magnificent *Interstices,* my map, my road out of town, my treasure island. A week passed without sleeping at home or thinking about the

future of Michael or even Irene. I passed out on the scaffold
with a brush in my hand, dreaming of Philip Cleary in his
studio, mirroring me. The only person I spoke to was Tony.
He appeared at one and five to bring me downstairs for the
two fifteen-minute breaks I took in the afternoon, quick
walks around the perimeter of the park. Tony had the best
idea of what my job was like, the solitude.

"You're my collaborator, Tony."

"You're my inmate." He cracked up.

Dreams of the future crept up on me: swimming in the
sun, walking along unfamiliar streets, surrounded by
strangers. Philip Cleary. I put a final layer on the white-
washed church.

Frederich Hecht arrived unannounced with the daughter
of a Berlin dealer, an aspiring painter.

"I greatly regard Freiburg," she said.

"She wrote her thesis about him. Look. She brought
along a copy," said Frederich.

She was tall, slender, beautifully dressed in black silk,
black cashmere, black leather, and thoroughly disappointed
to find me alone, surrounded by food debris and cigarette
butts, listening to Caetano Veloso songs at full volume.
Frederich sneered at *Interstices* and me but ogled the other
completed canvases propped against the walls, ready to be
signed and sold.

6

IT WAS SPRING and the city felt like a different place with new faces and cars and shops on each street I walked. I punctuated every move I made with the acknowledgment of its finality: This is the last Wednesday, Thursday, Friday, the last stroke with this brush, the last time picking up this palette knife, climbing off the scaffold, touching this wall, flipping this switch, locking this door. The peacefulness of the final days felt like getting away with murder. I worked alone up until the end. Sometimes I heard Michael or Gerda on the stairs at night. I had not seen him in person since I quit. He only left me polite, or mostly polite, notes. I finished the paintings in record time and Michael would never want to acknowledge the feat. I wished he would say something about it, even something annoying that I could understand as a thank-you. Michael never thanked me for my work, but this time, foolishly, I wanted him to. I was waiting.

Patrice had brought the final pictures up to the office and Michael had signed *Phu Quoc* and *Interstices* without me. Things were changing quickly. Hideki came to visit before I left for the last time. We sat at my desk while I threw old receipts and exhibition cards into the trash can.

"I saw one of Michael's paintings at a party the other night. It looked sort of like Lake Powell," said Hideki.

"*Bad News,* 2002."

I momentarily forgot who owned that painting and defied the urge to look in my notes to find out. Then it came back to me: an architect friend of Michael's and her husband. All those details were stored in my head for now but I was beginning to lose them. All my painting notes would be there for Michael's next assistant.

"How did you come to be admiring my handiwork in an Upper East Side townhouse?"

"I went to a party. With a photo editor."

Hideki got miffed because I had no quick response.

"Feeling righteous? I bet you have no reason to," he said.

I tried to stare him down so Philip Cleary would not become a topic. Hideki was the last person I wanted to confide in, he would tell everyone, beginning with Therese.

"Who's the editor? You like him?"

"I really like him right now."

"I keep thinking about your new paintings."

"Too bad I don't have anyplace to show them. I spoke to the gallery director last week. She said she didn't like how my work had changed. I should have known this. They don't want you to change. Ghis said they're too complicated."

"More abstract."

"But not too much more. She was really honest with me. She said people who buy paintings don't tend to want to spend a lot of time thinking about them. They want to match the sofa and curtains."

"Hasn't she placed a ton of your stuff?"

"Sixteen paintings and works on paper in the last eight months. Beaucoup bucks. But she's not going to show my paintings again. I thought I finally had some momentum. She wants the work I've been doing on paper. Better than nothing." He was close to tears.

"What are you going to do?"

"Finish these paintings. Hustle around for another gallery. What else can I do? I approached a few galleries in Brooklyn, even though it would be a step down for me. Fuck." Hideki tapped a pencil on the edge of the desk. "Fuck, I am so pissed. My gallery dumped me. I am too old to be living like this."

"Someone else will take you on. What about galleries in Manhattan?"

"There are places that would be good for me." The pencil fell to the floor and rolled under the desk. "But they're full. No one is looking for painters unless they are making slick little canvases in small, medium, and large and are willing to crank out whatever size the dealer asks for. Do you remember the one of the willow bush? Ghis wants that one, but one-third bigger."

"If you were twenty-two years old with a thirty-month painting career ahead of you, you would be a good boy and do what you're told."

"My paintings changed because I am a better painter than I was a year or two ago. The gallery is punishing me for that."

We discussed the photo editor's various skills in a whisper, which included Bikram yoga, French kissing, and baking lemon meringue pies.

"Michael will take you back if you explain that you're exhausted and need a break." He looked at *Phu Quoc* and *Interstices* leaning against the wall.

"A permanent break."

"Think of how great the work is because of you. You can't stop now."

I loved *Interstices* already. I put my hand in this one like I never had before. The lines had nervous, intense energy and the brushwork was fucking sublime.

"I should have stopped ages ago."

"How can you leave him? If you'd only been with him a year or two it would be different. But you're connected. What will happen to his work? His legacy?"

"I'm a laborer and Michael can find a new laborer. His legacy is not my problem."

WHEN THERE WAS nothing else for me to tidy up or empty out I knocked on Michael's door upstairs but no one answered. I wanted to see him, even if it was uncomfortable and we were both angry and hurt. I sat outside his door and smoked a cigarette, half hoping for him to return.

I decided if Michael came back I would make out with him. I smoked another cigarette, leaving the butts and ashes on the top step. He would like it if he found me waiting for him, even a sign that I had waited for him. It would make it easier for him to thank me if I did something nice for him first. If he came back in the next five minutes I would fuck him goodbye, but only in the stairwell, not in the house. But he never showed up. And that was it. My last day at work.

7

EVERY PAINTER AND her mother had work in the Armory Show except for me. Hideki's gouaches were up somewhere so I needed not to be a killjoy.

"I love that everything is for sale," said Hideki. "Everything and everyone."

We paused to take in the fray and the noise of voices and piano music, a spiky rendition of something by Gershwin.

"I like that it's all purposeless. Even the meaningful stuff is purposeless. Do all these people care about art?"

Hideki took his cell from his hip pocket, spoke for a few seconds, and then tucked it away again.

"That was Jennifer. She's already done Pier 90. She said she'll find us on 92 somewhere."

I scanned the faces and the walls of pictures ahead of me. Hideki groaned and took off his jacket.

"How's your back?"

"My back is old." He pulled an exaggerated face. "Do you read Jennifer's *TimeOut* column?"

"I did when she first got the job."

"Two years ago."

"Is someone playing the piano nearby?"

"That's recorded music. I'm going to see Maya perform. She's frying eggs on a hot plate to celebrate the traditional practice of home cooking she learned from her great-great-grandmother."

"Great-great sounds serious. I'm going to celebrate the traditional practice of taking a pee, smoking a cigarette, and looking at pictures. I'll find you and the yakuza in a while."

"Booth 304," he said.

Frederich's wares were set up in a space three times the size of the standard booth, not too close to the entrance but not too far. A similar gray carpet as he had in the gallery had been laid and the temporary partitions had been taped and painted. In the measured center of the carpet a gleaming rectangular table and four chairs beckoned visitors to come and have a seductive chat with Frederich or one of his associates. Michael's aquatints hung along the rear wall, looming over the slightly shorter L-shaped walls that bracketed the space. Therese's diptych was on the left, lithograph, etching, woodcut, and screenprint in an edition of seventy-five, and on the right were six original paintings by three other gallery artists.

I found Ghislaine Belcourt's booth where one of Hideki's gouaches hung salon-style amid an array of works on paper and paintings on canvas and board. Ghis had built a desk of plywood and fluorescent tubing and she sat, barefoot in a tangerine silk shift, talking on the phone to a gallerist in another booth somewhere, about the taste of feta cheese that was not made from sheep's milk, how it was not really feta but that she liked to eat this fake feta for dinner with an avocado and a few glugs of oil and vinegar. She handed me a book Hideki had made on Long Island last summer. Each pair of facing pages had been painted in a single day with various pared-down views of the ocean and the sound where he and Shiro splashed around in the waves and picnicked. He had described this book to me. Hideki was not sentimental about things he made, it was all meant to be sold.

Tony Wight Gallery's cramped booth featured three of Idris's sculptures. Tall plywood trees, eight or nine feet high, had flat boughs covered with canvas screenprinted with degenerated images of bare city streets, no people, no cars, just the building façades at the far side of wide stripes of blacktop. I walked around and between the towering trees, committing them to memory so I could tell Irene about them one day.

"What's happening, Emma Dial?"

Idris appeared before me. With a girl. A girl who laid her hand on his shoulder. No introductions were attempted.

"Just looking around. I like your trees a lot. Hideki has some stuff here at Ghislaine Belcourt's."

"What about you?"

"Maybe next year." Last year Idris and I had come to the Armory Show together and I had said this year would be the year for me.

"Sounds like a plan," said Idris.

Catherine and Lewis Breslauer made their way through the streams of people with their art advisor steering them in the direction of big-ticket items. In the four months since my stupid comment to them about my studio in Williamsburg I had been there only once. I harbored a fleeting fantasy that I could attract their valuable attention to Idris's trees. But the Breslauers were in demand and they were delivered to Vincent Bencivenga, who was showing Lucy Trost's new color prints of herself lying spread-eagled on the hoods of various muscle cars. Hideki had been to the Breslauers' house in California once and Lewis told him the Picasso paintings were kept in a vault except for one of Marie-Thérèse Walter from 1932.

Idris said goodbye and sauntered away with his new girl. I was touched by sadness that he was not in our lives anymore, as though there had been no friendship between us. Irene barely spoke of him.

The whole pier smelled like cigarettes although I had not seen anyone smoking. There must be some place out of view where people lit up. The Armory Show began to remind me of the AIDS Action Alliance benefit at the Waldorf.

Marcella, one of Jeff Koons's assistants, grabbed my arm.

"What do you think of it this year? You look dazed." She had come from art school in Düsseldorf a year ago and landed a job in Koons' studio straightaway. "Or have you not made up your mind yet?"

"I like those trees." I pointed to Idris's sculptures.

"I hear you quit Michael. Yes?" She cocked an eyebrow with interest.

"Are you looking for a change?"

"Always, always, always. The grass is greener, you know?"

"Call the studio. Michael will talk to you. He likes you."

I made my way around to Frederich's space again where he and Michael chatted with the Weisses. Michael had one arm across Maurice Weiss's shoulder and the other around Karin Weiss's waist. They had bought paintings from Michael's last two shows at Frederich's.

"I would be honored to visit and see how the painting looks in the schloss," said Michael. His eyes darted between the Weisses and Therese, who kissed her husband goodbye on the mouth. Hideki waited at her side.

"I hear you are lighting off on your own." Therese rushed at me. "Congratulations."

"Your prints look fantastic."

"Let me know if you want some work." She spoke loud enough for Michael to hear.

Michael shifted his weight back and forth repeatedly and bobbed up and down, trying to stay afloat. He inched closer to Therese and her diptych.

"Emma's 'taking a break.'" He made quotations in the air around the words "'taking a break.'" "It's time for her to do something different."

"Oh, Michael, come on." Therese gave him a mirthless smile. "See." She turned to me. "He can't stand to be without you. Total denial."

"I am in 'denial'." "Denial "in quotes. "For years I have been in 'denial' about Emma."

His angry tone surprised me. I had been stupid to think he was going to let me off the hook easily.

"Emma's loyalty and her abilities are dubious."

Hideki looked disappointed in me, which was outrageous. No one spoke. Michael had everyone's attention and he was going to keep talking. I could not believe he was going to do this to me.

Then Jennifer materialized, wrapped in a throng of artists, including two of Frederich's up-and-comers, one of whom wore a T-shirt that said "Let Me Putty Your Windowpanes." The Weisses perked up, trying to figure out who was who. Jennifer almost made it over to me but was waylaid by Chris Cagnasola, his wife, and their daughter. Jennifer and Chris had not seen each other since we were at SVA. His wife was doughy and unfashionable and looked as though she never lied about anything. I had to look away when he tried to make eye contact with me. I may have deserved this, but I had no clue how I was going to bear it. They were all close enough to hear Michael.

"Hello, Jennifer. We were just talking about how I had to release Emma from her responsibilities." Michael's voice was loud and manic. "Do you know about this?"

"No, Michael. I don't know." She whispered something to Chris Cagnasola, filling him in, I supposed. Jennifer would be able to write about Michael's diatribe and whatever turned out to be my reaction to it in her weekly column.

"Emma, physically and mentally, if you don't mind my saying so, can't do the work anymore. We barely made it through this series of paintings and the final picture, '*Interstices*,' is badly compromised." He put "*Interstices*" in quotes, which made me wonder if he would disown the painting altogether. He might not include it in the show or his catalogue raisonné and that would make it worthless to me.

"What are you talking about?" Therese looked ready to mix it up with him, for sport, not necessarily in my defense.

Michael bobbed again. Waiting for him to continue his lashing was excruciating.

"I was duped. For seven years I entrusted my work to an unstable person." He pointed at me in case there was any doubt.

No retort occurred to me. Crying was out of the question and I fought it with all my strength. Jennifer had told Chris Cagnasola something funny and they held each other's forearms and giggled. There was a one-in-a-billion chance that they were reminiscing about art school.

"My assistant tried to jump ship before she was jettisoned, but I told her, Emma, it is time for you to move on. Maybe it was burnout. As an artist I can't burn out. Burnout is for amateurs. Maybe it was too many late nights at Remiz or partying in Miami. Your friend Irene has a drinking problem, I know."

"Okay." It was the only thing that came to me. That I had harbored a cockamamie idea about being thanked was going to be my own little secret. That was one for the vault, as my grandmother used to say.

"Frederich, what is Emma talking about? What is she trying to say to me?"

The Weisses watched this scene like it was theater.

"You can see here in the prints that she was already slipping. These were made about six months ago. The carelessness has reared its head. Maybe no one can see it except for me. No. It's obvious Emma's problems are surfacing."

Frederich seethed. An uncontrolled episode in his domain meant heads would roll. He stamped his foot and an assistant materialized. Frederich whispered directions and the assistant moved toward me. I was going to be ushered away.

"I would never do something like this to you." I meant this for Michael but it applied to the entire group. I would like to maintain that even though I tried to take Chris Cagnasola for a fool, the lies I told him were not mean-spirited. I sidestepped Frederich's assistant; let her chase me if she had to.

Michael commanded everyone's full attention, including Therese's. He would have to capitalize on her nearness. It was precious to him. His head whipped back and forth between their two sets of prints, conceiving of a way to pull her into this more deeply.

"Frederich, did Therese use my printer for her thing?" It made sense that only Therese could derail him from taking me apart.

"No, it is not the same person who printed for you," said Frederich.

"Think twice before you let Emma Dial into your studio, Therese. She could ruin you."

Karin Weiss's mouth hung open.

"Please stop." I was desperate.

"I don't know what you're talking about, Emma." Michael bent his knees and then bobbed up to his full height to stress the syllables. "Who understands what Emma is talking about?"

My skin burned. Gerda walked up to Michael's side and gave me the stink eye. Without another word to anyone I fled to Pier 90. Before I reached Susanna Mackie's booth I doubled over and covered my mouth to stifle a cry and the sick feeling that had risen up. I had witnessed some nasty scenes between Frederich and his employees, collectors beating up their advisors and other hired help, and I suppose, like them, I never thought it would happen to me. I felt a painful pounding in my head, chest, across the entire surface of my skin. Jennifer had notes. Was it possible to avoid Chris Cagnasola forever? I took some of the deepest breaths of my life and kept moving.

Two leather-clad assistants leafed through the newspaper, impossibly blasé given the streams of people passing by and staring at them. Susanna stood in the busy aisle, her arms folded across her artificially tanned cleavage, blocking the way of everyone trying to pass. She spoke in semiprivate business tones to an elegant woman in a trench coat. "He painted for Peter Halley and she printed for Richard Prince. Now they make this fascinating work together. Bridget Riley meets Sigmar Polke."

"Oh wow," said the trench coat.

Behind Susanna's assistants hung two paintings of Yessenia standing on a gleaming six-foot aluminum ladder,
slashes of heavy ivory and gray paint interrupted sections of
her face and body so that she was missing, variously, an eye,
her nose, the left side of her face, her left arm, hand, and
hip. My anger welled up. Philip Cleary painted Yessenia so
sensually, and then obliterated her image in such an easy
way. This might have been the only way to distract me from
Michael's attack. My jealousy surged.

Before I could work myself up into a full-blown lather, I
spotted a folding chair across the aisle. Sitting down to take
another look and attempt objectivity seemed like a worth-
while challenge. Not that I was in any state to actually pull
it off. Then an orange light flickered in my peripheral
vision. I found the secret smoking section, was my first
thought. I touched the cigarettes in my coat pocket in anticipation. But I could not have been more wrong. It was a
painting, a tiny jewel-like painting. The Armory Show was
causing me more upset than I could have anticipated but I
already felt a kinship with that orange color. I had to get
closer.

The booth belonged to Apartment 1R, a Los Angeles
gallery. Four canvases, aflame with rousing colors and rich
snappy lines, hung in a row. From left to right:

Two shepherd mutts digging a massive hole, dirt flying
through the air behind them.

Maria Ostrovsky sitting across a table from her boyfriend,

the writer Lamont Pierce, the orange light on the wall behind them.

The same room packed with people drinking and smoking and dancing.

The room again, clean and quiet, a newspaper open on the table, the chair pulled back.

109 S. 8th St. (Where It Began), Maria and Lamont in Mount Washington, Birthday Party, The Next Day, all dated 2005.

Meredith Davies was not in New York nor was she a quitter. What else did I need to know?

8

When I reached the deli on Avenue A Irene was outside with the buckets of cut flowers. Our meeting felt portentous. She pointed to the stargazers wrapped in cellophane. "I want some of these."

Each bouquet had three stems and some stems had blooms that were not yet open. Irene's preoccupation with flowers was annoying but I could not criticize her for it or try to stop her. We had never tried to correct each other. I chose a bunch that looked like all the blooms would open even though I preferred tiger lilies.

Inside, I poured our coffees from a fresh pot while Irene paid for everything.

"I know what you're thinking," said Irene. "You hate it when I do this with the flowers but it makes me feel better."

"You're right. But that wasn't what I was thinking. I went to the Armory Show today."

The scene had gone hazy but when the details returned to me later I would be faced with my frozen, dumbfounded silence while Michael had his way with me. Chris Cagnasola must have thought I had lost my mind, trying to pass myself off as a painter showing with Susanna Mackie. Public humiliation, my bête noire, had bitten me on the ass. No one stuck up for me, and most disconcerting I had not been able to defend myself against Michael's attack. Even Irene had been dragged in. Things had to change. Things were already changing. Why had no one spoken up on my behalf? His prints looked great. I was not slipping. He only said that because the Weisses were not print collectors and he risked nothing by badmouthing the aquatints in front of them. Otherwise Frederich would have reacted differently. *Interstices* was still a viable painting. I think.

"Did you see Idris?"

"His sculpture."

She waited.

"It's great. You should go."

"I can't."

"Sorry. About everything. Meredith Davies was at the Armory too."

"How is she?"

"She's painting."

I watched my doppelgänger cross the avenue. Probably the last time I would see her.

"I've been watching that woman grow old. Do you have people like that, who you have seen around the city for years."

"I end up sleeping with most of them."

"What a novel idea."

"Don't go to work tomorrow. Let's stay home and do stuff," she said.

"I don't have a job to go to tomorrow."

Irene stopped. She laid her palm sweetly on the back of my head. "A lot has happened."

"We got in a huge fight at Frederich's booth today, except I failed to put my dukes up. It was a nightmare."

"You fought like a girl?"

"Yuck. Exactly. I should have ripped his throat out."

We climbed the stairs to the apartment. I tore the opening off the plastic lid of my coffee, spilling some of it over my hand and down my sleeve. Inside there were already half a dozen anemones and yellow tea roses in a Mason jar on the table. Irene dragged her feet over to the kitchen.

"Do you have a tan?" She squinted at me.

"Maybe." I tried to stifle any expression. "I don't remember making all these decisions." Where could I begin to tell Irene what happened in Florida? Where was the beginning?

"I know what you mean. I feel so old all of a sudden. You know, I have this idea for an alien abduction film. Maybe shoot it in Chicago."

"All I want to do is eat and watch television." I sank to the floor. The prospect of listening to Irene pitch a film idea made me nauseous. "I went out of town."

"I'm realizing that. Let me guess." Irene licked her lips. "Air travel was involved. Domestic, business class."

I thought of Philip Cleary's breath on my cheek and ear and how he made me writhe on the hotel bed.

"Michael must be out of his mind. Now what happens?"

"That's what I'm trying to tell you. I know I want more."

"Of course," said Irene. "Why stop now?"

We watched a nature program titled "Autumnal Bird Migration Over Miami," which posited that nocturnal birds are capable of compensating for wind drift on flights up to twenty or thirty miles. The mink coat covered our laps. When Irene tried to change the channel, I snatched the remote.

"What do you think, they're going to fly over Philip Cleary's house?" said Irene.

I was rapt before the soaring seabirds and gulls, the sound of their wings beating the air.

"We match now." Irene pointed to the coat and my silver hair and then she pressed her fingers into the white fur.

When we were roommates we had shared everything, all the food, the money, many of the men, and most of the clothes. We had shared a voice. On the telephone our friends guessed who had lifted the receiver. All the hours making pictures side by side, we had shared a purpose. That had not been true for years but I did not feel sentimental about it the way I used to.

I had a DVD labeled IRENE SHOOTS that I used to watch

when she was away. It was unedited footage, short segments
Irene made during travel time or after a day's work. Conversations with people she met, several with an Ethiopian
woman who ran a restaurant and rented *cabañas* north of
Palenque, on the ocean. Irene asked how she ended up on
the Yucatán and the woman told a long tale of moving with
her boyfriend to Washington, D.C., where they ran a
restaurant with his aunt in Adams Morgan. Irene had the
camera beside her on a tripod, judging from the woman's
eyeline and how freely she spoke about her travels and dis-
appointments and ambitions, uninhibited by the record-
ing. Irene could bring people to that state, where they
forgot themselves. Even I used to talk endlessly with her,
every story relayed in minute detail, hours and hours of
conversation. But silence had crept up on me, I had
become mostly unwilling to give anything away. She had
hung the camera from a tree in the jungle and trained its
eye to record her jumping into a deep swimming hole, a
cenote called Emerald Skull, alone at dusk. Irene's pale
body dropped down the screen, shouting before she hit the
water.

"In Florida they assumed I was an artist."

"What?"

"They knew I wouldn't stay with Michael forever."

"Okay."

She said okay but she got up and started rearranging lily
stems and making more coffee.

"I can't afford to live in New York anymore," she said.

She was supposed to have been out in March, along with

the other tenants who had not paid rent for a year and a half. Stranded without a plan, Irene was the only one left in the building. The landlord had lost his patience, now he was angry.

"Mr. Fontana lets his old Dobermans shit in the halls and all the stairwell lights are out. I carry a flashlight in my bag."

"What do you want to do?"

"I don't want to live in a depressing little apartment. I shouldn't have bought the damn coat."

"You can live in my studio. Hire Patrice to haul your stuff."

"The art handler?" she said. "You don't understand. I can't go live in Brooklyn. Let's get a new place together. It'll be great, better than when we lived here." She sat in the windowsill and looked down at First Street.

Flakes of plaster fell from the kitchen ceiling and it seemed very clear to me what I had to do. For starters, stop regretting the time I had spent with Michael, the years I let my studio languish, the disappointment I had caused my parents. My mother did not make things, she studied people who did, and I think they frightened her because work could take them so far outside themselves, away from the people who loved them, to places where they did not need anyone else. My grandmother had shown me the pleasure of being taken far away by a painting. She was the adult who had the greatest understanding of my mother's exacting disposition. Maybe she should have backed off a little. I needed to stop minding my parents and their lameness of twenty years ago. Of course they were imperfect. Perhaps I could call them up and demand that they be proud of me. Or warn them that I would be making them proud soon.

On top of it all, disliking my apartment and having an affair with my married boss seemed more asinine than ever. Though it was safe to say everything between Michael and me was kaput. Now Irene and her decrepit First and First, shrine to our art school days, were driving me nuts.

"Are we going to get jobs?" This was a fairly innocent question coming from her.

"I'm not getting a job. The point, *for me,* is not to get a job." I was already practically shouting. "I don't know what the point is for you. What are *you* going to do?"

"What the fuck? Why are you being so mean to me?"

Nothing kept me in New York anymore. Irene had no way to be prepared for my assault; there was no precedent in our friendship.

"I don't want to get a place with you. I don't even want to be here with you now. I guess that's why." I laughed, an ugly involuntary sound from the back of my throat.

"Because of that stupid painter?"

"Because I can't live with you like we're in college. I'm going to Miami." A month ago I had told Isabelle Cleary I meant to move there, and lo and behold, it would soon be so.

Irene scowled. "Do you think you're going to have some big art career in Miami? The American painter Emma Dial. You're too old. Too fucking lazy," she shouted. "You're a shadow, an outline of a person."

"That's exactly true." I had never bought a one-way plane ticket before.

Irene searched the room, thinking. I wondered if First and First appeared to her as it did to me, an old trap that no longer did us any good. Not that we should be living in tidy condominiums, but violent dogs, angry from neglect, shit in the hallway. Surely there was a middle ground.

"How am I going to see you?" Irene poured coffee for both of us.

"I'll meet you in neutral territory in five years."

"Five years? That's how long it will take?"

"Owens Valley, California." I had seen a photo of a woman running along the edge of a forest of salt cedars in a Föhn catalogue. She could have been Irene, or me, or someone like us. This was one of my romantic notions the likes of which Irene hated.

"Wherever the fuck that is." Irene shook her head dismissively. "I get it. I knew you'd end up on your own." Irene dumped a few teaspoons of sugar in her cup. "I understand, okay?"

Preoccupied, I nodded. I pictured pools and conch shells and deco detailing, gas-guzzling American cars and pink Spanish-style houses with banana trees and red bougainvillea in the garden. Whether or not these would be my ultimate desires or even available in Miami I could not have said. Travel throughout Latin America. I would figure out the details as I went along.

FIVE

1

ON APRIL 30, I looked at a one-bedroom apartment in a yellow courtyard building. The superintendent told me the tenants would be out by the second week of May.

"They're moving back to New York City."

Two gray cats followed me through the four crammed rooms. A sectional sofa took up the entire living room. I counted nine unmatched wooden chairs, pushed into corners, one in the bathroom, two at the foot of the bed. Piles of old newspapers and magazines and wet towels covered the seats.

"I need something sooner than that."

I opened and closed a closet door.

"Check this out." He turned the shower on to show off the water pressure.

The new issue of *Artforum* with *Sea-shadow* on the cover lay on the kitchen counter.

"I want to move in today. Or tomorrow, at the latest."

People drove to work. A line of women waited at the bus stop, each with a folded umbrella under her arm. The air was already humid. Miami Beach had plenty of empty apartments. A woman passed me pushing a stroller with a pink blanket draped over the front, shielding her baby from the sun. I walked three blocks until I saw another for rent sign outside another pretty Spanish-style building. The fourth place I looked at was white stucco and had a pool in the courtyard. White oleander trees surrounded the building and grew high above a metal fence. Silhouettes of a palm tree and two flamingos, painted white, were attached to the bars of the gate. Palms, red hibiscus, and passionflowers filled the yard and potted fuchsias hung on the terraces outside each apartment. I decided to take the place if it was vacant. No more hotels. No matter what it looked like inside I would sleep there tomorrow.

2

AFTER DINNER AT A French restaurant in Coral Gables, Philip Cleary brought me to see his home.

"This is my first winter in years without a construction crew in here." We crossed the threshold into a rectangular two-story glass and teak house he designed with an architect friend from Pasadena. "Finally, no one is working here except for me."

"I didn't know you had done this. Built a house."

"My nephew's construction company built it."

"I did not figure you for a pretty house, I expected it to be more utilitarian."

"Come look at these."

An arrangement of bonsai trees filled a picture window in

the living room, delicate beaded lamps sat at either end of the mantel, photographs of Isabelle and her cousins on each table and shelf. Unlike every place I had lived, there were no towers of junk, books and magazines and clothes anywhere. Paintings and drawings and antique maps hung salon-style. There was an immense wall of books. A shelf of globes. A piano. The aesthetic was opulent yet haphazard. The longer I looked the more clear it became that everything was purposefully arranged. Appreciate that you get to see this, I thought. I took a step toward the bonsais.

"Chinese elm, juniper, Hawaiian umbrella tree." He pointed toward each pot. "That is a sago palm, it's an exotic plant. Tolerates neglect but thrives with attention."

I imagined him holding a silly miniature watering can. Naked.

A door off the kitchen opened into a studio roughly the size of the rest of the house, 25 by 75 feet, with one wall of floor-to-ceiling frosted panes and an adjacent wall with three covered square windows. A powerful air conditioner purred. He raised a window blind to reveal a eucalyptus that was too close to the house and brown smudges all over the glass panes.

"Look at that mess. That thing has to go."

"Gray kingbird or a mangrove cuckoo?"

He looked at me like I was nuts.

"I'm going to chop that fucking tree down."

"Can't you trim it? Top it?"

"Nope."

Philip showed me the guns he collected. I held a semiautomatic pistol for a few minutes and dropped it on my foot when I tried to twirl it between my fingers like a cowboy.

"Okay, give that back to me." He took it out of my hands and locked it up again.

I sat on the edge of his long wooden desk below three tiger skins and the head of a large cat with serious teeth.

"That's a black-faced impala and a cheetah. You use impala meat to trap a cheetah. And that's a black wildebeest," he said.

"I know about large mammals. You killed them?"

"In Namibia."

I would have preferred not to know. A hazard of becoming acquainted with one's painting hero turned out to be discovering that he murdered animals and kept tiny potted trees. Who wanted to know the object of one's adoration was determined to control nature even by destroying it? I hoped never to meet Luc Tuymans or Peter Doig. Let them exist perfectly in my mind.

"I've been drawing since I got down here. It's been a winter for drawing," he said.

I liked the sound of that.

A six-foot aluminum ladder leaned in the corner.

"When did you paint Yessenia?"

"Right after Susanna told me she needed work for her booth at the Armory. I like to get those extra commitments taken care of right away. Not let them stack up, you know? Otherwise they take over my whole life. I thought they came out all right. Didn't you?"

"Yeah, they're really nice. I was surprised you painted her. I don't know why."

"Jealous."

"No."

"Liar."

"Egotist."

He shrugged.

He used an old wooden school chair with a black-and-white-striped cushion on it for his painting chair.

"That looks uncomfortable."

"It's not so bad. Try it."

I searched his face to see if he was kidding but he put his hand on the chair back, inviting me to sit down.

"I wouldn't want to sit here all day."

"Good thing you don't have to." He kissed my neck.

"I meant the chair is no good."

He said things that seemed innocent but were also slights. I did not have to sit and work all day and he did, or that was how I understood him. Before I could protest he had pulled my shirt over my head and kneeled down in front of me. He kissed my collarbones.

"I want to see you paint." I had become fixated on the idea that seeing him work on a canvas would tell me something I needed to know. Or it might have been pseudo-girlfriend behavior: only someone close to him could see him at work. If he painted in front of me it would prove there was closeness between us. Either way, this desire of mine was a perversion and I knew it.

"Have sex with me right now, Emma Dial."

"Only if you work on that fresh canvas right afterward."

"Get up and take those jeans off."

But afterward he was lazy and hungry and not in the mood to paint.

"Another time." He yawned.

"It's sick how irresistible you can be." I yawned too.

I WOKE IN THE DARK remembering my old life. In particular, the last summer before Michael Freiburg found me:

I read a newspaper on the subway uptown, arriving before the morning heat and the worst of rush hour, though not before the rest of the crew. The Russian brothers had filled the room with cigarette smoke by the time I clicked on news radio and dumped the *Times* or *Post* in a yellowing pile against the wall.

I worked in the Museum of Natural History all summer, painting an equatorial sky on the entire ceiling of the new Hall of Human Biology and Evolution, the first permanent exhibition mounted in over twenty years. My painting there could last forever. The Russians stepped into their diorama of prehistoric man while I studied the curators' plastic sleeve of slides of 360-degree views of African skies. I worked in denim coveralls and a knit ski hat, close beneath the air-conditioning vents, lying atop the electric scaffold I leased from a rental house on Wythe Avenue in Brooklyn. My back was in knots so I kept a bottle of ibuprofen at arm's length, three pills every four hours. The Russians argued while they worked. My earplugs muted them and NPR to the right pitch, the distant voices kept me company. It was like being underwater.

I batched my paints in plastic deli containers, quarts of blues and whites lined my worktable, a scrap of plywood laid over two garbage cans. The Russians paid me to mix their colors too. I did it after work for a couple of nights. They stood over me, chewing on their mustaches, nodding as I added tints from my tray of bottles.

The Met was stuffed with tourists but I visited the galleries of nineteenth-century European art every few days. I lowered my scaffold at four, changed back to my T-shirt and trousers, and hurried across the park, weaving through ultimate Frisbee players, running, jumping, salivating dogs, sweaty bodies lying on striped towels and tartan blankets, solitary magazine readers watching each other from behind black sunglasses. The museum galleries closed at five-thirty.

Weekday evenings I rode the L to Bedford Avenue and swam a slow mile in the Metropolitan Avenue pool. I shuffled south along the hot sidewalk toward my studio. My wet hair soaked my shoulders and back.

I was painting on squares of Masonite, repetitions of images, possibilities of a figure's movement and expression: my mother reading on the porch; Jennifer with her graduate school friends, preening like cats, their hands brushing at their faces and hair; Irene trying to fix a camera she found or stole and then dropped; versions of Irene tinkering or looking hungrily through a lens. Always outside. The subjects of my pictures existed out of doors. Hours working in my studio disappeared. My parents were waiting for me to go to graduate school. They never specified what I was supposed to be but always the idea hovered that I was performing at a sub-par level.

Saturday mornings Irene drove us out to Robert Moses Beach in a borrowed car. By nine-thirty we were on the road. She sang over the wind in the backseat. That summer "The Lambeth Walk" was her favorite song. We set up camp around a cooler of fried chicken, chocolate cake, seltzer, and beer. Irene kept her camera safely wrapped in a towel until after her first nap. *Ev'rything's free and easy. Do as you darn well pleasey. Why don't you make your way there? Go there, stay there.* I got my shorts off and went swimming, out past the buoys, then south along the coast. I called these swims my Olympics, racing imaginary competitors and beating them in the final lengths before riding a wave back in.

PHILIP CLEARY BEGAN to stir beside me. He turned to run his hands along my arm, over my hip to my stomach. His skin was warm and dry. It was still dark outside but the air was already hot. He planned to go out on his friend Luis's boat. Luis fished every weekend and stayed on the water all day.

"We have to get up and meet Luis." His mouth was beside my ear, against my cheek.

I felt his voice on my skin. His hand slid down my ass and between my legs.

"You want to stay in bed a little longer?"

I told him yes. I put my arms around him when he moved on top of me. I imagined the ocean between his breaths. He woke before each dawn horny and alert and bloodthirsty. He wanted to kill some fish or shoot target practice or, like that morning, fight with his neighbor who moved the garbage cans from the side of the house.

"You have a garage and a driveway, why do you have to park where I put my garbage cans?" Philip said.

"I don't want to block my wife's car. She leaves for work first," said the neighbor.

"I don't want to look at the garbage cans. That's why I keep them over there. Don't touch them."

These were grown men who owned houses on waterfront plots larger than an acre.

When Philip came in the back door he was trying not to smile. I sat on the kitchen counter drinking the café con leche he made for me. He kissed my nose.

"Your nose is peeling." He wiped a flake of skin away. "I heard you laughing at me through the window. Move away from the window if you are going to laugh at me when I'm trying to be serious."

I kissed him. He sipped my coffee.

"Come take a shower with me, Emma. We can't be late to meet Luis."

The one time I had been fishing on the ocean I got sick watching my mother throw up over the side of the boat. I had had to lie down on a bench and try to sleep but could not stop yawning and retching.

"You don't have to come if you don't want to." He brushed another flake of skin from my nose.

"Okay. I'm not coming."

3

I LOWERED MYSELF into a flowered chaise beside the pool.
I pushed my pants legs up above my knees and my sleeves
onto my shoulders. I needed something to wear that was not
blue or black or brown.

A woman in a white bikini took a towel from around her
shoulders and laid it over a chaise down the row from me.
She straddled the chair, rubbed lotion on her arms, stomach, and the fronts of her legs, lit a cigarette, and pushed her
sunglasses up on her head. She inhaled noisily with her eyes
closed. I squinted to watch her. When she flicked the cigarette butt to the grass at her side I turned back to the empty
pool.

"Aren't you hot?" she said.

"Very."

"New in town?"

"Three weeks."

"Welcome to Miami Beach."

She had an accent. I was curious where she was from but before I figured out how to ask she fell asleep. I sat mesmerized by the pool until the still water blurred.

Irene had not learned how to swim with her face in the water until she was twenty-six. With friends we rented a house in the Catskills for the summer, an ugly ski house with a sleazy-looking brown hot tub and brown sofa and brown carpets and beige linoleum in the kitchen. Ten minutes up the road was a man-made lake where we spent the weekend days reading in the sun and drinking Genesee beer.

Irene dated a guy who could do the butterfly across the lake, nearly a quarter of a mile. All summer they swam along the uneven shore and he coached her freestyle. On Labor Day weekend she planned to swim across for the first time. I sat in the grass with Jennifer and two dozing friends, trying not to pay too obvious attention to Irene's swim. She had been preparing since June.

"Here I go." Irene walked into the shallow water.

When they were fifty yards out I folded up my newspaper and watched, shading my eyes with my palm. It had rained hard all night and the lake was cold but the day was bright. I had swum across and back right after coffee and my hair was already dry. Irene's pale arms lifted out of the water, her head turned for breath, her unsteady kick alongside her boyfriend's easy strokes. When she was halfway across she stopped and flailed, like she was trying to jump out of the lake and run away. I stood on the shore. The boyfriend shouted, "Irene, it's okay! Calm down!"

Jennifer jumped up and down beside me. Irene's arms fluttered like wings, her feet came out of the water, her fingers clawed at her boyfriend's skin.

"You are the strongest swimmer," said Jennifer.

I dove out. The sound of Irene's frightened voice pulled me. I had no idea what I would do when I reached them, only that I had to get to her fast. When I came up for my first breath and stroke, the water was still. Irene had quieted, her arms were draped around her boyfriend's neck and he was guiding her to the other side. The two of them walked straight back to the house, tired and disappointed. I stayed at the lake. Give Irene privacy. She would want to be alone. Soon no one was talking about drowning anymore and Jennifer and the friends went back to napping. But I thought all day: I'll never let that happen to me. I'll never need someone to save me like that.

After an hour in the sun the tops of my feet were burned and my back was in knots. I got up with a head rush and stumbled over the edge of the flowered chaise.

"See you later," the woman said, her eyes still closed.

4

PHILIP LEANED BACK on his hips, filling the doorway, looking confused. I stooped in the corner by the front windows, sweaty in a T-shirt and a frayed denim skirt I had sewn from a pair of jeans. Country music played on the radio. I had piled all the furniture against the rear wall. Half the wooden floor was painted blue, a color I mixed to match the sky, just before it turned dark and the horizon disappeared into the Atlantic.

"I thought you were renting on a month-to-month basis."

"No." We had never discussed anything like that.

He marveled at the wet floor. I could not believe my ears when he asked if I had permission to paint.

"Do you like the color? It's a fucking great color, if I do say so myself."

He watched me like I was doing something weird or naughty. I pretended I could not read his expression, but he let me down. He should be impressed.

"Won't the landlord mind that you've painted the floor?"

"Someone already painted it and the color has worn down. I did a good job. I sanded the entire thing by hand."

"It must have taken forever."

"I've been here all weekend."

"Don't be angry at me because I couldn't come see you. I told you I had obligations this weekend. I have to work," he said.

"Don't flatter yourself. I'm not angry. I've been busy."

His implication that it was only important for him to paint pissed me off. Michael spoke that way, so I was accustomed to a man holding that view of me and the rest of humanity, womankind in particular. But Philip should be different. I realized how badly I wanted him to like the room. I did not want to have a conversation with him about why I wanted to make my one room the way I liked it, after visiting his house, he should understand.

"Do you want to come for dinner with me?" he said.

"Let me put my stuff away first."

He glanced over his shoulder into the hallway, pretending to hear something, to make me afraid that someone would see what I was doing. But I was not afraid. The owner would either consider my work an improvement or she would keep my security deposit. Both scenarios were fine with me. He watched me cover the paint can and wrap my brush in a plastic bag and lay it on the windowsill.

"Do you need to change?"

"Where're we going?"

"I just thought you might want to change out of those dirty clothes."

"I'm fine like this, if you don't mind."

He watched me like I was a stranger. It made me feel even better about the room but I kept waiting for him to change his mind, be incautious, share my sentiment. He should see that what I had done was beautiful.

THE FOLLOWING EVENING I finished the second coat and ran the air conditioner on high and opened the windows all the way. I pushed my mattress into the corner. I found a table behind the building, beside the garbage cans, and dragged it upstairs and put it in front of the windows. I bought two wooden chairs at a thrift store on Alton Road. Philip had given me an orchid the first night he slept over. I sat at the table listening to the radio, playing with a dark leaf.

He knocked lightly at six and let himself in. I was on the phone giving the last four digits of my credit card number and the expiration date. He took glasses from the cabinet over the sink and opened one of the bottles of wine he had brought a few days earlier. He put a glass in front of me and placed his chair close to mine. He took the clip out of my hair and, when it fell, brushed loose strands away from my face. I put the phone down.

"Who was that?"

"The guy at the paint store."

"What's going on?"

He smoothed the hair at my temple.

"I just don't have anything to make stuff. I needed to buy some. They'll ship it all to me."

"From where?"

"New York."

"I have everything. Why don't you come over if you need something?" He turned the radio off.

"I don't know. It was faster to call the place I know."

He fiddled with a button on my shirt, to change the subject.

"I like this blue shirt."

"Did you see how good my floor is in the evening light?"

He undid the buttons from the bottom up and put his hands on me. His right hand was cool from the wineglass and the other hand was dry. I took a long drink and he kissed my throat. I ran a hand down the back of his hair and pressed his face to me. His open lips were warm against my skin.

"Can I take this nice shirt off?" He eased it off my shoulders and onto the chair back.

He expected me to say something about my plans but I did not have anything I wanted to tell him. We could sit quietly for hours and I liked to sit with him without speaking. It was unusual for him to want me to tell him something specific.

The bottle of wine was finished before dark and when the

rain began we took our own clothes off and lay down on the saffron sheets.

"Anything I say about painting is aphrodisiac to you. Don't think I don't notice."

"Huh?" he said.

I shut my eyes hard while he was on top of me. He reminded me of Michael too much and that was a problem that would soon need solving. All I saw was a swirling of deep purple and gray and then I fell asleep, my head in the crook of his arm.

5

I SWAM AN HOUR in the pool before the mail came at eleven, bringing a small package. Irene's loopy cursive in red Sharpie on the brown grocery bag wrapping. Inside was a postcard of a Cuban royal palm, the caption on the back said: *Several varieties of palm trees line the coast.* Irene had written: *I found these for you. Happy Birthday.* There were three presents wrapped in flowered paper: a Ñico Saquito CD, a fully exposed disposable camera, and a black-and-white-striped bikini.

In the afternoon I dropped the camera off at Walgreens to be developed and followed a young tourist couple out of the store to the beach, where they walked straight to the water. I stopped in front of a new hotel. The couple strolled

305

along the edge of the wet sand, out of my sight. The sun was high, too bright to read, too strong to stay out for long.

MEREDITH DAVIES' birch plywood bookcases out on the sidewalk

Irene's 8- and 16-millimeter projectors

Patrice carrying my sawhorses down the green stoop, the door propped open behind him

A man slamming the trunk of a blue sedan

A taxi heading east on South Eighth Street

Two men, both with buzzed heads, kissing

A row of tables on the sidewalk in front of my studio, all my art supplies laid out, for sale

A group of customers pawing over brushes and tubes

The spines of my books traced by an index finger with a crimson-painted nail

Patrice sitting on the rear fender of his truck smoking a cigarette

Two neighbors carrying the refrigerator down the block

A pile of empty milk crates

A scrap truck hauling away my plywood and sawhorses and stretchers

A teenage boy sitting in my painting chair, dribbling a basketball between his knees

Patrice making change from his wallet

Bills stuffed in a Café Bustelo can

Joyce Barnes, standing before the iron gate to her garden apartment, waving goodbye

Blurry Irene in the rain, damp hair around her mischievous face

Empty South Eighth Street

Empty First and First

The mink's empty hanger
A boarding pass for a flight to Mexico City

Twenty-two of the twenty-seven exposures came out.

I BURIED THE BIRTHDAY CARD and photographs in the Dade County phone book and shoved it in a cupboard in the kitchenette. Now all my stuff was gone. I had a pang of envy that Irene's new beginning could be more interesting than mine. I picked at charcoal under my fingernails and sharpened a pencil with a knife. I drew Meredith Davies striding through the crosswalk on Twenty-third Street. Pages of her running in the street, her legs like scissors. The lines were sure, my resoluteness on the paper. Irene's passion for going too far would not cost me anymore. She had saved me a trip to New York was how I ought to look at it.

I ran my dirty hands down my cheeks, across my fore-head, around my eyes. I sat in the lamplight, drew my face, drew Irene's face, crumpled all the pages up. Philip Cleary was a rapacious lover. I drew Irene again, at the center of the page, and me at the right edge. Maybe if my mother had joined in the morning ritual with my grandmother, not all of the paintings would have vanished. Together we might have been able to save them. I clicked the switch on the lamp I bought at Goodwill, on off on. The shade was opaque pink glass, like the inside of a shell. I had stripped the paint off the metal base, baring the iron, and then sealed it with a toxic solution that still stunk. He had left marks on my hips; his fingerprints were fading from my skin. I under-stood what made my mother so angry about me. No one wanted her daughter to need prodding or propping up. I should be able to make art without relying on anyone else.

I WOKE ROLLED into the sheet, sweaty, feeling like I had been far away, but rested, listening to the soft sound of a slow swimmer. I opened the blinds and watched a back-stroking neighbor reaching for the edge of the pool. Not someone I had seen before.

The conversations I overheard at Books & Books, McDonald's, and Publix were factual in a simple way: The sun is strong. The president is in town. My favorite show was canceled. I considered chiming in: I saw that. I heard that. I read that too. It could not be so difficult to get along with some of these new people. I clenched my jaw less and tried to look friendly, normal, unreclusive. Adjusted.

I SWAM TO AVOID being freaked out by blank sheets of paper and empty canvases. I walked to the museum and roamed around the galleries listening to my footsteps, trying to be calm. I turned thirty-two at an Argentine restaurant. Philip Cleary ordered veal but they brought him chicken. I ate filet mignon again.

"When I go back to New York—" he began.

"Can we not talk about that yet? I'm getting used to living here."

He must know how hard it was to come out from behind Michael's shadow.

"This will be a great year for you, Emma."

We went next door to drink sambuca with coffee beans

and watch the tango dancers. He said he would teach me and we held each other in the parking lot laughing. He explained where I should begin with my feet, the valets steering around us.

I missed Michael's opening. I sat at my desk measuring out a grid when I heard Hideki's message saying Frederich's dinner for Michael was a mess of celebrity and the paintings were a massive success. He sent a birthday card with half a dozen Polaroids of his new paintings, with more figuration, made at the house on Long Island.

I tried to get all cried out and then do some work. There used to be families of loons on my grandmother's lake, diving below the surface of the water. I swam for hours each morning and again in the lavender evenings. I missed Michael, the odd hours he came over excited about paintings he had seen or envisioned, the cadence of his voice, the way he ran his fingers through my hair, the way he said my name. The way he had pushed me to paint. I forced him out of my mind.

6

THE AIR CONDITIONER HUMMED at the highest setting while I read about abducted children in the *Miami Herald* and the *Times* and redrew patterns I was working out on a large pad. The room felt small but there was nowhere better to go alone in the heat. I tried to recall how I spent my days in New York. Eating at Remiz, sleeping too much, sprawling on the couch with a paperback or pacing around Elizabeth Street, walking to Michael's studio. A long time ago I sat in dark movie theaters waiting for Irene to resurface and make things happen. For years other people's pictures had composed my landscape.

Honestly, I felt too fucking scared to paint. I had never been a person who had to get into some existential state to work; I had been task-oriented about it—there is always a job to be done—but this was a big horse to remount. Away from Michael's studio I missed painting in a physical way, the way I would miss drinking coffee. I think I was waiting to be interrupted, for someone to stop me, no one in particular, though Irene was an obvious candidate. Someone I could blame later. But I knew painting was welling up and I drew to ramp up to it. My marks on the paper were too calculated, contrived even, but they were a pleasure for me because they were mine. Michael's influence could take some time to escape. I worked for an hour or so and flipped back and forth in the pages, cutting sections and adding them to different pages, trying to admire the slow progress of my work—a collage of monochromatic, syncopated lines. It was a relief to be away from all the artwork that was about things, complaint, finger-wagging, autobiography, support for dull theories, everything to do with the art market. Self-seriousness. The hours passed. A pile of pencil shavings grew on the corner of the desk. I sipped espresso and listened to a baseball game on the radio, just the voices keeping me company. I savored the possibility of many, many days like this: work, swim, radio.

At four, my legs were asleep. I considered swimming again, to get the kinks out before a big slab of meat for dinner. The superintendent had straightened all the chaise lounges on the far side of the empty pool. I enjoyed his daily ritual, a kindness. Liz Lerner stood on the pink sidewalk holding two takeout coffees and cradling a huge box of chocolate in her arms.

She tilted her face up to me.

"I was in the neighborhood. Why don't you have a hanging plant on your terrace like everyone else?"

"I killed it. Come up."

Liz surreptitiously searched the room for new artwork but my sketchbooks were out of sight. She knew I saw her; it was done in a friendly spirit and when I was ready, I planned to capitalize on Liz's interest.

"Let's sit by the pool."

"I like the apartment. Was it the teensiest place you could find?"

"I sit outside a lot."

"This isn't New York. You should have lots of space. Rooms and rooms opening into rooms and rooms."

"It's enough space to do what I'm here to do."

The neighbor with the white bikini came home from work and said hello. At dusk Liz and I walked to buy beer.

"You're alone all the time. Do you see people from New York?"

"Philip Cleary." I never talked about him with anyone, though.

"And how is that?"

"I like him. I think for now it's good."

From what I could see, Liz navigated the perils of being attached to a powerful man without losing herself. Whether or not she missed being an artist was unclear. I think she missed being young in New York, but that was different.

"On a scale of one to ten, how difficult was it to leave?"

"More than I can say. It's both ends of the spectrum, one

and ten. I wish I had left soon after I got there and I could have stayed forever. I don't even know who replaced me. It's been a month and already I don't know anything about what's going on there. The last seven years of my life got swallowed up."

"I remember that feeling. It won't take long for life here to be yours. If you're painting it will happen even more quickly. You should come and see me at the house sometime. I'm always there."

"I will. I'd like to see that boy leading a horse painting again."

"Come anytime."

Liz sat with her knees under her chin, a fresh cigarette tucked between her fingers. She told me a story about driving through the Everglades eating avocados. She wore a sapphire on her right hand. Such expensive things made her look older than she was.

"I'd like to see the Everglades."

When Philip arrived we were still in the flowered chaises. There was no awkwardness between them about meeting at my apartment, or that I had an apartment.

"Emma was just talking about visiting the Everglades."

"But you just got here. Shall we go in and toast her arrival?" he said.

But we stayed in our chaises watching the dusky sky until Billy called and Liz left to meet him at a party. Philip and I went down to see the dark ocean. Hotel guests were indoors dressing for cocktails. We sat in the sand looking out across the water at the horizon, at the shifting light and colors. A mangled gull carcass washed up on the beach and two guys from the hotel came to take it away in a white bucket. I picked the peeling skin from my forearms and the tops of my feet.

"Is the water cold?" Philip said.

"I have no idea. I haven't been in the ocean for years."

"I've become frightened of it."

"You?"

"Yes, me," he said.

Once Irene and I had spent a weekend on Fire Island in a tiny house Jennifer and her roommate had rented for the summer season. I tore *The Sun Also Rises* down the spine so that Irene could begin the first half when I was midway through but she misplaced it immediately. From the moment we arrived, Jennifer's roommate inhospitably cleaned up after us, I broke every glass I drank from, and the guacamole gave Irene diarrhea. We tried to wake up in time to see the dawn but overslept in the bunk bed and missed our ferry home. Everything went badly; I could not recall each mishap. But we had body-surfed, strolled on board-walks, insulted and been insulted by our friends, drank margaritas made with shitty tequila, and made it out of the hot city for a Fourth of July weekend.

"We'll put it on the to-do list," said Philip. "Conquer fear of the ocean."

"No more lists for me."

He shrugged.

"I'm sorry. Michael made so many lists for me over the years."

He shrugged again but said he understood. "It's supposed to rain."

I lost sight of the horizon. We huddled together until the hotel lights were too bright to be able to see the clouds moving. A few people appeared on the beach in evening clothes. A woman dangled open-toed shoes from the end of her pinkie. Two men smoking cigars and carrying drinks spoke in loud voices to make themselves heard over the breaking waves.

FROM MY TERRACE we watched the rain break the pool's surface and the palms clashing over the apartment building next door. Philip spoke to Isabelle in New York for an hour while I tried not to listen.

"I think Isabelle is tired of painting," said Philip after he hung up.

"It goes in waves, don't you think?"

"Isabelle doesn't go in waves, though."

"That's different. Maybe when she's down here she'll get back into it. Art school can make painting damn uninteresting."

We were hiding from the mess I made inside cutting up the bundles of magazines I had lifted from the garbage dumpster of the hair salon around the corner. Ray Johnson's collages made me want to make my own. I arranged piles of pictures and half pictures of women's faces, eyes and lips, brows and curving jaws, and long white yachts on Caribbean seas and details from plates of holiday food. The blue floor was littered with scissors and cuttings and short

rows of repeated images: five stuffed turkeys, a dozen
beaches viewed through a woman's bare legs standing
shoulder-width apart, arrangements of variously prepared
eggs, impressionistic views of rooftops, like Bonnards.
Michael subscribed to these magazines. I used to leaf
through the editorials on Tuscany and Provence and Bali
when they arrived in the mail. I scanned them now like I
was the one who had been to all the resorts they advertised
because Michael had called me from spas and villas and
safaris all over the world to say he wanted to come home
and work in the studio with me but Gerda was determined
to stay away another week.

I reached over the railing to wet my hands.

The couple across the courtyard turned off their lights
and rushed through the downpour to their car. The whole
neighborhood seemed to be going out to dinner. My syncopated lines played in my mind, jutting into space, breaking
long and short.

Philip went in and fell asleep on the floor before the rain
stopped and I stepped over the carefully clipped curving
rivers and remote lagoons that surrounded him. When the
palms quieted outside I clicked the lamp off and lay on the
mattress under the window breeze, drifting in and out of
sleep. Philip woke in the last dark and tripped over a metal
straight edge on his way to shut the window and turn on the
air conditioner. He said he despised the smell of chlorine in
the morning, though I doubted he could really smell
anything.

He tugged some of the bed sheet away from me.

"Are you asleep? You're diagonal, move over."

Suddenly awake and mad that he was bossing me around in my own bed, I stalked outside and slept in a chaise beside the pool until the yard was in full sun.

7

INTERSTICES ARRIVED in a massive wooden crate built by Patrice. Leaned against the kitchenette, it dominated the entire room and basically rendered the apartment uninhabitable. The accompanying paperwork included a review: ". . . Mr. Freiburg's stylistic invention confirms his stature as one of the most interesting painters around . . . Of interest will be the tack his work takes since the recent departure of his longtime assistant." And this note written in black ink:

> Emma Dial,
>
> If you are down in Miami making paintings Hecht Gallery gets to see them first. Talk to me if you would like to place this picture of Michael's. Good luck to you.
>
> F. L. Hecht.

SUDDENLY I WAS in possession of a major work of art that needed climate-controlled storage, interest from Frederich Hecht himself, and acknowledgment from the *Times*. Only an idiot fucked up an opportunity like this one. Why move all the way to Florida? Why live in a Republican state making secret drawings in a sketchbook and keep this quasi-record of my life? No more tinkering around with half-assed collages. My days of procrastination ended.

PHILIP SAT at my table, naked and relaxed, the blazing sun bleached his tanned face, his back a thick curving shadow. He was unself-conscious when he was naked. I wanted to be that way. Our empty beer bottles from the night before were pushed to the side, on top of a pile of humanitarian junk mail from Planned Parenthood and Amnesty International for the previous tenant. I had opened those envelopes and thought of giving money but was already sick of having the paperwork around and wanted it thrown out.

A few murmuring voices in the courtyard caught Philip's attention. He rubbed his eyes and then returned to the *Herald*.

Three women stood close together beside the pool. No one was swimming. The women stared down at the water.

Last night I cleaned up before he came over. I threw tools and wood scraps into a milk crate and wiped down all the surfaces. Since his last visit I had built a stretcher and prepared my canvas and then finally started. How it happened exactly was unclear to me even while I spread paint on the dinner plate I used as a palette. A new visual vocabulary gained strength in me, nothing in Florida resembled New York, beginning and ending with the light. I mixed the colors with a butter knife. I had spent the day creating an elaborate pattern of finely weighted russet-colored lines and shadows, swimming in pale violet. I did not take a break until my mind was empty of the delicate lace. That first day reminded me of many other days of work, balancing on a tightrope, timid until I had a few easy paces behind me. Then bounding along without caution.

The women in the courtyard bemoaned a dead bird floating in the pool. They could not stop looking.

"Where is it from?" one of them asked. "How did it get here?"

Obviously, it came for me because I was finally ready to make a painting of its mangled little body soaked in chlorinated water.

Philip moved on to the *Times*. An empty to-go cup was on the counter beside the sink and he drank from the US 1 mug I had picked up at a thrift store. Coffee tasted good from that mug. I liked the colors of his skin against the wooden chair, his bare feet on my blue floor. If I stood right against the desk he was in perfect profile.

My bird slowly floated toward the deep end. Someone's former pet. A pet that got away.

The notebooks and pencils were in a desk drawer. What was Philip reading in the Friday paper? What was going on in the world? He leaned his elbows on the front section, which meant he could spend two hours sitting. Maybe more. I pressed my hipbones against the table. I forgot about what Philip might do and thought about the shape of him and how he felt to me. I liked him in my apartment. But what mattered now was the morning light and how the neighbors would remove the dead bird from the pool, the victim of a brutal cat attack, I decided. Blood and guts were leaking out into the water and the pool-cleaning brush and net had been misplaced.

So there was nothing else to do. I had no choice. All I had was the pale violet canvas, which seemed small at 26 by 20 inches, but it was a perfectly good place to begin.

Don't look up. Don't move around. Don't thwart me now! I did not want to make small talk or have any kind of conversation. I selected a brush from the cup, grabbed my colors: carbon black, phthalo blue-green, cobalt blue, plum violet, lemon ochre, cadmium red, alizarin crimson, titanium white.

My brush darted with confidence. My paint, my line, my color were right where I wanted them to be. I thought I was on an entirely different course with this first canvas, something related to the music I had been listening to and leaving New York and all the traveling I had not done. But here I was, outlining the bird's broken body and stabbing its feathers in plum violet, butter knife in one hand, cheap paintbrush in the other. Meredith Davies said Matisse painted intuitively, like an athlete.

Philip must have smelled the paint and heard me moving but he peacefully made his way through the A section and read the editorial page, the letters, and the op-ed page. The op-ed page used to publish Sue Coe drawings. Certainly he thought I was painting him.

"You know what I was thinking, Emma? I have a great idea."

I had to keep him from ruining this. It would be an accident but I would hate him if I stopped working now. Plus I had a sick feeling that his idea related to his bonsai plants, which I could not bear to hear about. Those stupid things.

"You know, I just started something here. Would you mind taking off? I have to keep going."

"Let me tell you quickly before I forget." He got up and started coming toward me. He had to be stopped.

"No, later. It has to wait. Go write it down so you remember." It required effort not to apologize to him. Tonight would I lean my tired head in my hand while he laid out a scheme involving the rearrangement of his bonsai plants? I knew I was right. They got too much sun where they were now in the picture window. Michael used to buy me nice dinners and talk nonstop about Therese's paintings or something she once said in her sleep. I would avoid repeating this type of scene, even if it meant staying home alone forever.

Philip dressed. He gathered his shoes, his wallet and keys. He sensed my urgency. If I pressed too hard he would resist and I just wanted him to get out. Being asked to leave was unusual for him. I wondered if a woman, or anyone, had ever asked him to leave before. Get out! in my mind I yelled.

"I can't wait to tell you, Emma."

"Kiss me goodbye."

"Okay. Keep going, Emma." He kissed both my shoulders on his way out the door. I complained about him being like Michael, and he was, but he understood on some level. Or maybe he humored me. Being by myself had never felt more imperative. One thing I knew: seeing Philip paint would be a letdown. Holding the brush again made me know this. Wanting to see him work was another stall tactic, a waste of my time. I was done being enthralled with other painters for a while.

Time slowed down; I slowed down; I switched brushes and poured thinner in yesterday's coffee cup. In Wellfleet we always painted in the morning, on an empty stomach. My parents might like to visit Miami. They would respect my humble one-room house. They might think I was suffering for my work, alone with no sign that someone else had prompted me to paint. They would bring me something practical and mundane to make life more comfortable, new towels and a toaster, and then feel I was doing okay. My mother might like this picture.

A red cloud filled the far end of the pool, a few steely feathers floated on the surface, and other tenants began to gather and mourn the animal. "How old was the poor little thing?" they all wondered. I did not wonder.

The orange light in Meredith Davies' painting reminded me of the beam that impregnates Mary in Fra Angelico's *Annunciation*. Did Meredith do that on purpose?

I stopped looking out the window and worked in a completely new way: standing, without the radio, without any planning, without a human subject. My strokes landed with perfect force, the soft brush slid smoothly across the light pool, my colors grew deeper and heavier, one oily wing outstretched, rising slightly above the surface of the water. Everyone else, everything else, got kicked out of the picture—no neighbors in their pajamas congregated on the sunny path, no mown lawn, no striped beach towels draped over the railing of a first-floor terrace. The dead bird, its insides streaming into the bleached-out water, a few yellow flowers beyond the tiled edge.

I CHUCKED the T-shirt I used for a rag in the empty sink and left the apartment. The pool water was already draining.

It was the hottest part of the day, when no one was on the street except construction crews and the police. I noticed buildings and faces and traffic for two blocks and then my attention wandered away. I watched my feet, my bony feet in Irene's old flip-flops. Dust and sand in the cuffs of my trousers. A couple of blocks ahead on the opposite side of the street there was a diner with a freshly painted sign. I stopped on the hot sidewalk. Since I had been in Miami I was continually nodding and waving at drivers when I stepped into intersections, excusing myself, thanking them for not running me down.

I was beginning to remember things. Hues. My arm passing over a canvas, a wide brush in my steady hand. The pleasure of my repeated gestures, making marks on sheets of heavy white paper. My voice. Saying yes and no. My will. I laughed again, might this even be fun? And now a small canvas.

I noticed the quiet. An aluminum ladder was propped against the air-conditioned diner diagonally across the street. The shiny cursive letters on the new sign spelled *Serafina's* in a sweet lavender latex. The sun would bleach it out by next summer. An elderly couple paused near the ladder; a pack of police officers came out of the diner and ambled to their cars, parked and double-parked at the hydrant. The old woman touched her husband's arm and they continued walking along.

I oriented myself on the bright new streets and hurried to a gleaming hotel I remembered from my first visit, singing the same line in a whisper, *I keep my eyes wide open all the time.* Not exactly true. The line was impossible; it ignored a usual progression, a normal sequence, and that held my attention.

Not every day would include time on a canvas. There had to be gestation periods, time hanging around, living with pictures I started and thinking about them. I had to get *Interstices* into storage so I could cook at home again. My way of working might not turn out to be like other painters

I knew; I had to be ready for that, gain ease with it somehow.

I pushed the glass door open into the cool air. The lobby was abuzz with air-conditioning and statuesque women being appraised by one another's boyfriends and husbands. I smiled at the concierge as though he had reserved a dining table for me moments ago. He could not care less. I easily passed for a new visitor in loose dark clothes and peeling sunburn.

The beach teemed with oiled bodies, topless and well toned from disciplined yoga and consistent mileage on a treadmill. German emanated from more than one direction. I plunked down my bag on a striped chaise and pulled my shirt over my head. In the seconds my eyes were covered by gray cotton, a trail of young feet ran past, kicking up sand. Adolescents shrieked and parents tried to stave off reprimand and banishment by hollering at their kids to stop what they were doing and be quiet.

This beach was postcard-pretty but the surf left much to be desired. I walked in up to my stomach and turned to see how far out I had come. Quite a way, maybe fifty yards. The still water shimmered and brimmed with waders, a few of them holding mimosas. I thought the tourist season was over but maybe this place was always popular. When was I last on a crowded beach? I dove under. It was warmer than the courtyard pool. My strokes were quick and powerful. The pool would be cleaned and refilled by tomorrow afternoon. The superintendent was absurdly diligent and non-confrontational. He would not want tenants to complain.

My body glided along, rising slowly and disturbing very little water when I broke the surface to breathe. Meanwhile,
here I was: the American painter Emma Dial, back in the
Atlantic after a busy morning in the studio, making the picture happen. I looked over my shoulder at the towering
hotel, blindingly white in the midday sun. The tide had
moved me along. No matter how calm the water seemed I
always ended up a staggering distance from where I first
dove in.

ACKNOWLEDGMENTS

MANY THANKS to Rebecca Beegle; Carol Anshaw and Sara Levine at The School of the Art Institute of Chicago; Robert Guinsler at Sterling Lord Literistic; Jill Bialosky, Adrienne Davich, Winfrida Mbewe, and everyone at W. W. Norton; and my family, especially my mother.

THE AMERICAN PAINTER EMMA DIAL

Samantha Peale

AN INTERVIEW WITH SAMANTHA PEALE

Among the artists you assisted in New York during the nineties is Jeff Koons. To what extent are the artists you encountered as an assistant an inspiration for The American Painter Emma Dial?

Artists working at the ground level—the ones who make paintings in their living rooms, put together exhibitions, and struggle to get dealers to look at their work—were the greatest inspiration for the novel. When I worked for Jeff Koons he encouraged me to do my own work. He always had the time and interest to find out what I was up to and serve up some uncanny insight. Watching him work, doing research for his projects, and being introduced to new art by him was a gift.

People immediately recognize Koons's name, as he's a significant figure in the art world, but could you tell us about other artists for whom you worked? Were they painters? Sculptors? How did they differ in temperament? What did you take away from your experiences with them?

I did some menial work for three other artists, all painters. I washed brushes, mopped floors, stretched canvases, labeled slides, wrote letters, fetched coffee, cigarettes, and dry cleaning. I maintained a sense of humor. The first painter I assisted was quiet and brooding, the second vociferous and strident, and the third seemed not to work at all. I wondered why I was even there. He read the newspaper, did the crossword, and listened to music. Then he would make a stunning painting. Maybe two. Then no more work for weeks or longer. What I took away from being an assistant was the imperative to be patient, find my own rhythm, and keep working with determination.

Tell us about the New York City art scene in the nineties. Is there anything you look back upon and see as particular to the era? What were the pressures? What kinds of changes were underway?

I participated in the art scene as an observer. I moved from Manhattan to North Brooklyn in 1989. When I got there, along with my three roommates (two writers and a theater producer), a community of visual artists had already been working in Williamsburg for well over a decade. Some of these artists started galleries such as Four Walls, Minor Injury, Brand Name Damages, and Annie Herron's Test Site. Unemployment was high and no one had any money, which made people resourceful and inventive. People lived in really crappy situations, sometimes illegally, in close proximity to Superfund sites and radioactive waste transfer stations. The jobs artists did weren't flashy or meant to be any sort of career; you worked to buy time and space. Bartenders, bike messengers, adjuncts, housepainters, carpenters, welders, strippers, administrative assistants. I saw a lot of people face the struggle that Emma Dial faces: how to build a life around art with so many opposing forces at work. They sacrificed comfort, stability, a known path. At that time, the perception that Brooklyn was in a different time zone than Manhattan made it hard to get the art establishment to venture out and visit studios. This was a tricky battle—the excitement of this rich community and its need to woo the establishment and also maintain its independence, assert its uniqueness, capitalize on its own resources. Galleries like Pierogi 2000 and Roebling Hall were founded and began doing great shows. The Museum of Modern Art merged with P.S. 1. Emma Dial comes along at the end of the nineties. She experiences a different city with a larger, wealthier art establishment. Like the artists who inspired her character, she must write her own ticket.

Are you a visual artist as well as a writer? If so, what is your favorite medium and why?

I love to draw. At The School of the Art Institute of Chicago (where I earned an MFA in writing) I took a lot of printmaking classes. When I worried to my first lithography instructor that I didn't draw well, he replied, "You can hold a pencil, can't you? If you can hold a pencil, you can draw." I like drawing and painting on giant litho stones and working the machines. Lithography holds plenty of room for experimentation and play, but you have to learn a mechanical process and more or less get it right. An essential part of writing the novel was drawing all the pictures made by the characters. It was important to determine Emma Dial's influences, to develop the work for hire that would challenge and excite her, as well as art she'd see and wish she'd made herself or find less interesting. Conceiving of her work—what she made before and after working for Michael Freiburg—required a lot of trial and error. Emma had to have an idiosyncratic and particular way of thinking about art, with a meaningful history and an uncertain future.

Many people would like to read The American Painter Emma Dial *as a roman à clef. How do you respond to this desire of readers?*
I'm all for indulging one's desires. People looking for Jeff Koons in *The American Painter Emma Dial* will be disappointed not to find him. The novel tells a more exciting story: the Herculean efforts required for a young woman to stake everything on her talent and interests when all the people in her life think she ought to be doing something else.

DISCUSSION QUESTIONS

1. How were you affected when you understood that Emma Dial executes all of Michael Freiburg's paintings? What was your initial impression of their working relationship?

2. The novel is populated by a variety of powerful women—Emma's grandmother and mother, her teacher Meredith Davies, painter Therese Oller, Gerda Freiburg, Irene Duffy, and Isabelle Cleary. How do these characters reflect and deepen your impression of Emma?

3. Emma Dial is defined by her uncanny painting skill. "I could copy any mark made by a human hand, though I never let on how proud I was of it." Many characters in the novel have opinions about what Emma should do with her abilities. Therese Oller would like Emma to paint for her; Therese's assistant, Emma's friend Hideki, thinks Emma should continue to work for Michael Freiburg. Discuss some of these points of view. Does anyone want for Emma what she wants for herself?

4. *The American Painter Emma Dial* is written as a "quasi-record" of Emma's life, taken down in a sketchbook intended for drawings. What is noteworthy about how she constructs this record? What story did you discover in the paintings she describes?

5. What picture emerges of Emma's friends, her peers who are also artists? What role do the characters of Irene, Idris, and Hideki play in the novel? How do they regard Emma?

6. Emma spends a lot of time looking at all kinds of pictures: the paintings she makes for Michael Freiburg; reproductions of work by contemporary, modern, and Renaissance artists; art made by her friends as well as pictures on the Web—nature photography and the lovely and mysterious Föhn clothing Web site, a secret pleasure. What do the types of images Emma describes tell you about her interests and desires?

7. Emma says that she has admired Philip Cleary's work since college. Discuss the aspects of Philip Cleary's art that attract Emma and inspire her admiration. Is it meaningful to you that he makes his own paintings?

8. What begins as a heavily freighted visit to The Armory Show results in Emma's public dresssing-down by Michael Freiburg. Does anyone get what they deserve in this pivotal scene?

9. Emma's friendship with Irene seems to be a source of strength for her, yet she chooses to distance herself from her closest companion. Is she envious of Irene? Do Irene's scattershot passions threaten to derail Emma's ambition? Why must Emma keep Miami to herself? Will their friendship survive?

10. What kind of relationship do Emma and Philip Cleary have? What draws them together? What will separate them? How does Emma's relationship with Philip compare to her earlier relationship with Michael?

11. The New York City that Emma inhabits is purposefully small, restricted to a few adjacent downtown neighborhoods. When the story moves to Miami, how does the change in geography affect Emma?

12. Discuss the novel's title. Emma and Irene played an interview game when they were roommates. What does the game reveal about Emma's aspirations and fears? What does it suggest about her sense of a public and private artistic persona?

MORE NORTON BOOKS WITH READING GROUP GUIDES AVAILABLE

*Available only on the Norton Web site: www.wwnorton.com/guides